GAME OF RISK

risqué three

SCARLETT FINN

Also by Scarlett Finn

GO NOVELS
GO WITH IT
GO IT ALONE
GO ALL OUT
GO ALL IN
GO FULL CIRCLE

TO DIE FOR...
TO DIE FOR TRUTH
TO DIE FOR HONOR
TO DIE FOR VIRTUE
TO DIE FOR DUTY
TO DIE FOR LOVE

KINDRED SERIES
RAVEN
SWALLOW
CUCKOO
SWIFT
FALCON
FINCH

MCDADE BROTHERS NOVELS
ALL. ONLY.
ONLY YOURS

THE EXPLICIT SERIES
EXPLICIT INSTRUCTION
EXPLICIT DETAIL
EXPLICIT MEMORY

LOVE AGAINST THE ODDS STANDALONE COLLECTION
SWEET SEAS
HEIR'S AFFAIR
RESCUED
MAESTRO'S MUSE
GETTING TRICKY
THIRTEEN
REMEMBER WHEN...
RELUCTANT SUSPICION
XY FACTOR

WRECK & RUIN
RUIN ME
RUIN HIM

MISTAKE DUET
MISTAKE ME NOT
SLEIGHT MISTAKE

THE BRANDED SERIES
BRANDED
SCARRED
MARKED

RISQUÉ & HARROW INTERTWINED
TAKE A RISK
FIGHTING FATE
RISK IT ALL
FIGHTING BACK
GAME OF RISK

NOTHING TO...
NOTHING TO HIDE
NOTHING TO LOSE
NOTHING TO DECLARE
NOTHING TO US
NOTHING TO SAY
NOTHING TO YOU

EXILE
HIDE & SEEK
KISS CHASE

LOST & FOUND
LOST
FOUND

THE FORBIDDEN NOVELS
FORBIDDEN DESIRE
FORBIDDEN WANT
FORBIDDEN WISH
FORBIDDEN NEED

ONE

RUGER WARNER WAS SITTING at the bar of his brother's strip club, Risqué, waiting for his brothers' attention. The twins, who looked and acted nothing alike, each had their strengths, and right then he needed both.

Blaser finished filling a drink order and came over. When he saw that his twin, Colt, was a few feet away whispering to his fiancée, surrounded by Risqué girls, Blaser whistled for his attention.

"So is the meeting setup?" Blaser asked.

Leaving the gaggle of women to their business, Colt moved down a couple of stools to sit next to him. "Are you sure you want to do this?"

"It's a trip to Jersey," Ruger said. "I'll make it back intact."

"It's not your safety we're worried about," Colt said, sharing a look with his twin.

"I know I laid it on pretty thick," Blaser said. "When I found out that you were mixed up with the people who took Bri, I wasn't exactly thinking straight."

"You and me both," Ruger said. "Bri is the love of your life, Blase. She was abducted, held captive, raped—"

His brother flinched.

"Bri can say it aloud," Colt said to Blaser. "Maybe you should try it too."

"That's thanks to Doctor Lyssa Cutler," Blaser said. "Your wonderful fiancée… Is she keeping her name by the way?"

Colt indicated he wanted another beer and Blaser delivered. A distraction or Dutch courage?

Colt slurped the liquid. "We haven't talked it out and it's not her name, it's her ex's. If I have my way, she'll be a Warner."

"Your kids will be Warners," Ruger said, "so it makes sense."

"We're not talking about my relationship with Lys tonight," Colt said. "Or Blaser's with Bri. We've spent too much time getting distracted recently. Did you find who you were looking for, Ruge?"

"Had to get in touch with some old contacts. I've been trying to track down the man we owe Bri's life to. The man who saved her. A guy named Drew Jansen."

"The meet in Jersey?" Blaser asked. "It's actually him?"

"Yeah, my contacts have set it up. I'm leaving tomorrow to meet him."

"And when you do?" Colt asked. "What do you plan to say?"

"I plan to say thank you," Ruger said. "And then figure out a way to repay the debt. He gave us back Bri. He can pretty much ask me to do anything."

Colt and Blaser looked at each other, their concern palpable. They were right to be worried and he'd be the same if the situation was reversed. He wouldn't want either of them walking into a possibly dangerous scenario without backup.

But he didn't like owing anyone anything. At the very least, Jansen deserved a handshake. Rushe and Flick, his contacts, had been tight-lipped about Jansen's motivation. The info from Flick had been sparse.

This meeting was important. Nothing his brothers could say would keep him from going to that hotel room and looking Jansen in the eye.

TWO

WAITING WASN'T RUGER'S strong suit. From the moment he'd learned of Bri's ordeal, and that it had been his fault, setting things right preoccupied him. That started with getting the truth about what had happened.

In a hotel room in Atlantic City, fun was the last thing on his mind. Gambling was on the agenda. Just being there was a gamble. The Jansen guy might not even show. Setting up the meet took two weeks, the guy was reluctant, which made sense given some of the crooks they had in common. Being stood up wouldn't change his goal. One way or another, he'd track Drew Jansen down.

Dropping to the end of the bed, his head fell into his hands.

His work as a fence, a black-market trader, wasn't supposed to put anyone he cared about in danger. He worked away from his family and never revealed what he did to keep them safe.

When Colt told him about what Bri went through… it had plunged a knife into his heart. Blaser loved Bri and had since they were teenagers. Bri had given him a pass, which was the only reason Blaser did too. Despite that, Blaser had spent the last two weeks scowling at him. It wasn't over yet.

An abrupt knock on the door brought him to his feet. Striding the width of the room, he opened the door without checking who was on the other side of it. Only three other people knew his location and one of them was the man he was about to meet.

Jansen went into the body of the room while Ruger closed and locked the door. He didn't expect interruptions but didn't want Jansen choosing to make a speedy exit.

The lithe guy walked with purpose as he paced to the top of the bed then back to stand next to the TV. "Rushe and Flick have saved Serendipity more times than I can probably count," Jansen said. Serendipity was his girlfriend, the woman he'd intended to save when he saved Bri and Flick. "I'm only here now because Flick did the pouty face at Rushe, and he got pissed off."

No one was safe when Rushe got pissed off and he'd do anything to keep his girlfriend, Flick, happy, even if that meant attacking a friend. Rushe was Ruger's only link to Jansen, and the guy who'd put the meet together.

"I appreciate you making the effort to be here."

"Good, 'cause it is an effort," Jansen said, his hands rising to his hips. "I'm not a cop anymore, which means I work alone."

"Like Rushe," Ruger said, though Rushe "worked" with his girlfriend now.

That description was dubious because Rushe hated to see Flick get into any kind of jam and she managed to get herself into them frequently. Rushe would probably rather see Flick at home safe all the time, but Flick wasn't that kind of girl anymore.

"No, not like Rushe," Jansen said. "I leave Serendipity at home. And I don't have Rushe's rep or… manner."

Rushe's manner had a lot to do with scaring the shit out of people and showing no mercy. "All I want from you is information."

"About Victor?"

"Yeah," Ruger said. "I know he was working for someone higher up; the feds are dealing with that mess. I need to know, are Victor and his men dead?"

"You should've asked Rushe that question. He killed them."

Rushe hadn't offered information, the guy didn't answer to anyone and distrusted everyone. The only reason Ruger got that far was with Flick's assistance.

"Yeah, Flick told me how it went down. Victor's men died after the rescue."

"Look, I worked with Victor and his gang undercover, as a cop. Victor found out who I was, and he kidnapped Serendipity to manipulate me into feeding my superiors false information. I did everything he asked, but it didn't matter. Their trade was human cargo. They trafficked women to men all over the world; men who ordered what they wanted and had it delivered to them.

"I heard about a drop. I knew Victor and his guys were sending out a shipment of women. I had to get Serendipity. If I let her leave the country… I had tried everything else, tried to get to her from within, but Victor was too strong. So I intercepted them on their way to the cargo containers. The van full of women left Victor's mansion, and I knew the route. When the time was right, I rammed them off the road. I killed John and Victor's other guys and let the women go."

"Bri?"

"Yes," Jansen said. "I wasn't being a hero. I was there to get my girl."

"And did you?"

"No," Jansen said, slumping down to sit on the bottom corner of the bed. "Serendipity wasn't there, but Flick was and so was Bri."

"You've got Serendipity now, how—"

"Yeah, Flick and I went back in to get her out. They were holding Rushe too. Once we freed him and Serendipity, we took Victor and the rest of his guys out. That was the end of it."

That was far from the end if what Flick had told him was true, but that was irrelevant.

Ruger offered Jansen a hand. "Thank you. Whether you meant to do it or not, you got Bri out of there. She's back with my brother, Blaser, and they're working things out."

"You're welcome," Jansen said, frowning and getting back to his feet while avoiding the handshake. "Is that all you wanted to know?"

Ruger lowered his hand. "No."

"I didn't care about Bri. I didn't even care about Flick back then. I was there to get my girlfriend out. I turned a blind eye to a lot of suffering in the name of keeping her safe. I'm no hero."

"Regardless," Ruger said. "I owe you a debt."

Ruger had worked for Victor himself before he figured out what the thug was into. As soon as he learned they were human traffickers, he cut all ties and refused to work for them anymore. His abandonment of their cause led to Victor instructing his men to abduct Bri, and subject her to horrific treatment, in the name of revenge against him.

"You owe me nothing," Jansen said. "We've all moved on from that. Dipity, Flick, they don't deserve to go through that again, and neither does Bri."

"I'm not talking about putting them through anything," Ruger said. "There must be something you need. I heard you went into private practice. Are you a PI now?"

"No, I've got a kinda vigilante thing going on. Maybe it's my cop days chasing me, or maybe I still have guilt about what I did for Victor. These days, I spend my time investigating corruption."

"My brother, Colt, was a cop. He spends his time tracking stalkers," Ruger said. "I understand not turning your back on the job."

"Except my current job has the potential to get me and mine hurt," he said. "Serendipity works freelance as a reporter. She's uncovered… Ashcroft is crooked, and it looks like he's in bed with the DA."

"Governor Ashcroft?"

"That's right," Jansen said. "He doesn't know Serendipity is involved yet, but he knows I'm sniffing around. I can keep her safe. I'm much better at it now than I used to be."

Almost losing his love once would be enough to make Jansen more vigilant about it.

The ex-cop's pensive expression drew him in. "You're worried about someone else?"

"I have a sister in Miami," Jansen said, tensing as he made the admission. "I guess… once bitten, twice shy. I know what it is to have someone you love used against you. We lost our mom young, just a week after Layla graduated college. It's just her and I now… I can keep Serendipity in my eyeline almost twenty-four seven. Rushe and Flick are still in Jersey too. They've been helping me work through the possibilities and with surveillance…"

"Wow," Ruger said. "I didn't think Rushe was the type to give a rat's ass about politics."

"He's not," Jansen said. "The trick to Rushe these days is getting Flick interested and she knows plenty about moving in society's highest echelons. Her family is seriously old money. She and Serendipity were the ones who started asking questions. Rushe and I are just trying to keep up."

"If Serendipity and Flick are involved, aren't their families in trouble?"

"Flick's family can look after themselves and have their own influence. Plus Flick hasn't had anything to do with them in a long time. Serendipity doesn't have family of her own. Her father split when she was young, and her mom died a couple of years ago."

"And Rushe doesn't have anyone to worry about," Ruger said.

Family was a foreign concept to Rushe.

"I've been doing the digging. I'm the only one Ashcroft has seen ask questions. Rushe spends his time trying to keep Flick out of it."

"If you're the only one the governor has seen, you're the only one in real trouble."

Jansen dismissed the threat to himself with a shrug. "Which I don't care about, but I can't protect Serendipity in New Jersey and Layla in Florida."

No, he couldn't, which presented Ruger with the opportunity he needed. "I'll get her."

"You'll get her?" Jansen asked, wearing another frown. "What do you mean?"

"You're worried about your sister. I have two brothers, their women are practically my sisters. I get it. I can look after your sister."

"No offense, Ruge, you're a big guy and I sure wouldn't want to take you on in a fight…"

"But?"

"But you're not security, you're not a cop, you're a fence. What do you know about taking care of an asset?"

Good point. But he'd seen his share of action over the years, even if he wasn't specifically trained in combat.

"I don't have to fight anyone," Ruger said. "I can pick her up and bring her to you."

"You can't bring her to me," Jansen said, shaking his head. "That just puts her in the path of trouble. Ashcroft might not be looking for her, yet. Bringing her to me would put her in more danger."

"But you're worried about what happens when Ashcroft realizes you're on to him. If he thinks you and Serendipity have threatened his way of life, he might try to get to Serendipity or Layla to get you to back off."

"Yeah. I have Serendipity covered."

"Then I'll cover Layla," he said. "Do you have an address? Somewhere I can find her?"

"Why would you—"

"Because you took care of Bri, whether you meant to or not. Running that van off the road, getting her out of it, you saved her from being trafficked to God knows where. As far as I'm concerned, I owe you."

"You think you can take care of Layla? That you can look after her? You'd have to get her out of Miami."

"That I can do," Ruger said, fishing his phone from his back pocket. "Do you have your phone?"

"Yeah," Jansen said, taking out his own.

"Turn on your AirDrop and send me your most recent picture of her. If you give me her address, I'll track her down."

"She doesn't know any of this is going on," Jansen said, searching through his phone, doing as asked. "She's stubborn. Picking her up won't be easy."

"Oh, I know about stubborn women," Ruger said. "I'll keep an eye on her until I figure out the best way to approach her."

"Then what will you do? You have to get her out of Miami, but you can't bring her here. If Ashcroft decides to look for her, she won't be safe at her friends' houses or—"

"That's easy," Ruger said. "I'll take her somewhere safe. A place filled with guys who'll watch her back. They won't let anything happen to her. Trust me, this isn't just important to me. It's important to Blaser and Bri, and to Colt and Lyssa too. We'll keep an eye on Layla for you. No one will harm her. You have my word."

"Okay," Jansen said, putting his phone away once all the information was transferred. "I'm trusting you because Rushe does, because from everything I hear you're a good guy. Once you have Layla, get her to call me. I'll try my best to get her to give you a break. If I call her before you go down there, she'll be expecting you and will probably go into hiding before you get the chance to get her. Like I said, she's stubborn."

"I can handle it," Ruger said. "I'm not worried about picking her up or looking after her. I can be persuasive when I have to be."

"Layla knows every line in the book," Jansen said. "She's used to guys and their attention. She's had more marriage proposals than most guys have pairs of shoes."

"Proposals? Does she have a thing for engagement rings, or—"

"No, she never accepts. As soon as a guy gets down on one knee, she ends it and runs, usually moving to a different state, or at least a different city."

"Why's that?"

Jansen shrugged. "Beats me. She's always been independent and thinks she knows best about everything. If you ask her, she'll tell you she doesn't need a man."

"You think different?"

"I think she doesn't need any of the losers who've tried to coerce her into marriage. One day, when the right guy takes charge… she'll figure it out."

Ruger nodded. "Okay."

Her relationship status and attitude toward marriage was irrelevant to his mission. But when he glanced down at the picture Jansen had just sent, he saw sultry almond eyes and glossy dark hair. The allure that had ensnared the men who wanted to marry her was obvious. Looking after her was his job and that didn't involve cracking the code to break into her heart.

THREE

"IF YOU ENTRUST the launch to us, Mr. Potter, I can assure you your club will be the most popular hotspot in Miami before this week is out," Layla Jansen said. "Tickets to your opening night will be gold dust in this town."

"Your firm does come highly recommended."

The meeting in this cocktail bar on the waterfront was meant to be informal, but the sixty-year-old in his slick Italian suit wasn't from that part of the world. His choice of apparel betrayed as much.

"We have done a number of very successful nightclub launches," Layla said, pushing a glossy folder across the metallic table-top toward Potter.

"I was advised to speak directly with your boss."

"Mandy has assigned your account to me. I am a very trusted member of her team."

Actually, Mandy couldn't stand her, and Layla had to beg for the chance to take the meeting. She'd only been working under Mandy for six weeks but could already tell gaining any glimmer of respect would be an uphill climb. The only reason Mandy folded and agreed to let her have this client was because he insisted on a meeting so late in the evening.

"In the buzz of Miami" was apparently what Potter had said, but Mandy had a new boyfriend and her recent evenings were reserved for him, meaning Layla caught herself a break.

"I suppose that's acceptable," Potter said, his gaze falling to the slope of her breasts displayed in the V-lines of her spaghetti strap sundress.

She reached to the brochure and opened the glossy pages to show him images of clubs launched by her PR firm. "You can read testimonials here from—"

"Layla Jansen!"

Drawing her eyes away from the booklet and up to the man next to their high silver table, she was at a loss. He had to be six five and was built broad under his white vest.

"Do I know you?" she asked, sitting up straight to examine the tan under the stubble on his jaw.

His eyes were hidden under slick wraparound shades, nothing about him was familiar.

"Sure!" he said with an exuberant grin and turned to Potter. "I'm Ruger Warner, Layla and I are old friends."

"Are we?" Layla asked through her smile without moving her lips. The men shook hands, but Potter was as flummoxed as her. "Remind me."

"Always a kidder," Ruger said, dropping a heavy hand onto her newly exfoliated shoulder. "Layla and I go way back. She's a great girl."

"And it was great to see you again, Ruger," Layla said, hoping he'd take the hint and vanish as quickly as he had appeared. She'd never had a one-night stand in her life, but she began to mentally catalogue every creepy guy in a bar who had tried it on recently. "Maybe we'll see each other again."

"You don't mind if I join you, do you?" Ruger asked, rounding the table to seat himself in the vacant spot.

"Actually—" Potter began.

"This is a business meeting," Layla said. "I can't catch up right now."

"Oh," Ruger said. "How stupid of me. This is the nightclub guy, Potter, sure. You were worried he wouldn't like your pitch, but smart move with the dress." Ruger lifted his glasses to ogle her cleavage. "Guy won't hear a word you say." He winked and re-seated his glasses.

Trying not to have a heart attack, she pounced out of her seat and snatched Ruger's wrist. "Would you please excuse us, Mr. Potter?"

Ruger put up no resistance when she yanked him from his seat to drag him to the sidewalk. Behind the potted palm tree which stood at the entrance, she dropped Ruger's arm and spun on the spot to thrust her fists to her hips.

"An old friend who knows my current calendar?" she demanded.

He grinned. "Weird, isn't it?"

"I don't find this funny. At all. What is your problem? Who the hell are you? Stalking laws are strict in this part of the world, you know."

Layla had no idea about the stalking laws in Miami. She'd been living there less than six months. So far, that information hadn't been high on her research priority list. It was quickly moving up the ranks.

"You need to come with me," Ruger said.

"Yeah, right."

"Seriously," he said, and his grin disappeared. "I need to take you from here, right now."

"Not a chance. Do you know how long I've waited to have a chance at a meeting like this? If I can crack this guy, I can have my own accounts and… Wait, why am I explaining myself to you? Go away! If you come near me again, I'll call the cops."

She moved half a step to the left intending to return to her meeting.

He grabbed her arm. "I can't let you do that."

"Can't let me what? I'll call the cops if I want to call the cops."

"What are they going to arrest me for? Standing in a public place?"

"Menacing, disturbing the peace, something," she said.

"That will go down really well with your client," Ruger said. "I'll just tell them that we're having a lover's tiff."

"A lovers—what the…? Who the hell are you? We've never met!"

"Only you and I know that," he said. "I know a lot about you. One brother, your dad died when you were a kid, and your mom died of cancer the week after you graduated college. You've spent the last ten years living all over the country and you've never settled down… Your last boyfriend turned out to be a bastard who screwed your best friend… I guess she wasn't a prize either."

A complete stranger with information about her past? Those weren't things she would tell a guy in a bar. Either he was a stalker, or he got the information from someone else. There was only one person in the world who would know all those facts.

Her shock became resigned impatience. "You're one of my idiot brother's idiot friends, aren't you?"

His floppy grin was more charmed than she felt. "Idiot brother, yes. Idiot friend, no. I'm really smart."

"I'll reserve judgment."

"Hey, I'm giving up my vacation for this," he said, holding his hands open at his sides. "He's got himself into some trouble."

"Drew is always in trouble," she said, edging closer. "Since my brother has been so kind as to educate you on my history, let me educate you on his. He does this all the time. He gets the sniff of some ridiculous case he's sure he'll crack open. He did it when he was a cop and it's no different now. He chases it around like a dog chasing his tail and it never comes to anything. If I had a dime for every time he called telling me how he'd pissed off the wrong person…"

"This time it's different," Ruger said. "They're coming after you."

"My brother and his idiot case are in Jersey. I'll panic when the hitmen get on a plane."

She tried to pass him again, but he got in her way. "They got on a plane this afternoon. They're on their way now, and your brother can't beat them down here. He's got Serendipity to worry about up there too. He can't be in two places at once."

"My brother cries when he gets a splinter. Does he think he can face down some crooks intent on fighting?"

"That's why he sent me," Ruger said, flashing his grin again.

"I'll take my chances," she said, patting his arm. "Nice seeing you again, old friend."

Skirting around him, she muttered to herself about her brother, Drew, and his dramatic flair, then pasted on her smile and returned to the table with Potter. "I'm so terribly sorry about that. Ruger is troubled, very troubled, but I've dealt with him now and he won't bother us again. Where were we?"

Potter's focus wasn't on her, it was on something behind her. Without turning around to see what had his attention, Layla knew she'd spoken too soon. Just at that, Ruger materialized at her side again.

"I'm sorry that I have to do this, Mr. Potter," Ruger said.

Awaiting an apology that never came, Layla was confused when Ruger crouched at her side, though not for long. He took her wrist, gave her a tug, and tossed her over his shoulder. Keeping hold of one wrist, he locked his other arm around the back of her thighs over her dress. Layla screamed and kicked, but he was unmoved.

"What is this?" Potter asked.

"She's late to take her medication. I didn't want to say anything before," Ruger said. "But it's vitally important she gets it on time, or she becomes an outrageous lush. We can't have her embarrassing the firm like that again. I'm sure you understand."

Various patrons gaped at the sight of her being carried out of the bar over the shoulder of this giant. When she saw Potter in the distance, standing at the table wearing a look of shock and disgust, she flopped and stopped screaming.

"I hope you're happy with yourself for ruining my career," she said, trying to aim a kick at his groin.

Being upside down and back to front, judging the angle was near impossible.

"You'll get another one, Layla. You always do, honey."

He kept on walking, carrying her to the end of the block then turning up another street.

"I can walk, you know."

"No need," he said and entered a parking lot to stop at a large gunmetal grey pick-up truck. Its lights blinked and he opened the back door to toss her inside, on her face.

Clambering to sit up, he was in the vehicle, backing out of the space before she had flattened her skirt. "You just kidnapped me," she said, launching herself between the seats. "Dozens of people saw you carrying me down that street. Your face will be all over the news by dinner time."

"People have seen stranger things in these streets," he said, turning the truck. "This is Miami, honey."

"You can't just kidnap a woman off the street! You'll have cost me my job, my career..." Indignation was exhausting. Slumping back in the seat, she folded her arms. "Oh, just take me home."

"No need," Ruger said. "Your things are in the back."

Whipping around to look out through the small back window, all she saw was the flat bed cover. "My things? You've been in my apartment? What are you? Some kind of snoop?"

"Not exactly, no."

"You picked my lock? That's breaking and entering, that's illegal, that's—"

"Jansen called the super and I gave him a hundred bucks," Ruger said, referencing her brother by his last name. "No one broke anything."

The stranger was confident and attractive, but the idea of him foraging through her underwear gave her a chill. "Are you a pervert?"

"No way... though I am wearing your panties right now. They're not as comfortable as they looked."

"They do me just fine," she grumbled, aware of his not-so-hilarious teasing. "Where's your cellphone? I want to speak to my brother. I'm going to kill him! Where are we meeting him?"

"Don't know yet," Ruger said, retrieving a cellphone from the glove box. "Be quick, I'm out of long-distance minutes."

She took the phone to dial. "Bet your balls I'll take as long as I damn well please," she said and listened to the ring of her brother's phone.

"Did you get her?" Drew asked when he answered.

"Her? Yes, he got her," Layla said. "What the hell is going on? You sent a savage to come and steal me off the street?"

"Oh, sis," Drew said, with audible relief. "Thank God, I was starting to panic."

"Who do you think you are telling this weirdo about me?"

"Ruger is a good guy," Drew said. "Honestly, Lay, you can trust him. I'm told that he's got this overhyped sense of responsibility. He's going to look after you."

"I don't need anyone to look after me," she said. "Why didn't you call me?"

"I just found out what they were planning this morning and I've been trying to call you. Where's your cellphone?"

Reluctant to admit the truth, she lowered her chin. "Let's just say there was an incident in a ladies' room stall."

"You're the worst, you know that? You think you can take care of yourself? You can't even pee without cutting yourself off from the world."

Affronted, she straightened again. "You're the one who thinks the world is tumbling down. This is ridiculous, Drew. You can't do this. You can't order your friends to commandeer me just because you want to be dramatic."

"I know you're pissed. But you're my baby sister and I promised Mom I'd look out for you. I've got mixed up with some serious sons of bitches, and you're the only family I've got. They want to use you to hurt me."

"So give up on the case. If it's going to hurt me, or hurt you, just give up."

"I can't do that. I can't let them get away with the intimidation tactics and—"

"Spare me," she said on a groan. "So it's okay for you to trash my career to save yours?"

"Public relations isn't your career. It was just something you decided to try. You would hate it, trust me. You have to be nice to people all the time, and we both know you're not capable of keeping that going for long."

"Such a funny guy," she said, unwilling to admit her brother was probably right. When it came to her, he usually was. "Okay, so if I'm in such grave, horrible danger, are you going to tell me the plan?"

"Stick with Ruger, he'll keep you safe. He knows what to do. If you do what he tells you, exactly what he tells you, you'll be fine."

"I don't know Ruger," she said, noticing he was watching her in the rear-view mirror. "He seems a bit slow to me, you know? Special."

Ruger's smile formed and moved back to the windshield.

"Give the guy a break, he's helping me out. We're both lucky he was down there to bail you out."

"I don't need to be bailed out. You do. Once again, you've gotten yourself into trouble. You're a danger to yourself, do you know that?"

"I do, but this one is worth it. Trust me."

"And who is looking out for you?" she asked. "You're up there all by yourself. Is Serendipity there? If we get on a plane—"

"You're not getting on a plane," Drew said. "You can't use any form of public transportation. They're looking for you and these people have the means to access all kinds of information. Including flight manifests."

"My God, Drew, what have you gotten yourself into? Who is after you?"

"I can't say much, but this is big, bigger than anything I've ever got into before, and if I break it—"

"Yeah, yeah, you'll be hot property." She sighed. "Okay, brother, I'll do what you're telling me to do. But look after yourself because as irritating and frustrating as you are, you're all I've got."

"You won't get rid of me," Drew said, and she was pleased to hear the smile in his voice. "You stick with Ruger, and I'll be in touch soon, okay?"

"Okay. I love you."

"Back attcha," he said and the line disconnected.

When getting dressed for the meeting with Potter, Layla had worried her silk dress would crease and that her shoes might pinch her toes. She hadn't worried about being drawn into her brother's crazy world.

It was no wonder Drew had such a tight relationship with Serendipity. He had a singular kind of focus which made him the best kind of guy to commit to. At least he would be if he didn't get himself involved with so many shady characters. He'd take whatever risks were necessary to crack a case and to protect Serendipity from the peril she was so frequently put in by his work.

FOUR

"OKAY," Layla said, climbing between the seats to position herself in the front passenger seat. "Where are we going?"

"We're getting out of Miami," Ruger said, with a sideways look her way.

Smoothing her skirt with one hand, she sought out road signs trying to get an idea of which direction they were heading in. "That's... incredibly general."

"I'm hoping the mysterious thing will work for me."

"So far it doesn't. The muscles are panty melting," she admitted, giving him the once over. "The arrogance and condescension, not so much."

"Thanks for the pointers."

"How do we expect to learn if we're not willing to be educated?" she asked, tucking the phone back into the glove box. "Tell me about your family."

"Why?" he asked, frowning at her sudden re-route of the conversation.

"You know about mine and I'm not in the habit of traveling around with strangers. It will make me feel better if I know something about the guy who's abducting me."

Ruger wasn't really abducting her because Drew had given him permission to do what he did. Still, she wanted to know who she was spending her time with.

"Fair enough. My mom and dad live in a nice house and like to talk about the grandchildren they don't have yet."

"Only child then… explains a lot."

"Actually no," he said, retrieving gum from the door well and offering it to her before he took a piece. "I have twin older brothers in committed relationships. I come from a huge family, there are a million cousins."

Feigning her disbelief with a curious frown, her sass wasn't defeated. "Your dad is still around?"

"Yeah," he said, glancing at her to observe her expression of astonishment. "You sound surprised."

"I am. Huh…" she exhaled. "He obviously never taught you how to approach a woman."

"Never needed taught," he said with swagger. "Some things just come naturally."

"You're rusty, maybe you should think about polishing up some of those skills," she said, admiring a guy who could give as good as he got. "So you're from Jersey?"

That was where Drew and Serendipity lived, so she guessed this Ruger guy was from there too.

"North Carolina, actually."

"How did you end up mixed up with Drew?"

"That is a very long and complicated story probably best left for another time."

"So that's how it's going to be?" she asked. "You think you're calling all the shots?"

"I'm the driver," he said, pleased with his superior position. "I have all the controls, right here."

Taking his grip away from the steering wheel, Ruger opened his hands to gesture at everything the driver had access too. Reaching over, she blasted the horn before he could swat her hand out of the way.

"If a woman knows how to move right, she has all the control," Layla said. "Don't you forget it, Ruger."

The satisfied tilt of his lips prompted her to lean a little closer. He drew his attention around to fix on her for longer than a driver really should. His eyes were paler than his brown hair, but they were far from aloof, his whole being exuded refreshing warmth and openness.

Most of the men from her past had been guarded or weighed down by the trials life doled out. Ruger was sharp, she could tell that by his wit, but he wasn't cynical, something she'd been accused of herself.

"Are you going to tell me how you hooked up with my brother now?"

"I have to figure out how squeamish you are before I reveal all," he said, concentrating on the highway ahead. "I wouldn't want you to have nightmares."

Almost affronted by the suggestion she could be weak, her eyes pinched closer, ready to accept his challenge. "I have a strong stomach, Ruger, you can't shock me."

"Have you ever watched a person die?"

Yes, she had, and it wasn't an experience that she wanted to repeat. Ruger was trying to shock her and was just playing; she was sure he hadn't intended harm. Despite his benevolent intention, her memory conjured a mental flash of the life seeping out of her mother. That memory wasn't one she wanted to share with him, with a stranger, and it didn't fit the spirited mood of their repartee, so she decided not to answer.

"Will you at least tell me why you're doing this?" she asked.

His motivation would reveal a lot about his character.

"Let's just say that I owe your brother one."

"Figures that Drew didn't pay you. I'd guess you met him on one of his other cases. That guy just can't leave anything alone."

"He's tenacious," Ruger said. "But that's not a bad thing. Jansen's 'hang on and never let go' spirit saved a good friend of mine."

"Well, I'm glad my brother did you a favor." She switched on the radio and began to flick through stations. "What do you know about this case my brother is on now?"

"It's a big one."

"So he said… big in what way?" Ruger hesitated, prompting her to abandon the radio. "I think if these men are coming after me, I have a right to know why."

"It relates to Governor Ashcroft and rumors of kickbacks."

"Rumors?"

"That Ashcroft is as crooked as they come," Ruger said. "He's making decisions in favor of those who can pay him the most and he has a lot of sway with the prosecutors and judges in his state. Serendipity got Drew involved. He has the skills to get the information she needs to prove that the stories are true."

"She's still on this journalism kick?"

"Yeah," Ruger said.

Layla couldn't judge Serendipity for her recent change in career because she too often made abrupt changes in her life. Journalism did complement Drew's need to investigate with purpose, but Layla wished they would settle down so she didn't have to worry about her big brother all the time.

"I've been watching you for almost a week," Ruger said.

This statement jarred her out of her thoughts about Drew's safety. "You've what?"

"Yeah," Ruger said. "I told Jansen I'd look out for you."

"You said you were on vacation," she said, narrowing her eyes, but he was intent on the road ahead.

"I'm not being paid, and Miami is a party town. How else would you define a vacation?"

At least he was being honest, but if he'd been watching her, there wouldn't have been much partying going on. Her social life had been uneventful for a while. Drew had made it seem like Ruger's presence was serendipitous. She'd need to have a word with her brother about distorting the truth.

"You said there were hit-men on a plane, was that a lie too?"

"No," Ruger said. "Drew is putting the pieces together and Ashcroft found out he was on the case. The not-so-good governor decided to do some investigating of his own and his men discovered your location."

"Does Ashcroft know Serendipity is writing a story?"

"It's more than a story. There is a real crime being perpetuated here. Whether Ashcroft knows about Serendipity's involvement or not, I don't know. What I do know is Ashcroft knows Jansen is onto him. Whatever Jansen is doing, Ashcroft is freaked enough to want to scare him off."

"That's all you know?"

"Call your brother, he'll tell you more."

"No, he won't," she said, pulling in a long inhale and glancing out her side window. "My brother still acts like I'm a kid in need of protection. He acts like I couldn't understand what he does."

"You don't understand what he does," Ruger said.

This declaration was enough to offend her, so she whipped around. "Excuse me?"

"You were on the phone arguing with him. You talk about his work and Serendipity's with disdain."

"You're calling me narrow-minded?"

"Something like that," he said. "You told him you loved him, but other than that, I haven't heard any indication you support your brother in anything he does. Why would he tell you about it if all you're going to do is judge him?"

She had graduated college at twenty-two full of optimism. Her mother had been battling cancer for years by that time and she had been sure her mom would conquer it. Even when her mom and Drew lost faith, she had it in spades. No one had expected her mother to pass so suddenly. In the end, pneumonia claimed her.

Drew had tried to be the parent, tried to bolster his little sister, but it was too late. Since those days, optimism was a foreign concept. She always swore she would never be blindsided like that again.

"I just don't understand the purpose," Layla admitted. "There's nothing I can do about it, so I have to accept what he does. But I don't understand why he would choose to put himself in danger so often."

"Having a cause, fighting for what you believe, that's the purpose," Ruger said. "Being freelance, Serendipity has no conglomerate protection. She's out there on her own. Drew loves her, so he supports her no matter how desperate or crazy things get."

"And my idiot brother won't just go to the police because that might break the story before Serendipity is ready to release it."

"Jansen doesn't have a whole lot of buddies left on the force," Ruger said. "He sort of left in disgrace, remember?"

She didn't need the reminder of his ex-colleagues' treatment. Not one of them showed understanding for the impossible position Drew found himself in. "Isn't protecting Serendipity more important than some dumb story? And where do I fit in?"

"Ashcroft knows Drew has been asking questions. The governor is trying to scare him off the story. His men are tailing Drew, he's not safe, but offing the man working with the journalist who has evidence to corroborate the story… that could draw unwanted attention to the cause."

"And no one is looking at the investigator's little sister in Florida."

Sliding his hands to the top of the steering wheel, Ruger rested his forearms on it too and nodded before he carried on. "Drew found out Ashcroft's men got on a plane, that they were coming after you. That's why you had to come with me. We were out of time. There was no way to approach you softly. I had to get you out of public view in a hurry."

"Great news for me."

"You're safe now that I'm here," he said.

She wasn't entirely convinced. "Are you some kind of martial arts professional or something?"

"No, but I've been in my share of bar fights."

That wasn't encouraging. "Okay, so you're a firearms expert? A crack shot?"

"Crack shot? Could be, I usually hit what I'm aiming at."

"Usually? What are you used to aiming at?"

"Never met a skeet I couldn't take down," he said and grinned, briefly taking his attention from the road.

"Skeet?" she said, sitting up straight. "We have hit-men and possibly the Treasury Department on our tail and you're making jokes about skeet shooting?"

"Governors aren't protected by the Treasury Department."

Grinding her teeth, she tried to contain her fury. "You said Ashcroft had contacts, didn't you?"

"If the Secret Service are after us, I think you'd need Chris Kyle in your arsenal."

"He's unavailable," she said. "Just what exactly is it you do for a living that you think you're so qualified to take care of me?"

"I have two brothers. I've been scrapping since I was in diapers."

His jokes didn't encourage assurance. "Quit dancing around it. What do you do for a living?"

"I'm a trader."

"Trader? Like on Wall Street?"

"No," he said. "Not that kind of trader… I'm in product sales."

Shame? No, he was being elusive for another reason. "You're in sales? What do you sell?"

"Whatever my customer needs."

Just when she thought the situation couldn't get much worse. "You're kidding, right? This is a joke?"

"Nope," he said.

"Did you go to college? Spend time in the military?"

"I have a degree in communications."

"Wonders never cease," she said, wondering if she would survive a leap from a moving vehicle. "My brother sent a salesman with a degree in communications to save my ass? I think I need to get out of this truck now."

Her throat tightened. Despite his calm demeanor, she was overcome with anxiety.

"What? You've got something against a guy who uses brains rather than brawn?"

"No, no… no, I…" Bitter adrenaline brought bile to her throat. "I've been told there's a chance I'm going to be tracked down and murdered by unsavory thugs and my idiot brother…" The thump of her heart echoed to her tongue. "He sends a fucking retailer!"

"I'm not a typical salesman. I don't drive around selling products door-to-door."

"I think I'm going to be sick," she said, pushing the button to lower her window all the way down.

She stuck her face out hoping for a blast of cool air, but she was just struck by humidity.

Ducking back in, she fanned her face and tried to steady her breathing. Panic wasn't the cause of her near hyperventilation, anger did that. This was the man her brother had sent to make her feel better? To look after her? He didn't have the skills to do either.

"What's the problem?" he asked.

"This is just like Drew—save a buck and send a friend!"

"I was in Miami to look out for you. I travelled down because I owed your brother and I always pay my debts. You should be pleased I was already in position to pluck you up and save your ass."

"It didn't occur to him to send some kind of security guard, or a cop, or anyone remotely qualified?"

"I'm qualified," Ruger said.

"To do what exactly? Take commission on my purchases?"

"You're freaking out over nothing," he said, with a sloping smile.

"What qualifications do you have to save my life if it comes to it?" she asked, ready to have him prove her point for her.

"The way it was pitched to me, it's my job to get you out of Miami and to a safe place. Drew has a plan beyond that."

"Oh yeah, what?"

"I don't know," Ruger said. "I didn't ask. Get the girl out of Miami, that's my task, and I'm going to do that."

"Great," she said. "A license to drive, that's your qualification."

"Not only that," he said. "I'm a brother."

Opening her mouth wide to inhale, she was about to argue back, but stopped and closed her mouth. Somehow, the reminder actually made her feel better. "A brother?"

"Sure and I wouldn't let anything hurt my siblings. My brothers can take care of themselves and they're both involved with women I think of as sisters. I'm in the position of understanding Drew's concern. His little sister is in trouble, and he couldn't come to you himself. He'd do the same for me."

"If there was a case in it maybe," she said, calming down and folding her arms after she put the window up. "Getting out of Miami is a good start if that's where the bad guys are headed… do you know anything about who specifically is looking for me?"

"No, but they're not looking for me. These guys would never link us, which makes me a great person to help you. Drew will work this out. In the meantime, I'll make sure no one finds us."

If no one found them, there would be no need for fighting or shooting. "You have your own business?"

"Yes, you could say that," he said. "You know it wouldn't be out of line for you to show me a bit of gratitude."

"For cutting your fake vacation short and getting yourself pulled into an adventure that might get someone else killed? What kind of gratitude are you looking for?"

"You're in PR, right? Maybe you can draw a poster for my brother's business when this is over."

"Draw you a poster?" she gaped, ready to bite his head off when she read his mischief. "What kind of business?"

"He owns a strip club."

"Your brother owns a strip club?" she asked. In an automatic nod to her shock, her eyebrows rose. "And he has a girlfriend?"

"One he loves a lot." Layla wasn't sure what kind of woman would be happy in a relationship with a man who paid women to get naked. "Be careful, your judgment is showing again."

"I'm not being judgmental," she said, unsure what other word would describe her thoughts. "I just can't imagine what kind of woman would be happy with her boyfriend owning that kind of place..." Ruger said nothing. "Maybe you should just concentrate on driving."

"I understand. You have resentment toward a person with a stable career. Blaser is an entrepreneur. He's no sleaze. He knows what he wants from his life."

"I have no resentment. I'm a fully trained cosmetologist, I specialize in hair," she said. "I could have a stable career if I wanted one."

"You are?"

"Yes, I went back to school a couple of years ago to train."

"Let me guess, you were heading in a new direction after breaking up with a boyfriend or fiancé?"

Ignoring the haughty amusement he exuded, Layla carried on. "A trade is useful, and I respect that. But while my life is in danger, I'd like my protector to be equipped with more than a credit card machine."

His playful smile made his eyes dance. He didn't hide his enjoyment of her wit, although he delivered his line as if he meant it. "Do you know how lethal those things can be? Any weapon in the world can be obtained if you have the right amount of green."

At the end of her rope, she implored for some time to reflect. "Let's sit silently for a while and revel in the joy of our new friendship."

Friendship was a loose term; she was stuck with this guy. Maybe after some time to calm down and come to terms with this new Drew-caused development, she might be more receptive to getting to know Ruger. For now, one fact was glaringly clear: her new life in Miami was over already.

FIVE

AFTER HER EVENING drink with Potter, the plan was for Layla to return to the office to email Mandy a full report. That time had come and gone; Mandy would be seething. No doubt Potter had taken his business elsewhere already and had probably called Mandy to regale her with the tale of their meeting.

With darkness upon them, she didn't object when Ruger took them to a drive-through for food then pulled the truck into a motel parking lot. She remained in the truck listening to the radio while he went inside to pay for a room.

What had this Ruger guy packed for her? Did she have something to wear in bed? Shampoo? Toothpaste? The corporate account at the bar and her stashed apartment key meant she hadn't needed her purse. It would still be in her bedroom. That translated to no bank card, no ID, and not a cent to her name.

Ruger returned to the truck and opened her door. "Are you coming?"

Holding on to the food bag, she climbed out of the vehicle and waited for him to retrieve two cases from the back of the truck to take them inside.

"Left or right?" he asked, nodding at the twin beds.

"I don't care," she replied, closing the door.

He tossed one case onto the bed furthest from the door. "That's you." Putting the other case on the end of the other bed, he unzipped it and began to retrieve items. "Dig in and eat, don't wait for me."

On the table by the front window, she divided her food from his and dropped onto a hard chair to nibble at her burger. "What did you bring me?" she asked, eyeing the case he'd put on the bed indicated as hers.

"Check it out and see."

From his own luggage, he'd taken out a towel and a change of underwear, which he tossed aside with a razor and a couple of bottles. After another bite of her burger, she brushed her hands together and crossed to unzip her own suitcase. It was packed with clothes and toiletries too. He'd done a good job overall; except the only footwear she could see were ratty old running sneakers. She couldn't find nightwear either, but her disappointment was short-lived when she discovered her purse stuffed in the corner.

Screeching out, she threw everything else aside and pulled it out. "Ah! You brought my purse!"

"I have female relatives, including a mother, and I've had girlfriends," he said, planting himself in a chair at the table. "Guys know women value their purses… we just don't understand why."

Hugging her purse to her chest, she refrained from hugging him too. "If you expect me to bounce from motel to motel, I need my purse."

"We won't be bouncing from motel to motel," he said. "Getting off the road is the best way to make sure we're not found. I'm going to shower after we eat. Do you need anything?"

Layla wasn't sure what he meant about getting off the road, but she joined him at the table to finish her food. "Where are we going then?"

"Somewhere they'll never find you," he said, scooping up ketchup with his fries.

"You're trying to be mysterious again. If you won't be honest, I can just call Drew and he'll tell me."

"I didn't tell him where I'm taking you."

Drew didn't know where she was going to be with this virtual stranger? Safety wasn't her first concern. Having had some time to absorb all the new information, she found herself preoccupied with where her brother was and who might be after him.

"I don't like the idea of lying low while Drew is out there in trouble," she said, munching a fry. "We should be up there helping him."

"Helping him, how?" he asked with his mouth almost full. "He knows what he's doing. He has the support of friends way more lethal than me. Once Serendipity finds a publisher and releases the story—"

"Who cares about the story? Someone should call the cops."

"The cops don't care about a crooked politician who signs their boss' paychecks. Do you think they'll do anything to protect your brother? Half of them are probably on the take. Your brother burned a lot of bridges in law enforcement."

"You two watch too much television," she said, still eating. "He should go directly to the DA."

With a snort, he gave her a shrewd look. "Now who watches too much TV?" he asked, taking a bite of his burger. "You can't just stroll up to the DA and ask him to arrest someone. Anyway, the DA and Governor Ashcroft went to law school together. You're not going to see a traditional prosecution... at least not without public pressure."

"So you want a prosecution from the court of public opinion?" she asked, pushing the rest of her burger aside and slipping off her shoes. "Do you think Drew will be any safer after he reveals this guy's connections? Who is he connected to?"

"I don't know," he said. "Are you going to finish that?" She shook her head, prompting him to reach over his drink to pick up the remainder of her burger. "I haven't read his or Serendipity's notes."

"We need more information," she said. "Do you have a computer?"

"Not on me."

"Maybe Drew can email the details to us. If we can get to a café with Internet—"

"You think he's nuts for investigating this story, yet you want to investigate too?"

"If you can get me to Drew, you can go back to your life."

"Jansen told me not to bring you to him," he said, finishing off all the food left on the table, including her fries. "It's not safe to take you into the belly of the beast, and your brother wants to finish his work without distractions."

"You two spoke about that, but you didn't bother to ask about the criminality of the governor you voted for?"

"I didn't vote for him, I told you I don't live in Jersey," Ruger said. "Jansen is protective of this one."

"So the plan is to keep me out of it? My brother is your friend and you're happy with that? You're happy that he's up there and in danger?"

"They don't want to kill him, not until after they know what he knows and where he's stashed the evidence."

"I'm reassured," she said, going back to her suitcase to sort through the clothes again. "You didn't bring me anything to sleep in."

"I wasn't going to rifle through your underwear," he said, sucking grease from his fingers then crossing to retrieve a tee-shirt from his suitcase. "Wear that." He tossed the tee-shirt onto the pile of clothes in her case.

Maybe protecting her modesty had been his reason for not going through her underwear. But the truth was she didn't own jammies, so he would have struggled to find anything that could pass as nightwear.

She didn't object to the tee-shirt. "I want to take a shower first."

He bunched up the trash and tossed it in the can by the door. "Okay."

"What will you wear to bed?"

After glancing down at himself, he looked up at her. "Do you have a preference?"

"I don't want you getting any ideas," she said, pointing a finger. "You stay on your side of the room… and keep your jeans on."

"You want me to sleep in my jeans?"

"Yes," she said. "I don't want you stripping down and trying the old, 'Oops, sorry, I slipped and fell' routine."

His lips quirked. "Happened to you a lot?"

"Once," she said.

"You must date some classy guys. What happened to Mr. Clumsy?"

"He was a colleague, not a boyfriend. We were at a company conference, and he got my fist in the side of his face."

"I'm pretty steady on my feet, Layla. You've got nothing to worry about."

"Good," she said, snatching a motel towel from the end of her bed. "And don't think about making an excuse to come into the bathroom while I'm in the shower either."

"I have no interest in seeing you naked," he said, sitting on the bed to unlace and toe off his boots. "There's probably pay-per-view on the TV if I need relief with a view."

"You are not going to watch porn," she said. "I'm not sharing a room with a pervert."

Lying back on the bed, he stretched to reach for the remote on the nightstand. "You think watching porn makes a guy a pervert?"

She marched over to snatch the remote control from him. "A guy who watches porn while there's an unfamiliar woman naked in the next room taking a shower? Yes. A guy who gets himself aroused and plays with himself while there's a poor unsuspecting female trying to sleep in the bed beside his? Yes."

"Have you ever watched porn?"

She didn't want to answer that, his mischievous smile told her he knew it too. "Who asks a person that? We just met and you're asking me about porn? How would you feel if a man asked your sisters-in-law that question?"

"My brothers aren't married, but their girlfriends would answer that question. No problem. Lyssa makes a living asking questions like that and Bri's sexual history is synonymous with Blaser's. They learned everything together, I'd guess they tried porn together too. And this is about you. You don't look like the shy type. You look like the type who's got a few notches."

"Oh my God," she said, throwing the remote onto her bed and slamming her fists to her hips. "You are so insulting! Are you saying that I look like a slut?"

"You know what you're doing with men. You know how to play them."

"I do not!" she asserted. "What would make you say something like that?"

"You knew what you were doing when you put on that dress tonight. Your client could barely keep his tongue in his head."

Examining her dress, she pointed to the hem. "It's down to my knee... almost."

"You have great legs; those speak for themselves. But they were going to be under the table all night, so you used your other assets." He spoke to her breasts. "I'm more of an ass man myself, but those babies even caught my eye, good choice."

"Don't look at my chest," she said, taking her fists back to her hips. "That's a perverted thing to do when you're alone in a motel room with your friend's baby sister."

"I'm a red-blooded male, you don't think I looked? Doesn't mean I'm interested in touching." Rolling over, he reached for the remote on the edge of her bed and flicked on the TV. "I'm not paying for pay-per-view anyway. I'm tired. I'll stick to a game show or something, I promise."

Dropping onto the corner of her bed, she sighed. "Forget it."

"I thought you were going for a shower," he said, when she didn't make a move for the bathroom.

"I'm uncomfortable now."

His laugh took her off-guard, but he slid up the bed to sit on his pillows. "I'm really not interested in you and there's a lock on the bathroom door. Go for your shower. I promise I won't budge from this spot."

"You really don't try to put a woman at ease, do you?"

"I'm actually impressed you're being vigilant. But I jerked off this morning, so I can live without tonight."

Her mouth dropped open, but no breath entered her lungs. "You're gross," she said, getting up to head for the bathroom. "I hope your brothers know how gross you are and that they don't act this way with their women."

"I don't tend to talk to my brothers about that kind of thing but given they're both having sex with their women, they probably know each other's masturbatory habits."

"I can't believe you'd speak to me this way."

"I'm an open book," he said.

"Too open," she said with a scowl.

"You should talk to Lyssa about your sexual neuroses when you meet her. She'll really help you relax about it."

"I am relaxed about sex," she asserted. His remote-control occupied hand fell to the bed. Now she had his attention. Though she didn't want it in the way his lowered eyes and heightened brows suggested. "Relaxed doesn't mean I'm easy."

"Never said you were," he said, going back to his channel surfing.

"When I'm with a guy, I love sex. Lots of it. All the time," she said. His lips edged up while he flicked through channels. "You know exactly what I mean, you're just trying to rile me up."

"I'm sitting here not saying a thing, Legs. Take your tantrum into the shower and let a man rest up, huh?"

Drew said this guy had a great sense of responsibility. He seemed like a joker to her, a joker with low maturity. Despite being peeved, she didn't feel threatened, and retreated into the bathroom to wash off the day. She'd need a good night's sleep because tomorrow was going to be answers day from Ruger and more importantly, from her brother, Drew, too.

SIX

RUGER WAS ASLEEP by the time Layla got out of the shower. So much for him being there to protect her. Anyone could've walked in and delivered her to her very own *Psycho* shower scene because her protector was snoring as loud as a tractor—giving any prospective murderer all the audio cover needed to commit his crime.

Instead of waking him up and pointing that out, Layla changed into his tee-shirt, turned off the TV, and curled up in her own bed. Ruger might not be a Doberman when it came to ensuring her safety, but at least she knew he was there. As irritating as his snoring was at first, when she relaxed, the reminder of company in this predicament was soothing enough to help her drift off to sleep.

On the flip side, Ruger was out of bed, washed, and ready to leave, long before she got out of bed. He'd shaken her awake, almost literally tossed her into the shower, and got them on the road by ten a.m. They hadn't eaten breakfast, and she liked to have three meals a day, so was relieved when he said they were stopping for lunch.

As soon as she finished her last bite, Ruger was on his feet, paying the check and rushing her out the door again.

"That lunch place was really great," Layla said, rooting around in her purse for a napkin. "How did you know about that diner?"

"A sign on the highway told me about it," he said, concentrating on the road.

So he hadn't known about it before, he'd just come across it by accident. But it was a nice place. Their drive had been pretty quiet. She wasn't a morning person and liked to wake up in her own time. Apparently, Ruger was happy to greet the new day because he'd been chipper all day— annoyingly so. Only now, in early afternoon, was she beginning to feel her own buoyancy emerge.

"I want to pick the next motel," she said, wiping her fingers. "How long will it take to get to Jersey anyway?"

"We're not going to Jersey," he said. "Or to another motel."

She began to click through radio stations. "We're travelling north."

"There are places in a northerly direction other than New Jersey."

"Okay, where are we going then, Mr. Smarty Pants? Oh," she squealed, pausing on a Maria McKee song.

Objection to the song lingered on his lips, but he rolled his eyes instead of protesting. "We're going somewhere safe to stay with people I trust."

"People?" she asked between singing along. "What people? Who are we going to stay with? One of your skanky exes?"

"My mom," he said.

Having been about to hit a high note, she gasped in and choked on her own breath, which Ruger seemed to enjoy.

"Your mom? You're taking me home to your mother?"

"No one will look for you there. She lives in suburbia. You and I have no history, no connection. Ashcroft's men will never find you in my safe place. We'll be off the road and away from investigating eyes… we can stay there as long as I need to."

"You want us to move in with your mother? What if she thinks we're a thing? Do you take many women home?"

"My family know some of my exes," he said. "But I have female friends too. I don't have intimate relationships with every woman I know."

"Haven't you heard the adage that men and women can't be friends?" she asked, searching in her purse again.

"I've heard it, I don't believe it. I've been friends with a lot of women."

"Long-term, close friendships?"

"Some women I've known since I was a kid," he said. "We're not particularly close, I guess. I'm friends with the women at my brother's club."

"And you've never slept with, or wanted to sleep with them?"

"No."

"Same age bracket?"

"Some."

"I bet they wanted to sleep with you," she said, acquiring a brush from her bag to run it through her hair before she tied it back with the band from her wrist.

"You think I'm so hot women just can't resist me? Guess it wouldn't be the first time I've let a woman down gently. You're cute as a… no, wait, you're not cute…"

"Oh thanks, Mr. Picnic."

"No, I mean cute isn't the right word." He scratched his head like he was really considering what word did describe her. "You've got those legs and that sway in your hips when you walk… you're seductive—no!" Bolting up in his chair, he beamed at her. "Tantalizing, that's the word!"

"Tantalizing?" she repeated. Not the type to blush, she did squirm a little at that description. "Doesn't that mean I'm a tease?"

"No, not like that," he said, snatching her hand to give it a squeeze. "You torment a guy with your posture and your gait, you're self-assured and…" She didn't realize how much she relished his description of her until he glanced her way and stopped talking. He cleared his throat as though that was enough to clear his thoughts too. "You know you're fucking sexy. I would, that's all I'm saying."

"Last night you said you wouldn't."

"Last night you were worried I was going to attack you. I told you what you wanted to hear."

Lying shouldn't be encouraged, but it was sort of sweet that he'd tried to put her at ease, even if he didn't mean a word of it. "My point about friendship between men and women is that sex is a fact of life and it's something we all think about. But what do I know?" she asked. "Maybe life is different where you're from. I've never been able to figure men out."

"Don't play innocent, you know men. I bet you've had a string of them."

"Are you calling me a slut again?" she asked, zipping up her purse and tossing it into the backseat.

"No," he said. "You can have a string of men without banging them all. Are you telling me guys don't pay attention to you?"

"Is that a compliment?" she asked, propping an elbow on the shoulder of her seat.

"You know how to use your body, that's all I'm saying."

"Do both of your brothers live at home?"

Glancing at her and then the road, his eyes narrowed indicating he had no idea where the question had come from, but he answered it anyway. "No, neither of them does, but they live near enough to visit. I've got aunts and cousins who live in the same neighborhood I grew up in. I'm the youngest of my brothers, but one of the older cousins."

"I dread to think how you would influence youngsters. I hope your mother limits how much time you get to spend with the teenagers."

"I pass down my wisdom and they love it," he said, wearing a proud grin. "Warner kids are always light years ahead of the other kids their own age."

"Do you have a counsellor in the family? Most of the younger generation probably need it."

"We have a sex therapist," Ruger said. "If that counts."

"You're related to a sex therapist?"

"Actually she's marrying my brother, Colt. You'll love Lyssa, she says exactly what she thinks... like someone else we both know."

"I don't say exactly what I think, believe me, I censor myself more than you might think," she said, letting her interest drift to the side window. A worrying thought snapped it back to him. "You're not going to tell your mom and brothers about what's going on, are you? Did you tell her that we were coming? What story did you give her?"

"I didn't tell my mom we were coming."

Showing up unannounced was rude and she didn't want to draw unwanted attention. "Then how do you know if your parents are there or willing to accept visitors?"

"My mom always has space for me," he said. "They have a five-bedroom house, and my room is still my room."

"Aww, she keeps it as a shrine?"

Swooning at him made him grin, which hadn't been her intention.

"She can give you tips on how to start your own," he said, maintaining his swagger. "Do you want a lock of my hair?"

"How about a couple of liters of blood?"

"Typical woman, wants to bleed me dry."

"What should I know about your mom?" she asked, ready to change the subject.

The dumbest course of action would be to flirt with the man sent by her brother to kidnap her, especially when said man was so irritating and cocksure.

"Nothing, she's just a mom," he said, before letting a sly grin slink toward her. "You wouldn't be nervous, would you, Legs?"

"I'm not nervous, people love me."

"Do they?" He smiled. "I guess I'm the exception."

"You just said you wanted to have sex with me," she said, grateful of the chance to remind him.

"Guys can sleep with a woman they don't like, easy. I'd screw you. That doesn't mean I listen when you talk."

"What guy does?" she asked, not expecting an answer. "I can't help it if you're odd. I suppose you like to rebel against the norm."

"Funny, because your brother says you're a pain in the ass who speaks her mind too readily to make a decent first impression on anyone."

Verbally sparring was fun. Though her words could be scathing, she didn't mean any harm. Did Ruger really think of her as cold and bitchy? Did her brother? Wow, that actually hurt.

"He's entitled to his opinion," she mumbled, shifting in her seat.

"What?" Ruger asked, glancing at her. "That's it? No snarky come back?"

"We won't get to your mom's until after dinner, will we?"

"No, we'll be on the road for a few more hours."

"Good," she said, going back to her radio flicking. "Do you have any requests?"

"Have at it, Legs."

Something curious in his tone discouraged her from looking at him. Could he sense her discomfort? If he could, she didn't want to face it. She needed time to gather her composure again so cranked up the music and began to sing.

SEVEN

THEIR DESTINATION WAS CLEAN, and the people appeared classy. Without a sign of poverty or graffiti anywhere, it was an unblemished suburb not too far from the neighboring city. They drove down residential streets flanked by beautiful homes with green lawns and cherry trees. She even saw a white picket fence around one house.

All her adult life, she bounced from city to city. It had been a long time since she'd absorbed suburban living. Her mother had done her best for her and Drew. They lived modestly yet hadn't wanted for anything growing up. After medical bills and the cost of college, her mother had nothing left to leave them when she died.

Winding through the streets, Ruger swung the truck into a wide driveway facing a double garage. The red brick house with pristine windows and glossy white eaves dried her mouth. The gleaming lawn of the front yard finished off the picture-perfect scene.

Ruger got out and came around to open her door. He took her hand and pulled her out, then slammed the door.

"We'll get the bags out after we've said hello," he said, and led her up the drive to a gate between the garage and house.

Through the gate and down a path, they ended in a vast backyard. He took her up four shallow slate stairs and opened a white door.

"Hello! Hello!" he hollered.

Someone screeched. "My baby is home!"

Ruger was pulled into the arms of a woman Layla couldn't see. All she could see were two arms trying their best to hold onto Ruger's form. On the other side of the hugging pair, inside the house, was more activity. Layla was happy to stay right there on the external stairs, hidden behind Ruger. Wonderful smells of wholesome food drifted out; her stomach rumbled.

"I'm ovulating and your brother isn't home," a female voice said from inside.

"Give me a minute to get in the door before you demand my seed, Lys," Ruger said. "You should ask your fiancé's twin. Their sperm has got to be interchangeable, right?"

Ruger was taken further inside, leaving her open to viewings. A woman with blonde hair and little pearl earrings caught sight of her and beamed. Layla couldn't remember a person ever being so immediately happy to see another person.

"You brought a girl!" the woman said with Disneyesque enthusiasm. "He brought a girl home!"

Layla was grabbed and yanked further inside. The blonde woman turned her around three hundred and sixty degrees to scrutinize everything about her.

"Uh, hello," Layla said.

Two other women sat on stools positioned around the kitchen's central island. The huge room contained a large range and had wooden countertops with glossy cabinet doors.

"This is my mom," Ruger said. "Prudence Warner. Pru to her friends. And that's my sister, Lyssa, and her best friend, Suzette."

"Your sister?" Layla asked. Ruger had corrected her that neither of his brothers were actually married. Deducing from other things he'd said, she took a guess at who the "*sister*" was. "Oh, the sex therapist."

"Have you been talking about me, Littlest Warner?" Lyssa asked, which was funny because Ruger was like six five and much bigger than the others in the room.

"This is Layla," Ruger said, concluding the introductions.

"She's beautiful, Ruger," Pru said, hugging her then joining her hand with Ruger's. "She's just gorgeous and perfect for you. She's wonderful."

Before they'd arrived, she'd assumed there was no need for a cover story. The gleam in Pru's eyes reminded her of what Ruger said about his mother's desire for grandchildren. Though she tried to extricate herself, she failed. Pru was holding on too tight, and Ruger was happy to curl his fingers around hers, encouraging his mother's exuberance.

"Wait until you get to know her before you make that judgment, Mom," Ruger said.

"All of my boys are finally matched," Pru said and leaned past the couple to close the back door. "We've had dinner, but there are leftovers if—"

"Not right now, Mom," Ruger said. "We've been driving all day. Is Dad home?"

"Bowling," Pru said, going to the furthest countertop to retrieve the coffeepot. Pru poured two new mugs of coffee and carried them to the center island where there was cream and sugar. "Come and sit down with us. We were just chatting."

"Girl talk," Ruger said.

His hand fell out of hers and landed on the small of her back to urge her forward. Despite her attempts to resist, he propelled her on until she stumbled and had to catch the island for support.

"How do you take your coffee, Layla?" Lyssa asked, standing up to lift one mug of coffee.

"Just like that is fine," she said, with little choice but to accept the hospitality.

Lyssa smiled and put the cup in front of a stool beside Suzette.

"She looks terrified," Suzette said to Lyssa.

"She'll be fine," Pru said. "We'll look after her."

"Good, 'cause I have to get the shit out of the car," Ruger said.

And now she wished she'd kept his hand. She'd hold on and never let go. Was he really just going to leave her with these strangers? There was no time to reprimand him, or beg for his company, because his mom stood up again.

"You watch your mouth around the ladies," Pru scolded her son. "You might get away with that around your father and brothers, but you know I won't tolerate—"

"Okay, Ma, I'm sorry. I'm tired, it won't happen again."

"Hmm," Pru said, locking her evil eye onto him.

Turning around to see if the glare worked, she was horrified to see him retreat from the house. The back door swung shut, leaving her with no choice except to turn around and face the truth—she'd been abandoned with his family.

"Sit down," Pru said, pointing at the stool Suzette had pushed out. "Tell us about yourself."

"Where did you meet Ruger?" Suzette asked. "Have you been together for long?"

Edging along to the stool, she wrapped her hands around the mug Suzette positioned for her. Taking a drink bought her a little time. What should she say to these women, who were clearly close to each other and expecting her to become a part of their harem?

"Well, uh…"

"Don't pressure her," Lyssa said. "This is a daunting environment. She's coming home to meet the family of the man she's in a relationship with. The last thing she needs is to feel like she's under the microscope."

"Thank you," Layla said, pleased someone understood the intimidating situation. "But Ruger and I, we're not… I mean… he's not…"

"He hasn't made his intentions clear?" Pru asked and tsked. "That boy, he thinks the answer to everything is a joke.

I'm sure he cares for you a great deal. He has never brought a woman back to spend the night with him before."

Sure she would drop down dead right here, Layla struggled to take in a breath. "No, we—"

"Don't talk to her about sex, Pru," Suzette said. "Don't get Lyssa started. She'll have the whole relationship dissected in ten minutes."

"Ten minutes? It's hardly going to take me that long," Lyssa said. "Ruger makes jokes to prevent himself confessing truths that may get him hurt. He's human. He needs love in his life just as much as the rest of us, but he's afraid of getting hurt. He's afraid of commitment."

"Find me a man who isn't," Suzette mumbled and lifted her mug to drink her coffee.

"Colt isn't," Lyssa said.

Though the therapist's smile didn't quite reach smug, her pride in her partner was clear.

"Your boyfriend?" Layla asked.

"Fiancé," Pru said.

Lyssa held out her hand to show Layla her engagement ring. It was beautiful, no doubt about it, but she'd seen her share of diamonds. None of them had tempted her into making the commitment.

"Hey, watch what you're doing with that thing," Ruger's voice sounded at the same time the back door squeaked. "Those things make Lay turn on her heels and run for the horizon. I need to keep her in one place for now."

He carried on across the kitchen with their luggage and disappeared through a swinging door on the other side of the room. Drew's History of Layla course obviously covered more than just the basics. When she turned back to the women, their piqued curiosity made her bristle.

"I have no idea what he's talking about," Layla said, finding solace in her coffee again.

"Did Ruger propose to you?" Suzette asked with an audible inhale and an open mouth. "I don't believe it for a second."

"Ruger? No," Layla answered. "But I've been proposed to before and I haven't accepted a man yet."

"Fascinating," Lyssa exhaled and pushed her cup aside. "How many times have you been proposed to?"

"Total, technically… six."

"Six!" Suzette and Pru said in time with each other.

"Technically," Lyssa said, so intrigued that she leaned closer. "That's an interesting distinction, why did you use that word?"

"Because three times were the same guy," Layla said. "That should just count as one, right?"

"Four different men have proposed to you?" Suzette asked. "How do you do it? How do you get them to propose?"

"I don't," Layla said, lifting her shoulders. "Things are always going good. We're having a great time, and then they ruin it by… you know."

"Ruin it," Lyssa said. "You think a proposal ruins a relationship?"

"It changes it," Layla said. "It becomes a different thing entirely. It becomes this monster. As soon as anyone knows you're engaged, there's all the pressure of meeting the family. Everyone wants to know when it's going to happen and what kind of wedding you want. Then they want to grill you about your values, how you envision your marriage, where you'll live, how many kids you'll have." A shudder of revolted anxiety fluttered through her. "No, thanks. You can keep all that."

She took another mouthful of coffee, but the silence was conspicuous, so she had to take a look at the faces around her. Pru was frowning and Suzette gaped, but Lyssa was grinning.

"Could I tempt you onto my couch?" Lyssa asked her.

"You on that already?" Ruger strode into the room and propped a hand on the counter beside her to scoop up her coffee and gulp down the rest of it. "She doesn't want to be on your couch and neither do I."

"Everyone else has had a turn," Suzette said. "I've been getting free advice from Lyssa for years. Bri's been on Lyssa's couch, and she got Blaser there too. Even Colt has—"

"He doesn't count," Ruger said. "He's been on her couch for a whole different reason. One that nearly got both of them arrested."

That was a story Layla wanted to hear, but for now, she just craned her neck to look up at him. "Where did you put my things?"

"Upstairs in the bedroom," he said. "There's a bathroom down the hall, I'll show you—"

"We're not finished getting to know each other yet," Prudence said. "If you whisk her up the stairs, we won't see either of you again until morning."

"You won't see me until morning anyway," he said. "I'm going out."

"Out?" Layla said, glad that this time she got to speak first. Apparently, you had to be fast if you wanted to be heard in this family. "You are not going out and leaving me here."

"You'll be safe," he said, stroking a hand between her shoulder blades. "My dad has four hundred weapons in the house. You should see the closet in the basement. It's like a military bunker."

"It is not. Don't scare the girl," Pru said. "She'll think we're crazies."

"She's dating Ruger," Suzette said. "He's as crazy as they come."

"Are you going to Risqué?" Lyssa asked, returning to her drink.

"What's Risqué?" Layla asked.

"Blaser's club," Ruger said.

"His strip club?" she asked, trying to crane her neck to gawp at him. But he was so close she couldn't make eye contact. That didn't stop her shock coming out. "You're going to leave me here to go stare at naked women?"

"The jealous type," Suzette muttered.

"Jealous and yet scared to commit to a man," Lyssa said. "Fascinating."

"You think everything's fascinating," Ruger said, sounding jaded. The cynicism left his voice when he gave the women his next instruction. "Don't hassle Layla, she's had a hard time."

"A hard time?" Prudence asked.

The matriarch's question was forgotten because Lyssa spoke. "You're protective of her. Why did you bring her here, Ruger? What do you think introducing her to the family will do?"

"Distract her," Ruger said.

"Distract me while you go to drool over other women?" Layla asked.

"*Other* women?" he asked, dropping his attention to hers, increasing the pressure of his hand on her upper back. "Have you got a problem with me admiring the female form, Legs?"

"Didn't we have this conversation last night? About you being a red-blooded male and your proclivity for admiring what you should keep your corneas off?"

"She's feisty," he said with another smile as though explaining her behavior to the rest of his family before he addressed her. "You are jealous."

"I am not jealous," Layla muttered, keeping the conversation private from the trio of women around the island would be impossible. "I'm telling you it's inappropriate and it makes me uncomfortable. You can't leer and expect women to be happy with your reaction to them."

"Ruger frequents Risqué and knows the women," Lyssa chimed in. "You don't need to concern yourself with him becoming aroused at the sight of the women there. Any who had an interest in him, or who he had an interest in, would've staked their claim long ago."

"What about Destiny?" Suzette asked Lyssa.

Layla was intrigued by the mention of the woman who made Lyssa nod.

"He and Destiny are close," Lyssa said with a slight nod. "But he's sent no signals that he returns the interest she frequently shows in him."

"Destiny is not interested in me," he said. Modesty didn't come naturally to him. "We're friends, that's all."

"You've never slept with her? You've never thought about it?" Suzette asked. "The way you guys flirt..."

"What about it?" Ruger asked, opening his hands. "We flirt, it's harmless."

"We'll see how harmless it is when she hears you've moved a woman into your mother's house," Suzette said.

"Which I wouldn't have to do if someone wasn't taking up residence in my apartment, would I?" he said, eyeing Suzette.

"You can stay with Colt and me if you would prefer that, Littlest Warner," Lyssa offered.

"Are you kidding? The way you two are going at it with the baby-making thing? No thanks."

"I'm sure you'd rather overhear Colt and I making love than you would hear your parents being intimate."

"Yeah, okay," Ruger said, holding up his hands. "Now you're crossing a line."

Layla liked the way Lyssa and Pru shared a smile. "He's just the same as Colt," Lyssa said. "They're so narrow-minded about intimacy."

"Oh," Layla said, swiveling to Ruger. "Now who's narrow-minded?"

"About my parents having sex?" he said. "Yeah, check that off the list, Lay. That's one thing I'll always be intolerant talking about."

"We all have boundaries I suppose," Layla said, subduing her smile.

"Okay, you ladies spend the night putting the world to rights," Ruger said. "I'm going to where the men are."

"Colt isn't at Risqué," Lyssa said when Ruger pushed away from the counter. "He's working… It's a favor for Chavez, and I'm telling you it better be worth it."

"Chavez?" Layla asked.

"My nephew," Pru said. "You'll get to know the family in time. He works for the police."

"And it was him who hooked Lyssa and Colt up," Ruger said. "Are you forgetting that, sis? I think you owe him one."

"And I'd be happy to pay," Lyssa said. "But does it have to cost us our future family?"

"So go find Colt on his stakeout," Suzette said.

"It's hard to be discreet about watching someone if your fiancée is riding you in the front seat," Lyssa said, dipping a finger in her coffee then sucking it dry. "I'll give it another hour and if he's not home, I'll find out where he is."

"You want to get pregnant before you're married?" Layla asked.

"Colt wants kids," Lyssa said. "What's important to me is knowing they'll be born into a loving family, and you don't get much more loving than the Warner clan."

"You're not afraid that… that you'll get pregnant and never get down the aisle?"

"No," Lyssa said.

Each of the women were amused by the question.

Ruger rubbed her back again. "Wait until you see the two of them together, then you'll know she has nothing to worry about," he explained, bowing close. "Colt is cuckoo-crazy in love with her."

"They got their marriage license," Pru squeaked, then covered her lips with her fingertips.

"Excellent," Ruger said. "Have you set a date yet?"

"We were talking about that tonight when something else came up," Lyssa said.

"Something else what?" he asked.

Pru and Lyssa turned their attention to Suzette, who hissed at them both. "Nothing."

"Okay," Ruger said. "I'm going out, everyone, be good."

He patted her shoulder and spun around to stride out.

Layla wasn't going to let him run away that easily. "Excuse me."

Rotating on her butt and bouncing off the stool, she hurried after Ruger and caught up with him on the path between the house and garage.

Grabbing his arm, she pulled him to a halt. "What's up, Legs?" he asked.

"You can't bring me here and then run off to get drunk with your brothers," she whispered.

"You think that's what I'm doing?" he said. Taking hold of her elbow, he nudged her back to the wall and rested his forearm above her head. "Look, my brothers know everything about the favor I owe your brother. But like I said, I've been in Miami all week and haven't filled them in on the latest developments. I'm going to Risqué to talk to Blaser because your safety means as much to him as it does to me."

"It does?" She didn't get it. "But I've never met either of your brothers."

"It's a long story. Just stay here and lay low. It's late and like I said, Ashcroft's men won't put you and me together, so you're safe here with my mom and Lyssa."

"They think that we're together," she hissed. "They asked me if you had proposed."

He flashed a smile. "My mom wants her boys to be taken care of. You can tell them we're not together. Tell them the whole truth if you want, I trust them."

"So why didn't you tell them all about it before we arrived?"

"Because this is not my story to tell. The mess Jansen helped out with involved Blaser's girl, Bri. Blaser knows what's going on because Bri told him, and if I know them, they're not far away from each other tonight. Knowing you're safe and that we're repaying this debt will make Blaser feel better. He has contacts who can help to keep you safe, so he needs to know we're back in town."

"So take me with you," she said. "Let me meet Blaser and Bri—"

"You will. But not tonight. I don't plan to hang around at Risqué for long. I'll tell Blaser what's going on and then I'll hit the hay."

"Can't you just call him? What's the point of leaving if you're just going to come back and sleep?"

"I will crash in Colt's office. He has an office at Risqué. You can take my bedroom upstairs here. I'll be back before breakfast, don't worry."

"You're going to leave me here all night?" Shifting her weight, she didn't want to reveal how uncomfortable the situation made her. "I'm not great with moms."

"You don't have to be great with my mom, she'll do all the bonding, I promise you."

"Why do we have to bond? I'm not going to have your babies."

"That's reassuring for both of us," he muttered. "Just be yourself. Think of her as a client you're trying to impress. You don't have to do much, just smile along with the conversation. My dad will be back in an hour. After that, Lyssa and Suzette will split."

"So I'll be left alone with your parents?"

"My mom will show you to my bedroom and give you towels. Just stay in the bedroom until I get back."

"In the morning?"

"Right. Are you going to tell them the truth?"

"Do you want them to think we're together?" she asked.

If she had to endure being there alone, she didn't want to break Pru's heart. Of course, she didn't want to feign a relationship with Ruger either.

"I don't care," he said. "I'll keep your secret for you if that's what you want. I love my mom and I'd trust her with my life, but she knows everyone in this town. If you tell her there's a hitman after you, she'll assume it's every stranger she sees. I don't want to upset her like that."

When she swayed side to side, she wiggled a finger into his ribs. "You really are a momma's boy," she said with a teasing slant to her mouth.

"Tease all you like, I love my family and I'd never do anything to endanger them," he said, removing her finger from his torso.

"Then I shouldn't stay here," she said, losing her ease. "I can go to a hotel and—"

"You can't use any of your cards, and you can't withdraw cash either. I already told you we're dealing with people who have connections."

Searching for an alternative, her focus flitted left to right. "I could transfer money into your account and you could withdraw it for me?"

"No, that won't work either. If you transfer money from your account to mine, Ashcroft's guys might find the connection and our cover will be blown. We can't do anything to put us together. So for now, you stay here, you have to… And you can't call your brother either, just in case they're monitoring his calls."

"If they are, they heard me talking to him in your truck."

"My phone has a trace block and a scrambler," he said as though it was no big deal. "No one can hear me or see who I'm talking to."

"What kind of sales are you in?" she asked, wondering why anyone would have such elaborate security on their cellphone.

"I told you that my job wasn't typical, and I know some guys in electronics who like to share their gadgets."

"Can I use your phone?"

"Tomorrow," he said. "I have to get to Blaser. Once I've told him what's going on, he'll help me figure out the next step."

"You're not reassuring me. Again, you're making me worry."

"I brought you here, to a safe place, and now I'm going to make sure we have the manpower to keep you alive. I'll try to get a hold of your brother tonight, but it's getting late. I don't know if he'll answer his phone."

"He'll answer," she said. "Or I'll get on a train up to Jersey just to piss him off."

"Your revenge will be short-lived because you'll be delivering yourself to the people who want you dead."

"I see that your repertoire doesn't extend into optimism," she said, reminded of how dangerous optimism could be. "Fine, I'll go back inside and sit with your family, but I won't forget you dumped me here."

"Course not, how else could you pass judgment on people if you so easily let things go? I know a grudge-holder when I see one."

"Others might find you funny, I'm not on that list."

"I'm observant," he said. "And you, Legs, are a lady with a chip on your shoulder."

"Have you ever taken anything seriously in your life?"

Bringing himself lower, he fixed his eyes to hers. "There's only one thing I take seriously."

"Oh yeah, what's that?"

"In a place you'll have my complete concentration," he said.

Brushing his hand down her cheek, he pushed away from the wall and disappeared out of the gate to the driveway.

What did the intensity of those eyes imply? Probably best not to over think it. Ruger was a joker, a guy who sailed through life without a worry because he didn't care about anything enough to let it bother him. Except he'd said he loved his family and didn't mind when she teased him about it. There was something under his blithe surface, something he would never let her see.

EIGHT

"SO YOU JUST LEFT HER THERE?"

Ruger had been at Risqué for almost half an hour. That was the first chance Blaser had to come talk to him. The club was busy and while that was good for his brother, it meant waiting for attention. Usually he would come to visit the club after he got back in town, but he'd wait until the wee hours when Blaser was closing up shop.

Waiting until later hadn't been an option. If he had stayed at his parents' house until Risqué was closed, his mom would have stayed up to quiz him about the new woman in his life. He could have handled his mother's interrogation. What he couldn't handle anymore was being in close proximity to the legs that had teased him throughout their long drive from Miami.

"What else was I supposed to do?" Ruger asked, swirling the beer left in the bottom of his bottle.

That corner of the bar was reserved for family. Behind the bar was accessed there in the dark corner where the family enjoyed some privacy from the patrons admiring the women doing their work.

"Not leave her there," Blaser said, spreading his hands wide on the bar. "You left her with Mom, Lyssa, and Suzette. That's like leaving a lamb to the slaughter."

"Not this chick," Ruger said, looking down the neck of his bottle. "She can handle it. She can handle anything."

"Why are you looking out for her then?" Blaser asked. "If you think she can take on the world—"

"She'd sure try it. If these guys got a hold of her, they'd want to hurt her. They'd probably keep on torturing her until they got her brother to back off."

"And that matters to you?"

"You know why it matters to me," he said, making eye contact. "Jansen saved Bri's life."

A life that was only put in danger because he had refused to work for the gang's leader. He wanted to make amends, but no matter how many steps he took in that direction, he could never shake the guilt that curled itself around his shoulders and tightened inside his chest.

"Lyssa knows what happened with Bri. She knows what crap you're mixed up in. Once Colt knows about this deal you made with Jansen—"

"It wasn't a deal. I went to see him, just like I said I would. When I heard what he was dealing with, I thought helping him out with his sister was the least I could do."

"Yeah, and that's cool," Blaser said. "You're right, we do owe him. You know that Colt and I will do whatever it takes to repay the debt we owe him."

"Do I hear a but?"

"Taking her to Mom was extreme."

"Not the way I see it," Ruger said, pushing his bottle aside to rest his forearms on the bar. "I had to take her somewhere and Suzette is still in my apartment."

"That's another of your good deeds that's blown up in your face. I don't think she's ever moving out of there."

"You could talk to her."

"Oh no, that's your mess. All your mess," Blaser said. "I'm not kicking Suzie out. She's paying rent on time every month and you won't hear me arguing with that."

Blaser did have enough on his plate. He owned and managed not only the strip club but an auto garage too. Managing the apartment complex he lived in was another of his responsibilities. Suzette lived in Ruger's apartment in that same building. The offer to let Suzette stay in his place was meant to be a temporary solution and he'd done it under heightened circumstances. Being a nice guy wasn't meant to cost him his home.

"Are Dax and Ivy home?" Another couple who lived in the same apartment complex.

Blaser nodded as he wiped down the bar. "Got in last night and they're not the sort of couple to let you crash at their place either."

"What about Bri? You could talk to her."

"About what? She and Suzette aren't that close. If you want someone to talk Suzette into moving out, Lyssa's your girl."

"No, you could talk to Bri about staying with you until this is over. Come on, bro, I need to stash Layla somewhere. She can't stay with Mom indefinitely."

"I'd love to have Bri in my place full-time," Blaser said. "But you know what Lyssa says about rushing her."

The captivity Bri had endured after being taken by Victor's gang traumatized her. Rather the rape she'd been subjected to made her wary. Ruger understood that. His brother had been patient with the woman he loved and although everyone knew they were having sex, Bri still wasn't quite ready to integrate her life with Blaser's round-the-clock.

What else could he suggest? All ten apartments in the complex were one bedroom. He couldn't even ask anyone to put Layla up because there was no room for a houseguest.

"You know that Mom won't complain," Blaser said, tossing a bar towel over his shoulder. "She'll look after Layla better than any of the rest of us could. She'll have the girl fed and pampered every hour of the day."

"I'm not sure if it's Layla I'm worried about or Mom."

"Mom? Why would you worry about her?"

"Layla likes to speak her mind and doesn't pull her punches."

Blaser's lips quirked. "Is that so?"

"Yeah," Ruger said, taking a deep breath and picking at the label on his bottle. "She just opens her mouth and lets out the sass. She's not shy about telling someone when they're out of line. She voices her opinion about what Jansen's doing and calls me out on my behavior like she has the right to comment on our lives.

"Last night, we were in this motel, and she gave me grief because I made a stupid joke about porn. I mean, come on, it was a joke, and it's not like she doesn't have enough sass to go around. The girl is quick-witted and makes fun of me, but I don't think she likes it when I give it back to her and—" Lifting his focus from the bar, he was surprised to see Blaser rubbing a hand over his mouth, doing a terrible job of hiding his amusement. "What's the matter with you?"

"Nothing," Blaser said, quickly clearing his expression. "I guess you'll have to stay with Mom while this is going on too."

"Stay with Mom? No way, I couldn't move back in there."

"Mom's is always your first stop when you come home," Blaser said. "She loves nothing more than spoiling her baby. And now she knows Colt and I have women of our own to keep us in line, she doesn't have to worry about us."

"Where is Bri?" Ruger asked, scanning the room.

"She's at Ivy's," Blaser said, resting his hands on the bar again. "Bri was looking after the garage while Ivy was away, so she said she was going there to bring Ivy up to speed. I think it's an excuse to drink wine and make fun of guys, or whatever women do, but I'm just happy to see her smiling."

"She would have sympathy for me."

"Sympathy is going to be hard for you to find on this one," Blaser said. "All you have to do is stay at home for a couple of weeks. It's really not a big deal."

"Easy for you to say, you're not the one being subjected to it."

"Subjected to what? Mom's cooking? You love it. She'll do all your laundry, turn down your bed, draw you a bath, whatever the hell you want, because she loves taking care of you. You afraid of looking like a momma's boy in front of Layla?"

"No! I told her I love Mom, I'm not ashamed of that."

"So if Mom isn't the problem…" Blaser said, leaving the question hanging in the air.

"What?" Ruger asked, sitting straighter. "I don't have a problem with Dad."

"Which leaves one other person who's currently in the house."

Glancing behind Blaser, Ruger nodded to show his brother there were two waitresses waiting. When he noted them, Blaser left the family corner to go and deal with the orders.

So Blaser was implying he'd have a problem with Layla? Did he? He couldn't figure that one out. He was great with women. They loved his easy manner and his jokes. It didn't hurt that he wasn't hideous to look at either. He'd never met a woman he couldn't flirt into submission, not that he took advantage of the opposite sex, he just found it easy to ingratiate himself with them.

"Hey, baby."

Destiny strutted over. Holding her arms wide, she draped one over his shoulders and the other around his chest. She was such a pixie of a woman that she almost couldn't reach the breadth of him to link her fingers. She hung them around his neck instead, pushing her breasts into his arm and pressing a loud kiss to his cheekbone.

"Hey, Destiny," he said, tipping his head back to finish off his beer.

"Why so blue?" she asked, laying her head on his shoulder. "You've been over here all night with that scowl on your face."

"I'm not scowling," he said.

Crystal rounded him to enter the bar and spun around to examine his expression. "Yes, you are," she said, dropping her elbows to the bar to prop her chin on the heels of her hands. "You want a private dance?"

"I'll volunteer," Destiny said, rubbing her nose back and forth on his ear. "Will that put a smile on your face?"

"I'm smiling," he said, forcing himself to do just that. "See."

"It's a girl," Crystal said to Destiny. "Any guy that determined not to let it show can only be smarting over a girl. Anyone we know?"

"Oh, you are hooking up?" Destiny straightened but kept one arm around his shoulders. The other hand went to her cleavage. "My heart is breaking."

He might have worried about Destiny's statement after what he'd heard at the house about others' opinions on his relationship with the stripper. But Destiny was wearing a smile as wide as her face, so she obviously wasn't being serious.

Crystal laughed and leaned over the bar to rest a hand on his shoulder. "You Warner boys never will let one have something that the others don't, will ya?"

"What does that mean?" Ruger asked.

"Colt is getting married, and Blaser has Bri," Crystal said. "You're not going to be far behind."

His laugh loosened his shoulders. "Not me, sweetheart. I'm avoiding that particular abattoir."

"Poor thing," Crystal said to Destiny.

"Denial," Destiny said to Crystal's nod.

"Why should I tie myself down when I have such a delectable buffet to sample right here?" he said, looping an arm around Destiny. "There's plenty of me to keep all you ladies happy. I care about all of you. I'm not a one-woman man."

"You're not allowed to sample the women in here," Crystal said. "Colt's rule, remember?"

"Hey, both my brothers hooked up with women who were waitresses in here."

"Man's got a point," Destiny said.

"You ladies get in line. I'll show you how much love there is to go around."

"Room three is free," Crystal said to Destiny who took his hand.

He hadn't exactly meant to imply that he wanted a private dance. But it wouldn't be the first time he'd auditioned a girl who ended up working there, though he had never slept with any of the Risqué girls.

Rising from the stool, he figured it couldn't hurt to let Destiny strut her stuff. But before he turned around, he caught a glimpse of a familiar form coming in the main entrance on the other side of the bar.

"Fuck," he whispered, crouching to get a better view of the woman suddenly lit by a bright pink flare from the stage. "Rain check, sweetheart."

Ducking to kiss Destiny's cheek, he put a hand to her waist and pushed her into the bar to get past her.

Twisting and weaving through men and employees, Ruger got to the opposite side of the bar to meet the woman wearing the dress she'd had on when they met.

"Layla," he said in a stern tone he didn't recognize as his. How did his father's voice get into his throat? Layla spun around, her glittering eyes pleased with themselves, which only made his brows clamp down. "I told you to stay at home."

Grabbing her arm, he hauled her to the wall behind the last booth in the row.

"Yeah," she said, clutching her purse to her hip. "Then I remembered, you're not my father, my brother, or my parole officer, so you have no right to dictate my movements."

"No right? I'm the guy keeping you safe, that gives me plenty of rights over you."

"Does it?" she asked, tilting her head. "I haven't seen any danger yet. In fact, if my brother hadn't verified your story, I'd think you're keeping me around for another reason."

"What kind of reason?"

Noticing that his grip was still around her arm, he dropped it to his side. His body was cloaking hers from the rest of the room. With the booth to his left, he could angle his body to keep her exactly where he wanted her. The physical contact was unnecessary, touching her was an indulgence.

Her dark hair swooped to one side and was held in place by a clasp that sparkled when the light from the stage cast over them. It was hypnotizing, but he didn't remember packing it with the rest of her things. The swathes of glossy hair reflected the light too reminding him of being parked outside her apartment complex, in the Miami heat, seeing her for the first time in the flesh. All he'd seen were long, tanned legs, and the reasons for being there in Miami completely fell out his head. He hadn't bothered to look at the face connected to those legs hurrying down the external stairs of the apartment building he'd been staking out. The sandals with the skinny heel accentuated the sculpted calf and the svelte thighs under a short, see-through skirt that gave him a clear view of the outline of the rest of those thighs.

"Hey!" Layla said and smacked his chest, bringing him back from that memory.

For a few seconds on that stifling day, he'd considered pursuing those legs, but then he'd caught sight of the face attached to them.

The same one pouted up at him right then.

"What?"

"Move aside," Layla said. "I want a drink."

"You can't use your cards. Didn't I say that already? Repeatedly?"

"I have cash in my purse."

"Which you should ration because we don't know how long it has to last you. Do you think booze is the best way to spend your meager funds?"

"Drew will get money to me if he has to," she said. Opening her fist, which was still on his chest, she pushed her palm into his pectoral muscle. "Will you please move?"

He had no good reason not to move, not now she was there. With Blaser and security, it was actually easier to keep her safe there than it was to leave her unprotected at his mother's.

Doing as she asked, he side-stepped. She wiped away her glare to replace it with a warm smile baring no resemblance to the harsh, judgmental woman he'd accused her of being. Full of confidence, she sashayed across the room. More than a few of the patrons took their eyes away from the dancers on stage to watch the clothed woman make her way to the bar.

He hated that anger visited him at the sight of men ogling the same legs he could be accused of ogling himself. She went to the bar and slapped a hand onto it. Anyone in proximity who hadn't been looking at her before was looking after that. She didn't mind though; she was focused on Blaser who left the order he was filling to cross to her.

Starting toward the bar, he reached Layla's side in time to hear Blaser laughing at something she said.

"Bet you're glad Bri's not here now," Ruger said.

Blaser's laugh faltered to a frown. "What?"

"Nothing," Ruger mumbled.

He'd been a second away from berating his brother for flirting with a woman in spite of the girlfriend he had waiting at home.

Jesus.

Blaser and Bri weren't jealous, they only had eyes for each other. That was the reason Bri could help Blaser run a club full of half-naked women without ever complaining or being insecure. Blaser didn't notice any other woman when Bri was around. No amount of flesh would distract him from his love for his high school sweetheart.

Ruger knew that and didn't really think Blaser was making a play. For some reason, his instinct to get between Layla and another man was overwhelming. So much so that he hadn't recognized he was going to do something about it until he'd already spoken.

"Someone missed dinner," Layla said to Blaser in explanation of Ruger's behavior. Leaning back to put an arm around him, she patted his stomach and pouted at his brother. "If Ruger hadn't been in such a rush to ditch me, he might have enjoyed his momma's leftovers. He was in too much of a hurry to come out and play."

"Playing sounds like Ruger all right," Blaser said. "But my baby brother has never been accused of being in any kind of a hurry."

"Ah, you're Blaser," Layla said, holding a hand across the bar, Blaser shook it in introduction. "I should've known. I'm Layla."

"I'd figured that out," Blaser said, giving her back her hand.

"Has Ruger been talking about me?"

Blaser's mouth opened, and he inhaled in prelude to speech.

Worried what his brother would say, Ruger was quick to shut him up before he started. "Just get the girl her drink, will you?" he said, not appreciating the smirk on his brother's face as he withdrew to fill Layla's order. Ruger pulled up a stool beside hers. "You could have raided my mother's liquor cabinet if you had a habit you haven't clued me in about."

"I don't have a habit," she said, closing her hands over her purse on the bar.

Blaser brought her drink and she nodded in thanks.

She was too busy trying to catch the straw with her tongue to notice the look he and Blaser exchanged before Blaser went back to filling his waitresses' orders.

"Why did you come?" Ruger asked. "Why here? You could've gone to any bar in the city."

"Because Lyssa and Suzette said this was sort of a family hang out, for the younger generations at least. Your mom says she's never been here."

"Not while it's open, no," Ruger said, regretting leaving Layla alone with such a wealth of information and women who enjoyed sharing it. "You told her you were coming here?"

"Lyssa dropped me off after she took Suzette home. Colt got his man, so he's waiting at home for Lyssa. She was eager to get there for the baby making, I guess. Is Colt hot too?"

"He's Blaser's twin," Ruger said. "They're not identical, but we all have the same kind of look about us." Though Ruger had a couple of extra inches of height on his brothers. "You said 'too.' You think I'm hot, honey?"

"I think your brother is," she said, widening her smile around that small black straw. Twisting to face him, she held her glass in one hand and the straw between her fingers with the other. "This place isn't as bad as I thought it would be."

"It's not seedy. There are no drugs on the premises and the women make a wad of tips, which they keep. Blaser makes enough in drinks and door admission to cover his overheads."

"They didn't charge me admission," she said.

"You're a woman."

"I'm glad they noticed. So can anyone dance here?"

"You are not getting up to dance," he said.

It was possible she'd already raided the liquor cabinet at his mother's house if she was considering twirling with the pole herself.

"Not me," she said, putting down her glass and taking his hand. "Will you dance with me?"

"Oh no, not a chance," he said. She bounced back after leaping off her stool to try for the center of the room. He remained on his stool and was happy to wrap their joined hands around to his back, forcing her to stand against him. "We're not dancing."

"Why not?"

"It's not that kind of place."

Turning her head, she checked out as much of the room as she could see. "I see other people dancing."

"Other women, you see other women dancing, and they're on stage or on tables. This isn't a nightclub. Have you ever been to a strip joint before?"

"No," she said. "Why would I go to a strip joint?"

"Look," he said. Spinning her around, he shifted in his stool and brought her into the vee of his thighs. With his head dipped, he rested his cheek in her hair to talk in her ear. "The women dance on stage, they dance on the tables, and if a guy pays enough, they'll dance in one of the private rooms over there." He pointed to the door to the private rooms, then flattened his hand on her abdomen. "The men watch. Some toss money onto the stage, some tuck it into a G-string, but do you see any of the men dancing?"

Her hair tickled him and caught on his stubble as she scrutinized the room. "No, and they all look…"

"They're happy to be watching the women dance, not a single complaint, and no man is itching to get up and join in. The point is to enjoy the view, not partake in the spectacle."

"Isn't that sort of boring for the rest of us?"

"Does anyone in here look bored?"

There were the usual grumpy men, some of whom didn't look particularly exuberant, but no one looked bored.

"No."

"This isn't a nightclub, if you want to go to a nightclub—"

"You'll take me?" she asked, flipping around so he found himself nose to nose with her.

"If our road trip is anything to go by, you're looking for a karaoke bar. You're not going to find me in one of those any time soon," he said. "You don't have the money to spend either."

"You know, you keep reminding me I'm nearly penniless and you keep reminding me you're the one supposed to be looking after me. Doesn't that make you responsible for bank rolling me too? Given you're telling me I can't access my own bank accounts."

"I only pay women who provide me with a service," he said.

"You pay for company? Ah, right, yes, that makes a lot of sense."

"I don't pay for sex," he said. "I didn't mean that."

"And I didn't say that," she said, her glossed lips tilted closer. "I said you pay for company. I imagine with your personality it's difficult to find willing friends."

"You ain't no picnic yourself, honey," he said, struggling to find a purpose for his hands that didn't involve touching her. "I don't see a line of friends and lovers forming to take care of you in your time of need."

Her frisky disposition sagged. Although she tried to disguise her hurt, he saw it spread throughout her self-conscious form.

"Aren't you a delight," she said.

Backing off, she snatched her purse from the bar and made for the door.

NINE

"AH, HELL," Ruger grumbled.

Keeping his back to the bar, he tracked her progress to the exit.

"What did you do?" Blaser asked, coming up behind his brother on his own side of the bar.

"I took it too far."

"Yeah, I guessed that. I've never seen a woman run away from you so fast. She didn't finish her drink."

He could be ballsy, but usually got away with his banter because he kept it light-hearted. He never went as far as to say anything personal or malicious that might upset a person, yet he'd done it with Layla.

"You better go after her," Blaser said.

Ruger didn't need Blaser to say it. Leaving his stool, he headed for the door and out onto the street. Hurrying to the edge of the sidewalk, Ruger looked one way and then another. Halfway along the block he saw her striding away from the club with purpose.

He quick-stepped to catch up with her. "Lay," he called out. She didn't turn around, so he ran up beside her. "Layla, I'm sorry."

"You don't have to apologize."

"Will you stop and talk to me?"

His legs were long enough that he could keep up with her without trying too hard, but he'd prefer to look her in the eye when he apologized.

"The guy at the door said there was a payphone a block over," she said. "I don't want to hang around on the street this late alone."

She wasn't alone, he was there with her. But he hadn't inspired confidence when he blew off her concerns about him being able to keep her safe. His words in Risqué no doubt made her believe she was an inconvenience he didn't really want to protect.

"Why do you need a payphone?"

"I have some change," she said. "I'm going to call Drew and then I'll get a taxi to the bus station."

"No, look," Ruger said, taking her arm, forcing her to stop. "I'm sorry, okay? I shouldn't have said what I did. I want to look after you and I'm glad it's me doing it and not someone else."

"You don't have to pander to me, Ruger. I'm a big girl. I get it. I do. You're right. I followed you and let you call the shots. It was easier and I didn't have to worry about being active in ensuring my safety. It was lazy of me, and it was unfair. You're right, we don't know each other and I'm not your responsibility. You're only doing this because you owe Drew a favor."

She tried to walk away from him, but he didn't let go and used his grip to guide her into a nearby alley. Putting her back to the wall, he penned her in so she couldn't run away again.

"You're right, that's how it started…" If he wanted to keep her there and fulfill his promise, he had to make her understand how important it was to him. "I told you I was in sales and that's not… it's not entirely accurate."

Her curiosity eclipsed her rankle. "What do you mean?"

"I'm a fence. Guys who have goods to move come to me and I find someone who wants those goods."

"You're a criminal?" she hissed and tried to push his arm away to escape, but he didn't budge—losing her now meant losing her for good.

"No, not like… Well, yeah, but I'm changing. What I did… I guess you could say what I did was against the law, but—"

"You think you can talk yourself into innocence? You're either law-abiding or you're not."

"The cops didn't care. I never got in trouble, and I never hurt anyone."

Except that wasn't entirely true. Bri had been hurt. He hadn't intended for her to get caught in the crossfire, but she had. It was because of his mistake, his error in judgment, that her trauma had happened.

"Why would Drew set me up with a criminal?" she muttered to herself. "Why would he—"

"You might be surprised how many of his friends are involved in illegal activities," Ruger said, thinking of Rushe and Victor.

Though few people could accuse Victor and Jansen of being friends.

"This isn't funny," she said, inching in the direction of the street, though his arm stayed in the way. "I've shared a bedroom with you. My God, did you touch me while I was sleeping? Drug me or—"

"I didn't have sex with you. Just because I sell knocked off goods doesn't make me a rapist. If I'd screwed you, you would know all about it."

"You're a cocky bastard. You're just through telling me you're a criminal. I'm sorry if my accusations make you feel type cast, but I'm wondering what else you haven't told me."

"There's a lot I haven't told you, Lay, and from the way you're reacting I'd guess there's a lot Drew hasn't told you either."

"Why confess now? Why tell the truth? I could call the cops or—"

"If you call the cops, you'll upset a lot of people and lead Ashcroft's men straight to you."

"Don't threaten me," she said, peering up at him as though she could squish him like a bug despite their disparate statures. "If you hurt me, Drew will hunt you down and—"

"Drew wouldn't have sent me to you if he didn't trust me. I'm going to keep you safe, Lay," he said, bringing his hand up to her face. "Even if you get on a bus and try to run away, I'll be right there beside you. If I have to keep you in my sight all the time, I'll do it."

"Why bother? If I walk away, it's not your fault, is it? Tell Drew I was unreasonable, that I was awkward and uncooperative, he'll believe it."

And with that statement, clarity came. "You're awkward and uncooperative because you want people to walk away from you. If I wash my hands of you, there's no chance of us getting close."

"Why would I want to be close to you?" she asked, pushing his hand away from her face. "Why would you want to be close to me? We barely know each other. We don't even like each other. We've been forced—"

"Enough, Lay."

Tilting her head back, curiosity took his mouth down to hers. Her abrupt inhale of surprise gave him the opportunity to slip his tongue into her mouth. With those legs she stood to around five eight and the heels gave her another boost. Perfect.

Denying his attraction to her ended with him hurting her. It was easier to tease than to admit the intensity of temptation he was fighting.

With his hand on her cheek, he directed their kiss. She tried to link their fingers, to pull it down, but he wasn't giving an inch.

The smart lips he'd sparred with were good for more than words. Their glossed plumpness tasted of cherry and strawberry mingled with the spice of alcohol on her tongue.

Snapping her head to the side, she broke the kiss. "How dare you speak to me like that and kiss me—"

"Enough, Lay," he said again and curled his thumb under her jaw to force her mouth back to his.

The legs he'd admired from afar appeared in his mind's-eye. When he'd first sighted them in Miami, he'd pictured himself kissing them, touching and caressing them. When he'd tossed her over his shoulder, he experienced how they felt under his hands. Next would be wrapping them around his hips as he slid himself into her.

As though his thought startled her, the thud of her purse hitting the ground preceded her breaking their kiss again. Nice. She'd lost her senses enough to lose hold of her purse. Damn, he wanted to touch her, but he couldn't push her too far. Neither of them had expected the moment. Not like… For her, it probably came out of nowhere. And the taste of her…

Yeah, okay, he wanted her, he admitted it… to himself. He'd give her some time to adjust to the idea fully before he pushed it.

Bending her knees, she crouched to snag her purse from the ground but stayed down there and brought her chin up to meet his eye. "If I stand up, will you make me kiss you again?"

"If you stay down there, I'll give you something else to kiss."

So he hadn't totally given up being a wiseass.

"Ruger," she said. Straightening her legs to stand at full height, she looped the strap of her purse around her arm and rested a hand on his waist. "Kissing me won't change my mind."

"About leaving or your opinion of me?"

"I have no opinion of you."

"Sure you do, and you're entitled to air it… Come on, let me have it."

"I don't have an opinion of you," she said and sighed. "You were right about me though, I am judgmental… I don't mean to be. I don't mean to come across that way. I suppose I've learned to focus on the bad stuff because when you do that, you can't be disappointed."

"I'm disappointed," he said.

"You are?"

Her desperate eyes shone with a need he couldn't quite put his finger on. "If you leave now…" he said, "I'll never get to see where this could go."

"This?"

"Your legs were the first thing I noticed about you. I thought your sass would be a turn off but wow honey, you take it to a whole new level, and I love it."

"Do you think flattering and seducing me will make me stay? That it will stop me from asking Drew why he chose you to watch out for me?"

"I offered to look out for you, that's why he chose me, and that was before I'd seen you in the flesh."

"You said you weren't interested in me," she said, prodding her finger into him.

"Yeah, well, you know what guys are like. Denial is easy. When Drew sent me to look after you, I don't think he had this in mind."

"This?"

"Me, feeling up his little sister in an alley in the middle of the night."

"You kissed me; you didn't feel me up."

Cradling her breast, he gave it a squeeze. "That better?"

"Probably not as far as Drew is concerned," she said, taking his hand from her chest and linking their fingers. "I'm sorry I was so sensitive in there."

"You had every right to be. I was a dick—"

"I'm apologizing and that doesn't happen often so just appreciate it, will you?" Sealing his lips, he gave her the time and space she needed to say her piece. "You hit close to home, that's all. Drew is my brother, I love him. He's the only family I've got, and I want to hold onto that, but… I've only ever had one really good friend and, as you know, she slept with my ex. Maybe I'm still smarting about that more than I want to admit to myself. Getting close to people means trusting them not to hurt you and hurting you is what people tend to do, in my experience."

His thumb traced across the back of her hand and his tone went softer. "You must have let some guys in. You've been proposed to a few times from what Drew says."

"Those relationships were supposed to be easy. I didn't mean to hurt anyone. But relationships don't come back from refused proposals. I tried to salvage things with one guy, but… It just never works out."

"Do you still care about any of your exes?"

"Care about them? Sure. Enough to marry them or sleep with them again? No. But I don't do one-night stands."

"I wouldn't ask you to," he said, hooking an arm around her. His father would remind him not to keep her out in the middle of the night. "The truck is parked a street over. I'll take you back to my mom's. I'm sorry I ditched you and ran."

Leading her out of the alley, they fell into step with each other, and she didn't try to move out of his embrace. "Suzette told me you let her take over your apartment after her fiancé turned out to be a psycho. That was sweet of you."

"I didn't let her take over the apartment. I said she could stay there while I was out of town. Now I can't get her out. I've had to stay with my mom or in Colt's office any time I've been back in town."

"Maybe it's time to start looking for a place of your own again, a new place."

"I'm not ready to give up on the old one yet. Whether Suzette moves or Bri does, one of them will move on soon."

"Bri?"

"Blaser's girl."

"They don't live together?"

"Not yet," Ruger replied. "That's another long story and we've had enough of those tonight. I'm starving. Let's go back to my mom's. I'll eat, we'll get some rest and then we'll tackle tomorrow, tomorrow."

"Okay," she said. "Take me to the truck. I'm exhausted."

She sagged against him, and he bent to scoop her up into his arms again. Instead of throwing her over his shoulder as he had in Miami, he went for a more traditional arrangement. She laughed and didn't put up a fight.

Looking after Jansen's sister was meant to be a repayment of his debt. Now the lines of the relationship were blurring, he might end up owing Jansen another favor.

TEN

FOR THE NEXT WEEK, Layla settled in at the Warner family home. Prudence was a wonderful hostess who couldn't do enough for her guest. The couple were so hospitable that, in an attempt to offset some of her guilt for intruding in their home, she tried to help out around the house as much as possible.

Ruger stayed true to his word and slept at his mother's every night. Instead of sharing her room and her bed, as she had thought he would try to do, he stayed in the neighboring room. Blaser's bedroom, apparently.

Despite them not sharing a bedroom, she was convinced Pru believed they were an item. It didn't help that he kept kissing the sense out of her, handsfree, so far anyway.

Sitting in front of the bedroom mirror, she ran a comb through her hair for a final time, checked her makeup, and then twisted around to look at the dress and underwear laid out on the bed.

Three days ago, Ruger had come to her with a wad of cash and told her to go shopping for what she needed. He was probably sick of hearing her moan about a lack of appropriate footwear. After promising to pay him back, he'd given her a line about Drew having sent him money. The way he mumbled and quickly walked away told her he'd probably made that up.

Just when she was about to untuck her towel to get dressed, the bedroom door opened, and in strolled Ruger. Lowering her chin, she waited for an apology for his unannounced entry, but the man had no shame.

"Are you nervous?" he asked, resting against the metal rail at the bottom of the bed parallel to her.

"Why would I be nervous?" she asked. "It's a family dinner. I've only been invited because I've been living here a week. I've met everyone before."

"You haven't met Bri yet, and you haven't had everyone in a group like this. It's okay to say you're nervous."

"I'm not nervous," she said, holding onto her towel as she stood to stand in front of him. "Ruger, honey, are you nervous?"

"They're my family. Why would I be nervous about eating dinner with them when I've done it so many times before?"

"When was the last time you had a woman at the dinner table who everyone assumed was your girlfriend?"

"Blaser and Colt know you're not, and there's no telling Mom. She won't hear it. Lyssa keeps telling me relationships are defined in different ways, which are not always immediately recognizable as a traditional union. I mean, what the hell is that supposed to mean?"

"Maybe she knows you've got the hots for me," she teased, bowing a little closer.

"Me? You've got the hots for me, Legs. Look at the way you strut around wearing almost nothing, desperately trying to get my attention."

His assertive poise was lessened by his preoccupation with her cleavage. "Did you just notice I'm naked?"

The smile he'd worn when he started teasing had become something more intense and less playful. "I guess I should've knocked, huh?"

"A few seconds later and you'd have gotten the full show."

"Can I go out and come back in again?" he asked, returning to his grin.

"You're nervous because you can't define this any better than I can."

If one of them didn't pull back on the teasing, they'd end up in a full-on sass-off. Often they got lost in their banter. If they didn't pull it back, they'd never decipher if there was anything serious or worth pursuing between them. More often than not, Ruger was the one telling her to stop pushing him away with banter. Today it seemed to be her turn.

His hands landed on her shoulders and drifted down her arms then back up. With his fingertips, he traced the width of her collarbone. When they met in the middle, they coasted up her throat, forcing her head to tip back, which was always his prelude to kissing her.

His first kiss had stunned her, she hadn't expected such a full-on display of affection. They'd only known each other a couple of days, yet there she'd been, pinned to an alley wall outside a strip club, desperately trying to remind herself of her no one-night stands oath.

Ruger was a powerful man to look at. Height, muscles, his presence in any room was striking. With pale but warm hazel eyes that lit with his impish moods and smoldered when his thoughts turned brazen, she'd noticed him. She had. But to kiss her to shut her up, to take liberties with her mouth, she hadn't expected that.

Now his kisses were familiar. Their rhythm matched hers, the way he teased her lips with his for a few seconds before his tongue got involved. Not that it asked politely, he always managed to catch her on an inhale. His tongue would meet hers, the greeting like that of intimate friends.

His touches weren't bold. She sensed he was holding himself back, though she didn't know why or if she wanted him to. Other than his tongue-in-cheek squeeze of her breast in the alley, he'd always kept the touching to her arms, shoulders, and above. He avoided making contact with her chest and anything below the waist was a no-no.

Her initial assumption was he was easing her in, taking things slow so he didn't come off as a sleaze. But for a week, he'd been kissing her, and she still didn't have any idea about his package or how quickly he became aroused. Maybe he was holding back because he was ashamed of the anatomy below his belt…

He took her shoulders and broke their kiss.

"Colt will be here in ten minutes. He's a stickler for timekeeping," Ruger said, moving her aside to pass her. "You should get dressed."

Catching his wrist, she made him turn back to her. If she asked him straight out what was going on, she might come off as a slut, the last thing she wanted. Of their own volition, her eyes drifted south seeking some evidence she influenced him in the right way.

"What you looking for, Legs?" he asked, swagger in his tone. "You looking for a show of your own?"

"Maybe," she said.

Having never been accused of being bashful, Layla folded her arms and leaned on the perch Ruger just vacated.

His hands went to his belt. "If I drop my pants, you've got to drop the towel," he said, sliding the leather from the buckle and popping the tooth from its hole.

"Says who?" she asked, wearing a grin matched by his. "Are you gonna make me?"

"When I show you what I've got, you'll beg to get naked with me."

"You wouldn't make me beg," she said. "You've been dying to get with me since the minute you saw me."

"Confident, aren't you?"

"You can't prove me wrong, Ruger Warner. It's why you've been grabbing me and kissing me all this week. You want me, just admit it."

"You admit it first," he said. "You've been kissing me back all week, showing off that sexy body, flaunting it around me, because you want me to kiss you."

"I know what I want, you're the one with the jitters."

"Jitters?" he said, prowling over, coming so close she had to breathe in to make space. Grasping the bar behind her, Layla steadied herself, her toes were barely touching the floor. "The only thing I'm not sure about is if you can take it."

"Oh, I can take it," she said, enjoying their mischief.

Most men didn't know how to respond to her gibes because they didn't know if her wry words were sincere. Ruger got it. He got her. These provocative taunts kindled their attraction and the fuel burned hotter with every exchange.

"Sure about that?"

"Mm hmm," she said, taking her sweet time about moistening her lips, reveling in the fact that the action of her tongue transfixed him.

"I think you'll regret telling me that," he murmured, still watching her mouth.

Easing away, he finished unbuckling his belt and yanked open his fly. Presenting his hand to her, butterflies reached her throat when she placed the back of her hand on his palm. Increasing his grip, he lowered it, enticing her hand into his underwear.

Guiding her fingers around his girth, a knowing smirk decorated his face when her eyes widened. She had never felt a man so large before, never experienced it first-hand. She shouldn't be surprised because he was large in every other part of his stature and attitude. A man that cocky had to have the goods to back it up.

"Still sure?" he asked as though he expected her to retract her hand, make her excuses, and never lay lips on him again.

"That will never fit in my throat," she said, squeezing her fingers around him.

Now it was his turn to be surprised, his eyes rounded as his form loosened, like she'd just given him the greatest gift womankind could give.

"But if it'll be happy in my pussy..." she whispered.

Swinging an arm up to catch the back of his neck, she pulled his mouth to hers, taking charge. Working her fist around his cock, still sheathed in his underwear, she dug her fingernails into the side of his neck and let a moan of curious pleasure escape into his mouth.

His hesitation was gone. He snatched her waist and lifted her onto the bottom bar of the bed. While she was still too low to welcome him into her body, she did part her legs to allow them to get closer than they'd ever been.

"Ruger!"

"Fuck."

His sudden curse was partnered by a glare that would've turned his mother to stone if she'd been in the room. Luckily, she wasn't. His mother's call came from the upstairs hallway, meaning there was no time to try accommodating Ruger now. His angry frustration distracted him. It was only when she squeezed him again and coiled her thumb over the head of his dick that she got his attention back.

"Colt will be here in a few minutes," she said, pleased to know his anticipation was hot. "Is that all the time you need to satisfy yourself in my body?"

"Right now? Probably, yeah," he said. His anger melted away and he rested his forehead on hers. Keeping her head in place, he joined their mouths again. "We'll get this dinner out the way. I'll make our excuses and we can come up here—"

"Can we have sex here?" she asked. "Is that allowed?"

In high school she'd been a bit of a prude, "*a late bloomer*" was what she told people. In truth, her mother's cancer and overprotective brother meant her house wasn't a place boys liked to come and spend time with her.

So having a tryst in Ruger's mother's house would be the first time she'd had sex with a parent under the same roof.

"Want me to get a hotel room?" he asked.

That would be just as bad as doing it in the same house as his parents. Everyone would know they were going there just to get it on.

With a shrug, she exhaled and finally took her hand out of his underwear. "It doesn't bother me to do it here if it doesn't bother you."

"Really? 'Cause I can just as easy—"

"No," she said. "That's just a crazy waste of money. We'll be quiet. It would be rude to ask your mother to listen to us doing that."

"I want to hear you scream," he said, almost pouting. "Let's just get down to dinner, I'll figure something out."

"Problem solving is kind of your thing, isn't it?"

She didn't begin to understand what being a fence involved. From their brief conversations since he'd confessed the truth, she figured out that people came to him with goods they wanted to sell. Often, Ruger had no idea about the purpose of the goods, or how to operate or utilize them himself. But if he wanted a reasonable cut of the sale, he had to figure it out and ensure that no one was short-changed.

"We could always do it in my truck," he said, sinking lower to capture her mouth.

Urging him back, she laughed. "It would be a shame to dodge the cops for all these years just to finally be caught for public indecency, wouldn't it?"

"Lady has a point," he said.

"Ruger! Your brothers are here!"

Again, his mother called for him and this time he rolled his eyes like a teenager.

Gripping his tee-shirt, she curled her legs around his thighs. "Your mom must know you're in here," she whispered. "Every other day she's come and knocked on the door to tell me it's time for dinner."

"You know I am a grown up and I've had plenty of sex before. Plenty."

"I'm sure you have, honey."

"This is so frustrating. You're right, I should just get a new place, shouldn't I?"

"Unless you're willing to ask Suzette to vacate, it might be your only choice. You said you were trying to change, didn't you? That you weren't going to do illegal things anymore."

"Yeah. I'm just not sure what that's going to be yet."

"You'll need a base somewhere. My guess is that it's here or Jersey, you'll need to take your pick."

"Jersey?"

"You know Drew, so you had to have met him in Jersey, that's what I figure."

"We have a lot to talk about," he said, sliding his hands under her hair to hold the back of her head and tip it so he could sample her mouth again.

She didn't like the way he said that, like there were things he had to reveal. He said it in a release of breath like the confessions were no more than an inconvenience; a boring routine they had to go through for him to make love with her under the guise of full disclosure. But he so often said things like that when Drew came up. What didn't she know about her brother?

For now, his brothers were downstairs. They were the ones Ruger had to worry about. Resigning herself to reality, she slid off the foot bar and pushed him to the door, walking him backward all the way.

"You've seen me, shouldn't I get to see you?" he asked when she opened the bedroom door, catching her towel to prevent it from falling.

"I haven't seen anything," she said, holding her towel together in her cleavage. "And when it's time for you to appreciate the view, that's when you'll get to see it."

"I'll appreciate it."

She gave him another shove to send him backwards over the bedroom threshold before closing the door on his protestations.

Her body wasn't flawless, but she wasn't shy about it. Getting dressed in front of Ruger would feel backwards when what they both really wanted was to stay naked and enjoy each other.

This was the part of relationships that she enjoyed the most. When it was fun and new and exciting. She could revel in this part because there was no pressure. Living in Ruger's mother's house was sort of a unique setup, but that wasn't a choice either of them were happy with. She would be out of there just as soon as Drew was finished whatever he was doing.

Each time she spoke to her brother on Ruger's phone, he was evasive. The story was the high he chased despite Ashcroft's people still watching him. From what he'd heard, the men Ashcroft sent to Miami returned empty handed. On learning that, she hoped that meant danger wouldn't be coming her way any time soon.

If danger found her, Ruger would keep her safe. He might not be a martial arts expert or a security guard, but he had a heart and guts that would keep them both safe.

Terrible as it sounded, she was in no rush to have Drew declare the all-clear. Yes, she wanted her brother and Serendipity safe, but spending time with Ruger was no hardship and the Warners were generous. There were worse places to be, and when it was all over, she'd miss every person she'd met.

ELEVEN

LAYLA WAS THE LAST ONE to make it to the dinner table. As soon as she stepped into the dining room, it was obvious something was wrong. Prudence was talking everyone through her process of cooking the meal, something she liked to do. Pru and her husband seemed unaware of the tension humming around the brothers and their girlfriends, at least they were pretending to be.

Ruger was the only one to meet her eye when she came in. Lyssa was busy trying to maintain the conversation with Pru, making all the right noises about how wonderful the food was. Colt was fixated on Blaser who was whispering to Bri.

If she had been nervous, that anxiety would've vanished when no one noticed her arrival. Pru welcomed her in. Ruger rose to pull out her chair, but the rest of the table was preoccupied.

It was only after dinner, when everyone moved through into the living room for coffee, that Layla found an opportunity to question Ruger while he was in the kitchen stacking the dishwasher.

"What's going on?" she asked.

"Don't ask," he mumbled.

Except she wanted to know and didn't like feeling as though she was the only one out of the loop. Though she wasn't actually part of the family, so didn't have rights to be involved in any of the intrigue.

"Are you okay?"

"Mom will be wondering where you are," Ruger said. "You should go have coffee."

"I told them I was coming to help you." And since she was there anyway, she went to the sink to rinse off the dishes waiting to go into the huge dishwasher.

"You don't have to do this," he said.

He'd seen her helping out all week and had given up trying to deter her a few days ago. Until then. The new grumpy attempt concerned her.

"I know it's none of my business, but I could tell as soon as I walked into the dining room something was wrong. If I knew it, then your mom did too, but she's acting as if nothing is going on. Did she give you news before I got downstairs? Is she...?"

She hesitated to ask about Ruger's mother's health. She wouldn't be the best person to give advice if Pru was sick. Her own heart seized at the notion of such a wonderful woman being torn from her family when she was so loved and involved with all their lives.

"No, it's nothing to do with Mom," he said. Putting a bowl in the dishwasher, he gave up on the chore and leaned back in the corner formed by perpendicular work surfaces. Sensing he was about to say something, she put down the dish she'd been rinsing and waited. "It's Bri."

The young vibrant woman at the table, whom she hadn't been formally introduced to, was a beauty. A meek one and she hadn't expected that. Maybe if Bri just got bad news, that wasn't the best day to judge her personality.

"What about her? Is she ill?"

"She's pregnant," Ruger said, locking his eyes on hers.

The seriousness didn't elude her, having a child was a life-changing thing. But Bri was with a man who loved her, and she doubted Blaser would turn his back on her.

"How is Lyssa taking it?" she asked. He frowned. "Her and Colt have been trying and it hasn't happened yet."

An accidental pregnancy could upset the couple trying in vain to conceive.

He exhaled. "Lyssa is great, I don't know… Colt told me before we sat down. I haven't had a chance to talk to them properly yet."

Though her hands were damp, she went to loop her arms around him and offer some comfort. "This is good news," she whispered. "It might be a shock, but they love each other, Ruger. Blaser and Bri, it's obvious from the way he talks about her how he feels."

"I know that," he said, catching her hand before she could touch his face.

Movement made her turn around. Colt and Blaser were marching across the kitchen toward the back door.

"Outside," Colt said without missing a step in Blaser's wake.

The two men went outside, and the screen door swung shut.

"Go on," Layla said. "I've got this."

"Thanks," he said.

Brushing a kiss on her head, he passed her to follow his brothers into the backyard.

Carrying on with the task was the only way to contribute, and she was happy to have something to do. Colt was level-headed and Ruger was loyal. They'd help Blaser process and do whatever was needed.

TWELVE

WHEN RUGER GOT OUTSIDE, Colt was on the edge of the slate patio watching Blaser stride around the vast yard in a tight circle. Leaving Blaser to his journey, Ruger stood beside Colt and joined him in spectating their brother. Blaser would talk in his own good time.

"I guess he isn't taking the news well," Ruger said. "How's Lys?"

"Lys?" Colt asked, shifting his concentration from Blaser. "Why would you ask about her?"

"Layla did," Ruger said. "She thought Lys might be upset that Bri tripped and fell into what you guys have been trying for."

"Shit," Colt said, rubbing a hand over the back of his neck. "She's fine, I think… I didn't think about that."

"Women," Ruger said on a tsk. "I guess you have to be a woman to think like one."

"I'll take her home early and take her temperature." Something he'd heard his mother and Lyssa talking about with regards to fertility and the correct time for conceiving. How would Lyssa feel about attempting conception after receiving Bri and Blaser's news…? Colt must have read his confusion.

"Not like that temperature, metaphorically. I'll check she's okay."

"How did you get out of there?" Ruger asked. "Mom has been on overdrive all night; she knows something is going on."

"She never asks," Colt said. "She just assumes we'll tell her when we're ready."

"Are they going to tell her?"

Colt shrugged. "I don't know. Lys and I went over there to pick them up and… they asked us to go inside. Bri did the talking, Blaser just kept staring at her."

"I guess it's a shock. They've only been back together a couple of months," Ruger said. "Is it definitely his?"

"You watch your mouth," Blaser snapped, stopping dead.

"I didn't mean like she'd cheated on you," Ruger said. "I didn't know if she was with anyone before you got together, you know."

Bri's rape had taken place more than a year ago. How was he to know what she'd done with anyone since then?

"She hasn't been with anyone," Blaser said, sliding his hands into his pockets, strolling to his brothers' position. He kicked at the edge of the patio and breathed out. "She's pregnant."

"I want to say congratulations," Ruger said. "You guys have been sort of coasting towards this since high school. I can't imagine you having kids with anyone else to be honest."

"This isn't about that," Blaser said, soft and shrewd. Blaser knew Bri better than anyone else and there was no doubt about their love for each other. "The woman I love is carrying my kid." He opened his hands to the heavens then let them swing up to link his fingers on the top of his head. "I'm thrilled, guys, really I am."

They relaxed and after the shoulder slapping and brotherly hugs, they were all smiling.

"If it's a boy, you have to name it Ruger," Ruger said, then pointed at Colt. "I called it first."

Blaser's happiness faded and again he became serious. "I don't know if she's ready for this."

"Bri?" Colt asked.

"Yeah, with everything she's gone through… us losing each other and last year. Plus, there's all this stuff with Gary. We'll both have to testify in court."

"He'll see that she's pregnant," Ruger said. "Has she been to visit?"

"A couple of times," Blaser said, bobbing his head. "Gary still blames her for everything that's gone wrong in his life, but he keeps sending her visit requests. He wants to see her, yet every time she comes back a mess."

"She did the right thing," Colt said. "Gary murdered a man, and he wasn't done. You could've been next on that list."

"I know and I think she knows it too," Blaser said. "That doesn't ease the guilt she feels at squealing on her own brother to the cops."

Guilt? Yeah, he could identify with that. It didn't matter how many times someone said a situation wasn't your fault or that you'd done the right thing. You couldn't rationalize your way out of guilt once it had you in its grip.

"Have you had it confirmed?" Colt asked. "The pregnancy test could've been wrong."

"She took three," Blaser said. "I hate that I wasn't there with her. She told me at the club. She took them at her apartment. And that's another thing, both of us are so busy all the time, how will we look after a baby?"

"You've got a babysitter on call," Colt said, tipping his head back toward the house. "You know Mom will look after the little guy all the time. Lys and I will have him too."

Blaser became more solemn. "Dude, I'm sorry that—"

"Hey, don't even worry about it," Colt said. "It's not like you planned this."

"Yeah, but you guys did, and… you know…"

"We'll get there," Colt said and smiled. "The practicing is a lot of fun. I didn't even think about it until Ruger asked about Lys. Apparently, his Layla is quicker than I am."

"My Layla?" Ruger asked after a double take. "What the hell did you say that for?"

Blaser and Colt jeered, and Ruger got a punch on the shoulder.

"You're wound tight about that, aren't you?" Blaser asked then looked to Colt. "What did I tell you?"

"Tell you what?" Ruger asked. "What are you two talking about?"

"Blaser told me on night one you were hung up on the girl and I think he's right."

"Not that it matters when a guy can't follow through," Ruger muttered.

His brothers began to heckle again.

"That admission puts our problems in perspective," Blaser said to Colt.

"Yeah, you should talk to Lyssa," Colt said. "She specializes in guys who can't satisfy their women."

"Guess we know why she's with you then, don't we?" Ruger teased and they all laughed. "The equipment isn't the problem, the location is. I can't exactly screw her under Mom's roof, can I?"

"Mom tell you that?" Colt asked.

"I didn't ask Mom's permission," Ruger said. "I don't know how that would go. 'Hey, Mom, you know the girl I moved into your house and told you repeatedly I wasn't in a relationship with? Yeah? How would you feel about me fucking her senseless in my childhood bedroom?' I don't think that would translate well."

"If Mom thought it would get you hitched," Colt said. "She'd probably be okay with it."

"Hitched? Just 'cause her legs go all the way to heaven doesn't mean I'll put a ring on her finger. Layla isn't into that anyway."

"Isn't into what?" Colt asked.

"Marriage," Ruger said, giving Colt a shove. "Anyway, enough talking about me, what about him? Blase, what are you going to do?"

The back door opened, and they all turned to see Bri coming down the back stairs towards them.

"What are you doing out here, Doll?" Blaser asked, shoving between his brothers to meet Bri halfway. "Get back inside, it's warmer in there."

"I won't get rid of it," Bri said, determined.

"What?"

"If you guys are out here talking about how best to… I'm not getting rid of our child, Blase—"

"Baby, I would never ask you to do that," he said, cupping her face. "This is our kid and I love you. This is a home run for me."

She faltered. "But you've been… I didn't do it on purpose if that's what you think."

"Would you stop talking," Blaser said. "I'm worried about you, that's all that I've been thinking about. You don't want to live together. You've just started spending the night and… this is a lot to deal with after what you've been through and—"

"This is the best thing that's ever happened to me," she said. "For all the darkness that's been in our lives, finally we have something to celebrate together, something happy. It's going to be difficult, and I don't know how we're going to figure this out but… we have nine months to make the big decisions. Can't we just be happy that this happened to us at all?"

"Yeah," Blaser said on an exhaled laugh. "Yeah, we can."

He kissed her so thoroughly that out of respect both Ruger and Colt turned their backs on the spectacle.

"I think they need a minute," Ruger whispered at Colt.

"I think they need more than that," Colt said. "Hope the neighbors aren't at their windows."

"Yeah, or they might blind a couple of kids."

"We can't tell your mom, not yet," Bri said. The couple were talking, so they turned to bring them into view again. "We're not telling anyone until after twelve weeks." Nudging Blaser aside, Bri glared at both of them. "That goes for you two as well, don't tell anyone until we're sure everything is going to be okay."

"Scouts honor," Ruger said, holding up his fingers, but she wasn't fooled.

"You were never a scout, Ruger Warner. Lyssa I trust completely, she takes confidentiality seriously. But I don't know your girlfriend, Ruger, so—"

"She's not my girlfriend," Ruger protested. From the way Bri glanced at Blaser, he'd guess she knew that. "You know what? All of you can go to hell."

Heading back to the house, Colt came along with him. After the taunting died down, Blaser and Bri stayed out in the yard.

Ruger got inside to see that Layla had finished with the dishes. The dishwasher was on, and she had hand-washed the ones that didn't fit in the machine.

Colt patted his back. "I'm going to take Lyssa home," he said to his brother. "Goodnight, Layla."

"Goodnight," she called as she finished wiping the counters.

"What are you doing?" Ruger asked, walking over to take the cloth out of her hand. "You didn't have to scrub the whole room."

"It was that or go and sit with your mother, who I'm sure is fitting me for a wedding dress."

"I'm surprised the idea didn't bring you out in hives," he said, linking his fingers in hers. "Want to take a walk?"

"I guess. How's Bri?"

"Fine, better than fine. I think they're really happy."

"It didn't seem that way at the table," Layla said, taking off the apron to hang it back up. "And Bri marched out of here with purpose, I don't even know if she saw me."

Ruger took her hand again and they exited through the back door. Blaser and Bri were at the rear of the garden, too far away to notice him and Layla going down the path and out of the gate onto the driveway.

"Why are we walking?" she asked, keeping time beside him.

"I just needed to get out of there. It's so intense. Blaser and Bri are having a kid; Colt and Lyssa want one, they're getting married."

"Everyone is growing up except for little Ruger."

"Little Ruger is plenty capable of growing."

"I wasn't talking about your dick," she said. "Lyssa was so right about you."

"That statement is usually a prelude to someone telling another someone what's wrong with them. So go on, what does Lyssa say?"

"That you're afraid to get hurt. That you make jokes to make people believe you don't need them."

"Interesting analysis, Doctor Jansen," Ruger said, curving his arm around her shoulders. "And what would Lyssa say about your tendency to aim your gibes at those you are most comfortable with?"

"I don't know what you mean," she said, shrugging his arm away from her body.

"I joke with everyone and yeah, maybe I do it to keep people at arm's length. But you, you're perfectly nice to my mom and dad. You never make fun of Colt or Blase. You aim your sass at Drew and at me, why do you do that?"

"I don't," she said, picking up the pace.

She headed to the corner and rounded to the next street, but he caught up with her without much effort.

"You do and you know why you do it. It's like I said, it's because you're pushing at us. You want to see how far you can push us. You want us to prove we're not going to walk away. Is that why you refused all those marriage proposals? You wanted one guy to stick around? You wanted one to really fight for you instead of creeping away with his tail between his legs?"

"You think you know so much," she said with enough anger to prove he'd hit a nerve. She stopped and squared her shoulders. "I don't need anyone to stick around, and I don't need anyone to fight for me. I said no because I didn't want to marry those guys. I didn't want to be with them. It's as simple as that. There's no underlying agenda."

"Okay," he said with his hands in his pockets. "If that's so then why are you shouting at me? Couldn't you just tell me that in the course of conversation on our lovely evening stroll?"

A couple walking their dog on the other side of the street called to him and he offered a wave in salutation. When she spoke again, her shoulders had lost their starch.

"You've lived around here a long time, haven't you?"

"We grew up in that house," he said. "So, yeah, I know most of the faces around here."

"I haven't been back home since my mom died," she said. "I was living in a dorm at college when she died, she'd been in the hospital for a couple of weeks. After she was gone, I… I just couldn't do it. I couldn't go back there and go through all our memories. Drew did it all by himself."

"You were a kid, and he was your big brother, it was his job to look after you."

"And whose job was it to look after him?" she asked. "I know why Drew does what he does. I know he's looking for something, and that he gets the distraction he needs in his work. I can't imagine what memories he fights with, what it was like going back to our mother's house, alone, packing up everything she'd ever owned. He dealt with the lawyers and the doctor's bills. You accused me of being judgmental when it came to his work—"

"I didn't mean—"

"I get angry at him because if he dies, I'll have no one left. No one who knew her or knew about what we went through as a family. All those memories will be lost."

"Babe," he said, offering her a hand.

She considered the gesture then slid her fingers between his and began to walk again.

"I see you with your brothers and their partners, and it's… it's a beautiful thing to see."

"I guess we take it for granted."

He'd always had his brothers looking out for him. Being the joker came easy. Colt took things seriously enough for everyone and Blaser was street savvy, he could see a threat coming. So growing up, he'd let them take care of what was important, and he spent his time enjoying himself believing his brothers would take care of the responsible things.

As he'd gotten older, he'd been wise enough to look after himself but still had his brothers to rely on. His parents were still together and in love. Despite his trade, he had security, he always had a home to come back to and people he could call on for help in a time of need.

"I'm sorry, I don't know what came over me there," she said, reinforcing her modesty with a laugh. "I never open up to guys like that."

"Maybe you should try it more often," he said. "As a guy, I can tell you I approve."

"You have a therapist in your family," she said, laughing. "From what I know of Lyssa's influence on all of you, she would be devastated to discover you'd dumped a woman just because she opened up to you."

"Dumped you, huh? Does that mean we're a thing now?"

Teasing with a brow raise, she let her expression morph into a smirk. "A thing?" she asked. "I had my hand in your pants before we ate at your mother's dinner table. Yeah, I think there's definitely some kinda 'thing' between us, don't you?"

"Yeah," he said. Her fingers were cold, so he pulled her closer to cradle her digits with his other hand too. "If you're cold, we should go inside."

"Not yet," she said. "Just one more block."

Searching for something positive to talk about, his thoughts were cut off when she moved against him. Following her lead, he let go of her hand and put his arm around her again. The softer side of Layla, the side open to being affectionate, was new to him, but he liked it just as much as the sassy woman used to facing life alone.

Blaser's future was carving itself out. All Blaser was doing was making choices and living his life. Colt and Lyssa were making decisions that weren't panning out as they'd hoped, but that didn't stop them trying.

Watching his family mature and grow was enlightening. He'd never given much thought to how he wanted his future to look and always assumed when the time was right, things would just happen.

But things wouldn't just happen if he didn't decide what he wanted from his life, and who he wanted in it. His career was non-existent. He couldn't rely on his illegal exploits especially not knowing they hurt people.

Maybe an aspect of moving forward in his professional life would mean making changes in his personal one too. Just like that, an epiphany, he made the decision to reserve a hotel room for the following night, proving choices weren't tough to figure out as long as you were decisive in obeying your instincts.

THIRTEEN

"YOU KNOW, dinner was a nice surprise, but your, 'Let's take this upstairs line' was cheesy," Layla said while being dragged down the corridor of the hotel she and Ruger just ate dinner in.

"How else did you want me to say it?" he said, turning to walk backward, bringing her hand up to his mouth. "You want me just to come out and say, 'Hey, baby, I booked a room, get your panties off' would that have worked?"

"Maybe," she said, grinning. The wine had been sweet, and Ruger attentive. It was a night of seduction to be sure and she should have figured out his intentions when he said they were eating in the hotel restaurant. "But just because you bought me dinner doesn't mean I owe you anything."

"No, that's true," he said, pulling her up to a room door and caging her against it while he fumbled in his pocket for a key.

He'd had a drink of his own but didn't need any courage. Capturing her mouth with his, he distracted her while he unlocked the door. It swung away from behind her, and he reached inside to flick on a light. Although he was still trying to kiss her, she turned around to emphasize her point and prove she wasn't a sure thing. Except her gusto abandoned her when she saw the four-poster bed adorned by gold pinstripe linen covered with crimson rose petals.

Maybe dinner didn't mean she owed him, but the trouble he'd gone to in order to create this surprise might leave her a little indebted.

"This is amazing," she said.

Seizing her hand again, he pulled her toward the bed. Layla was about to tell him off for his eager behavior when he surprised her by stopping and bending to retrieve a bucket of champagne on ice from behind the footpost of the bed.

"You thought I was going to stick my head up your skirt, didn't you?" he asked, sitting on the end of the bed and tugging her down next to him.

"I did not," she said, though her smirk would speak for itself. "Why did you do this?"

"I'm not going to propose if that's what you're worried about."

"Phew," she said and took the flute of champagne he poured for her. "I'm never going to live that down. I don't get what the big deal is. If I had married the first guy who proposed to me, I'd probably be living in a trailer park with six kids from six dads and a regular on Jerry Springer by now."

"Sounds like he was a keeper to me," Ruger said, putting down the champagne bottle when he'd poured his own flute. "I bet letting him get away keeps you up nights."

"Shut up," she said, making a face when he winked at her. "Just get on with it, will you?"

"Bodes well for the night ahead," he said, leaning over to kiss her cheek.

Holding his glass aloft, he waited for her to do the same.

"To what?" she asked.

"To debts that should be repaid," he declared then stage whispered to her. "This room and the setup cost more than a grand, Legs. You'll be working it off for months."

"Implying my skills aren't worth much," she said. "I said it wouldn't fit in my throat. I said nothing about how hard I'd work to ensure satisfaction."

"Hmm," he said, swigging his champagne then taking her glass away to put both of them on the floor. "You are a tease, Legs."

"So if this was a real date," she said, leaning back when he swooped in to try for a kiss. "What would we be doing now?"

"This is a real date," he said. "We dressed up, we ate dinner, what more do you want?"

She couldn't ask for more effort on his part or for more romance. He'd certainly set the scene. "Is there music?"

"As a matter of fact," he said, rising, he went to the corner and opened a large entertainment cabinet to show there was indeed a stereo. The CD unit appeared to be sealed, so whatever was in it was what they were stuck with.

Ruger pressed a few buttons and got the thing on. When it finally did spring to life, she was impressed by the slow, piano melody just right for the moment.

"Can you turn the lights down?" she asked when he started toward the bed again.

He stopped and glanced back at the light switch. "No, but…" He switched on the floor lamp in the corner, which was operated by a dimmer by the bed, then he turned off the overhead light. "Anything else?"

"Yes," she said. Her new high heels hurt, but with his height, she needed them to compensate. Standing up, she held out both hands and met him in the center of the room. "You still haven't danced with me."

He didn't make a joke. He just took her hands and guided them up to his shoulders then slid his own hands around her waist.

"You're right," he said as they moved together in the private space. "This is much better than getting you drunk and jumping you."

"You went to all the trouble of reserving the room," she said. "We should at least enjoy it."

"I reserved the room because I wanted to be alone with you." He brought her hand to his lips. "There's no pressure for there to be anything else… you know…"

"Ruger, I told you about the guy who tried to get into my bed without permission, didn't I? If I didn't want to be here, if I didn't want to be with you, I wouldn't be here. I'm not shy about saying no."

Putting her hand back on his shoulder, he kissed her and encircled his arms around her to bring her head onto his torso. Grateful he hadn't brought up the rejected marriage proposals again, she closed her eyes and lost herself in the seductive notes of the music and the sensual scent of the solid man holding her like she was the most precious thing in the world.

One song finished and another began. Still he held her close and swayed in their intimate slow dance. Ruger was no sleaze. He didn't try to hurry things along or grope at her ass. All he did was hold her and dance with her, just like she'd requested.

Layla was happy to give him the greenlight but was sort of disappointed he didn't seduce with a little more passion. He was clearly a man with confidence and wasn't hesitant in other areas of his life.

"Ruger," she said.

"Yeah, Legs?"

"Do you want to make love to me?"

A warm laugh, so silent she didn't hear it, misted her hair. "Yeah, I do."

"So tell me," she said, lifting her head to meet his eye. "Or better yet, show me."

The laughter faded into a growing intensity. The usually jovial Ruger ebbed, giving her a real sense of the power this man could wield. Someone of his stature could be intimidating, but she knew him too well to fear him.

"You're sure?" he asked, bringing his hands to her face.

"Very."

"Turn around," he said, his voice deeper than before.

The strength of his authority made her turn without thinking to refuse him. Sweeping her hair away from her back, he held it out of the way to unzip her dress. Her desire for him to be more dominant was being fulfilled. It wasn't a sweet seduction. He didn't kiss her from her clothes and segue into making love before she had a chance to notice what was happening.

When the zip was down, he pushed the fabric from her shoulders and let her hair fall to take hold of her and spin her around. Underwear hindered his view, but that didn't stop him from using his strength to force her back to drink all of her in. When he wanted more, he took it. Reaching around, he unhooked her bra with one hand and stepped away, absorbing more of her.

It was her choice to drop her arms and let the bra fall away. His moving back made that clear and her confidence soared when his breathing hitched in his throat. Oh, wow, the thrum of activity in her chest descended in a thick column of want that sank into her abdomen.

He hadn't even touched her. How crazy was that? The arousal, his seduction, came in the way he looked at her, his utter concentration on her body. Fair was fair and just as she was about to ask when she would see him, he began to unbutton his shirt. Until about halfway down, he kept scrutinizing her breasts, but that scrutiny moved up to her eyes in time with his shirt falling to the floor. Had she worried he wouldn't be able to protect her? The definition in his chest, in his arms, he wasn't a stranger to the gym.

On impulse, she lifted a foot to move toward him, but he held up a finger and she paused.

"Turn around and pull your panties down," he said.

Again, that gruff voice prompted her to do as told. Bending down to slide the satin of her panties to her ankles, the slick natural lubricant of her body blossomed.

The sound of her own gulp pulsed in her ears. As she cast the scrap of her panties away from the spike heel of her shoe, she straightened up, unsure if she should turn around again or not.

Ruger answered before she could ask. Sweeping her hair forward from one shoulder so it hung over one of her breasts, he urged her on to place her hands to the column of the corner footpost of the bed high above her head.

"Keep them there," he commanded, his face lost in the swathes of her hair he was inhaling.

His hands came around her body. One went for her breast while he used the force of his caress to hold her spine to his chest where she could feel the thump of his own want in the rapid tattoo of his heart.

He came lower, parting his thighs, impelling his colossus against their apex.

"Ruger—"

"Shh," he said. His lips breezed out of her hair to her unobstructed ear. "Say nothing."

His whispered words tingled in her ear and fizzed to her neck when his breath prefaced his kiss against her carotid. The suggestion of his thoughts enhanced his long, slow, incredible kisses on the side of her neck. Wrapping his form around her, he kissed her throat and collarbone, working her breasts and nipples with one hand while the other held her hands captive.

"Stay there," he exhaled, still kissing her neck.

The caress immobilized her. When his hand departed from hers, the prospect of its potential destination interrupted the rhythm of her breathing. She'd never thought about it before, but there she was, pacing each breath, getting more and more lightheaded as the seconds passed.

Everything zeroed when the length of his index finger met her Brazilian. Without time or thought for words, she handed herself to him as he angled her hips back, forcing her cleavage to the wood her hands were still splayed on.

Ruger's finger descended into the damp crevice of her body, begging for the attention he seemed happy to give. Of their own volition, her legs separated as he coaxed his finger through her, immersing the digit in her core to her absolute delight.

"Ruger…" she said again, working herself against the invader that came out of her to pinch her clit and spoil it with delectable devotion.

"Shh, not yet, Legs," he said, bringing his lips back to her ear. "Soon, you can make all the noise you want, but not yet."

When had she become the type to take orders? When Ruger gave them, they became her reason for being. Her compliance fueled his desire. She could feel it in the fervor of his finger when it slipped back into her, feel it in the increased pressure of his lips that parted on her throat to let his tongue taste what his heart desired.

Staying quiet was not her default. She wanted to talk, wanted to ask for more, yet she squeaked and writhed against the length of his digit that curled into her G-spot and then stayed put. The internal chant of her atoms vibrated. With a squeeze of his curled finger, he pushed the ball of his hand into her clit and boom, it was like the key had been turned and suddenly she couldn't keep her mouth shut.

A quaking gasp made her legs give, but his arm came around her ribs and he lifted her up to drop her face first onto the bed. She didn't care where she was, the connection of their bodies remained and when he repeated the maneuver, this time with a sideways rub of her clit, she was urged over the precipice into orgasm again.

From the distribution of heat on her back she knew he was kneeling over her, and the gradual increase of his weight led up to his mouth closing over her nape and her hair being pushed up, out of his way.

Still recovering from the surprise of her climax, she couldn't object when his hands slid away, and his weight disappeared. She didn't even have it in her to turn over and see what he was doing. Trusting he would come back and that he had a plan, she stayed put breathing in the clean smell of fabric softener and rose petals.

"I could take a couple of naked pictures now," he said, "since we're here."

Gasping, she flipped onto her back half-expecting to see him there with his cellphone at the ready. Instead, she saw a fully naked Ruger, such a breath-taking sight that humor and horror fled. She learned in that second, with that first glimpse of him, that Ruger had the brawn to back up his brains. Picking out each defined muscle group, it became clear that stamina wasn't going to be a problem for him either.

Lifting one knee onto the bed, Ruger brought the other up on the opposite side of her legs, sandwiching her form between his solid thighs. He was grinning now, probably pleased with his joke and her reaction to his physique. No doubt there was some pride in his swagger too, attributed to what he'd accomplished with her so far. But she was happy to stay on her back and welcomed his kiss when he bowed to placate her.

Beneath him, she welcomed his brief kiss. The density of his fist rested on her while the hot head of his member was squeezed between their bodies, his weight descending onto her.

"I'm wearing a condom, okay?" he asked, still holding himself in hand.

His other forearm was caught in her hair, so he curled his hand around to stroke her locks away from her forehead. She nodded, happy he was being so conscientious and avoiding the break in proceedings she might have otherwise made.

Initiating the next kiss, she gave him permission. "I'm ready."

"I know," he said, wearing a grin. "You've got a regular gush going on down there."

"You want me to apologize for being aroused?"

"Never," he muttered, descending on her.

Opening her legs for him was natural when his tongue cajoled its way into her mouth. Focusing on the softness of his tongue—its insistence on being joined with hers—she didn't think anything of the motion of his hips.

Spearing himself into her, she stopped kissing and breathing when she realized it wasn't going to be an easy job. She hadn't been with loads of guys, but she'd been with enough of them to expect this part of sex to be simple. Insert penis, easy, at least it usually was. Her past lovers had been a variety of sizes, some larger, some smaller, and some right in the middle.

Ruger wasn't like any of those men. He sensed her reaction and took his mouth from hers. "You okay?"

"Uncomfortable," she admitted.

"You want me to stop?"

"No. No. No. No," she said on one rush of breath. "Just, take it slow."

Easing back, he pushed in again, working the first inch of himself in and out of her until she was prepped to take more of him. Accommodating him sent a sting of discomfort zipping through her, the shock of it tensed her up.

"Easy, Legs," he said, freezing in position. "You've got this, you're okay."

"I'm so glad we didn't do this at your mother's house," she said, attempting a joke.

He laughed, probably just to be polite, then combed his fingers through her hair and caressed her cheeks. "Wrap those legs up around me, hmm? Fulfill my fantasy."

"Your obsession with my legs is not healthy," she teased and twined her fingers at the back of his neck while coiling her legs around him too.

"It's okay, I think I'm going to become obsessed with a different part of you pretty soon."

"I'm ready," she said. "Keep going."

As he urged himself deeper, he kissed and caressed her, softening her body, asking it to allow him inside. She hadn't realized they'd got all the way until his pace increased. He was in and out of her, faster and faster. Overjoyed she'd adjusted to hold him, she relaxed and basked in the enthralling sensations of this new experience.

Each thrust amplified the one before. This was a stronger, more addicting intimate encounter than any she'd had in the past. He slowed, attracting her attention to his frown. Pulling him down, she did her best to kiss it away. Something he'd seen in her put that expression on his face. Nothing in her was negative, she needed him to feel the way she did.

Apparently, it worked, because he sped up, and as he pumped in and out of her, she matched her rhythm to his. Whimpering, moaning, her climax was closing in. Goddamn, she wanted to hold out for him. He was too big. Touching her. All of her at once. Touching places inside of her that had been long neglected or felt newly discovered.

"Ruger," she said, gasping in to hold her breath as her muscles contracted.

The burst of release drowned her in the most powerful orgasm she could ever remember. So caught up in her own sensations, she missed the change in him, with another plunge into her, he growled out her name and then went still in the reverberation of his own pinnacle.

When his lungful of air came out in one long puff, she let go of her own held breath and they made eye contact for a few seconds before he dipped down to kiss her forehead.

"Wait here," he said, and rolled away off the bed.

She wasn't going anywhere; she wasn't capable. Watching him go into an adjoining room and turn on a light, she picked out the features of a bathroom in her brief view before he closed the door.

Her muscles ached. None more so than her most intimate ones. She'd never fit another man. Damn. Rolling onto her front, she rested her head on its side and closed her eyes, trying to calm her erratic breathing and thumping heart. The zing of orgasm-afterglow still buzzed her nerve endings. She should go to the bathroom to clean herself up. That would be the smart thing. But, oh, she couldn't bring herself to move.

Being with Ruger was an accomplishment. Not because of their anatomy, but because no other experience felt so right. Every part of it was right from their dinner downstairs, their banter, the way he took control, but valued her while sating his body and hers.

"You okay?"

He landed on top of her, but quickly moved and she switched her view from left to right to peek up from her pillow.

"I think okay about covers it," she mumbled, her mouth still half encased in the pillow. "Your dismount could use some work."

She loved his laugh. He slid down until his face came in close to hers, his arm resting on her spine. "I had to get rid of the condom," he murmured past his curled lips, then kissed her. "I'll try to be more romantic about it the next time."

"Next time?" she said, wriggling over to rest her torso on his and brush their noses together. "Who says you get a second chance?"

"That big, satisfied smile on your face, that's who," he said, bobbing up to catch her lower lip in his teeth before he kissed her. "And they don't rent rooms in here by the hour, I checked, so we've got this baby for the rest of the night. We'll need to do something to pass the time."

"Oh, well, then I guess sex is it."

"Yep, nothing else for it."

"There must be a TV," she said.

Before she could look over her shoulder, he lunged to the side of the bed to grab the remote, which he threw toward the door on the other side of the room.

"It's broken," he said, capturing her in his arms.

"I'm surprised the hotel didn't give you a discount on a room with a broken television," she said, not buying his ruse for a minute.

"I paid extra," he said, grinning. "Told them I wanted my girl's undivided attention."

"Well, Ruger Warner," she murmured, splaying her hands on his chest. "I guess it's time for me to hold up my end of the deal."

Joining their mouths, the bliss of this new intimacy captured her. Drew had sent her more than a protector. Ruger was someone different. A man who could change her perspective in so many ways; all she had to do was be open to the possibilities.

FOURTEEN

"WE COULD JUST MOVE IN," Ruger said, polishing off his breakfast bagel.

"Into a hotel?" she asked, sipping her coffee.

It had been touch and go whether or not they would make it down to the hotel dining room for breakfast. After their morning tryst, she'd barricaded him out of the shower because she wasn't sure her body could take much more of his attention. Enamored with the man, and being eager to please him, didn't negate her aching muscles requirement for recovery time.

"I got it for the night because I didn't want any interruptions," he said. "Now I've had you all to myself, I'm not sure that I want to share you again."

It was nice to be adored, she couldn't deny that and would love to spend some more alone time with him. But moving into a hotel seemed a little extreme.

"Wait," she said when she had an unsettling thought. "That wasn't it, was it?"

"What it?"

"Last night, that wasn't… you know… all I get. Is it like as soon as we walk out of here, you turn back into a pumpkin?"

His laugh was insensitive given her doubt. At least it would've been if she didn't know him; that display of amusement was enough to relax her. When he took her hand to kiss it, she slipped it out of his grasp and smoothed her napkin on her lap—a little embarrassed at revealing such dismay at the idea of their intimacy being over.

"No, that wasn't it, Legs," he said. "You said you didn't do one-night stands, and I don't want a one-night hook up with you either."

Hesitant to ask for clarity, her own uncertainty was sort of hypocritical. She couldn't ask him what it was until she knew what she wanted it to be. She didn't do one-night stands but didn't only sleep with men she saw a forever future with.

Sometimes she just trusted fate because the bigger picture often eluded her. She didn't know what she wanted her life to look like when she was forty, fifty, and beyond. So if Ruger couldn't put language to what was going on between them, she couldn't be hurt or angry because she couldn't put language to it either.

Saving her the trouble of explanations, Ruger's cellphone rang on the table, and he tilted it to read the screen.

Frivolity left his expression.

"Your brother?" she asked, hoping all was well at home.

"No," he said. "Yours. Hang on."

Ruger left the table. When he was a few paces away, he answered the phone and put it to his ear. Thank God he'd taken the phone away. Drew would hear in her voice that something was different, he always could. He had her signals down; he'd always been perceptive like that.

But Ruger's frown didn't change as he took the phone out of the dining room and into the lobby, so she couldn't judge his mood any further. If Drew was in trouble, Ruger would know how to help. If there was any danger to her or Drew, she hoped Ruger would be honest with her about it. Drew was a capable brother and cop. He loved Serendipity and had proved in the past he would do anything to keep her safe.

Layla liked Serendipity. From the very first moment they'd met, Layla had been able to tell that the woman was good for Drew. Serendipity kept him honest. At times she was sure Serendipity was the conscience Drew sometimes struggled to hear in his own head.

Having a love like that was not something she'd ever envied of Drew. As thrilling as it was to see him happy, she never imagined her future would contain such a secure devotion. That she would meet a man willing to put his life on the line to protect hers… as Drew would do for Dipity. No, she couldn't see it.

Giving Ruger the space to take his call, Layla didn't chase after him. She finished her coffee and was pouring another from the pot on the table when something tickled her awareness. What was that? The origin of her unease was unknown, yet when her attention rose to the vast glass frontage of the hotel dining room, her focus came to rest on a black car parked on the other side of the street.

They weren't in the center of the city, but this wasn't the suburbs either, so there was plenty of activity outside. Any number of different actions could have caught her eye from pedestrians and tradesman to cars and cabs on the street. But that one black car stood out for her. Why?

The tinted window of the vehicle glided down halfway. From inside, a man watched her as intently as she was watching him. Trying to convince herself he was just a guy checking her out, it wouldn't pay to be paranoid. Ashcroft couldn't know her location. Ruger protected her, and she'd followed the rules of not using any phone except Ruger's to contact Drew.

Still transfixed, she didn't notice Ruger approach the table until he sat down beside her. "I'm sorry, honey, we have to go."

"Okay," she said, dragging her eyes away from the car. "Why?" Reminding herself of who'd been on the phone, her panic levels rose. "Is it Drew? Is something wrong?"

"Nothing we can't handle," he said. Tipping the rest of his coffee into his throat, Ruger threw a tip onto the table and took her hand to pull her up. "Are you finished?"

She was already on her feet, so the question seemed moot, but she offered a smile to help ease his new burden and let him lead her away. Glancing back over her shoulder, she sought out the black car parked at the curb. It was gone.

A chill whispered across her shoulders like someone had stepped on her grave. The car being gone should reassure her but for some reason it set her more on edge. Ruger was determined in guiding her through the lobby, so it didn't feel like the right time to mention her heebie-jeebies. There was nothing out there for her to show him anyway. It was stupid. Benign. So something had unsettled her? It was nothing. She shrugged off her worries and caught up to walk at Ruger's side.

FIFTEEN

THE LAST THING he'd wanted to do that morning was rush Layla out of the hotel. Their night together had been more intense than he'd expected. Instead of sating him, it whetted his appetite for more.

Typical that her brother should be the one to put a stick in the spokes of their intimacy. Leaving her alone at the breakfast table to take the call was supposed to give him his chance to tell Jansen about what he felt for Layla, honesty upfront. Except, he couldn't be honest about feelings he didn't have words for yet. He could be honest about their actions, in implicit terms. He should've been.

But as soon as he answered the phone, Drew was talking. All thoughts of honesty vanished in the gravity of what he'd been told. The details had been hurried, and he'd returned to the breakfast table intent on getting Layla back to his mother's, a safe place.

Leaving Layla at his parents' house with promises of returning as soon as possible, he'd kissed her and got back on the road again. Tracking down Blaser was an easy objective. The best thing about that particular brother was he could be found without any trouble. Colt was always stalking something or someone out and could be in any number of locations. Blaser was only ever in one of three places, the apartment complex, Risqué, or at Warner's Autos.

Risqué wasn't open yet and unless Bri had tempted him into taking the morning off, Blaser was going to be at the auto garage. Speeding to that location, Ruger parked outside and greeted the men he passed.

Expecting Blaser to be dirty and under a car somewhere, he scanned the legs of the men he could see but didn't identify any of them as his brother. The tow truck had been in the yard, so it was unlikely Blaser was out recovering a vehicle.

Heading into the office, he intended to ask Ivy, the desk girl, for Blaser's whereabouts. But there he was. Blaser. Leaning against the file cabinet, wiping his hands on a rag as he and Ivy laughed about something.

"Oh, watch out," Blaser said when Ruger came in. "He's going to accuse me of flirting with you and then remind me I have a girlfriend." Ruger just scowled. Blaser shook his head. "I guess he only does that when I'm talking to his girlfriend."

"Oh, do you have a tinge of the green-eyed monster, Ruger?" Ivy asked.

Ruger didn't answer her question. He chose to respond to Blaser's accusation instead. "Ivy's married."

Blaser raised his chin while inhaling. "Ah, I wouldn't flirt with her because Dax put a ring on her finger, is that it?"

"Yeah, that and Dax would put you in a body bag if you touched his wife."

Dax would do that to any man who thought to put his hands on Ivy for any reason, so that wasn't really much of a joke. Ivy was the only one who laughed. From how she quickly returned to her work, Ruger guessed she was thinking the same thing about her husband and the truth of what he would do to any sleazebags.

"What brings you here?" Blaser asked, squeezing the rag between his fingers to clean off the grime.

His grey coveralls were smeared with grease and emblazoned with his name. The thick layer of black beneath his fingernails wasn't shifting. He decided there and then, auto-repair wasn't going to be a part of his future.

"Jansen called me."

"And?" Blaser asked, smart enough to know that all jokes were off.

"They had trouble. Ashcroft's men burst into their safe house."

"Wasn't much of a safe house then, was it?" Ivy chimed in, leaning back in her seat to look up at Ruger.

Ruger didn't know Ivy or her husband well, but they had been around to help Blaser. So when he looked to his brother, he wasn't surprised to see Blaser nod.

"She's fine," Blaser said. "We can trust her."

That was enough for him. Angling to include both Blaser and Ivy in the conversation, he carried on. "Shots were fired. A bullet got close enough to Flick to piss Rushe off, so he broke the guy's neck… with his bare hands."

"If it was Bri, I'd have done the same."

Blaser had been in his share of trouble when he was younger, but Ruger doubted he actually knew how to crack a guy's spine like that. Though if love was involved, men were capable of miracles.

"Anyway, they have more heat than they're comfortable with," he said. "Ashcroft now has grounds to send legitimate forces after him."

"Ashcroft knows about it already? What did they do with the body?"

"I don't know," Ruger said. "As far as Jansen knows Ashcroft hasn't got the evidence yet. But when the guy fails to show up…"

"It's only a matter of time before they put the pieces together," Blaser said. "And Ashcroft is cozy with the DA."

"Yeah, which is why Rushe and Flick are heading north. I have to meet up with them, help supply them 'cause where they are is secluded. We don't know how long they'll have to be there."

"This is getting dirty fast," Blaser said, folding his arms. "I don't like it."

"None of us like it," Ruger said. "But we're not going to turn our backs on them now. For one thing, Rushe will hunt us down if he takes offense to us cutting him and Flick off in their time of need. But beyond that—"

"Jansen saved Bri's life," Blaser said. "I haven't forgotten that."

"Good," Ruger said. "I have to meet up with Rushe and Flick tomorrow. But it will take a day for me to get everything together they need, and I have to see Lyssa."

"Lyssa, why?"

"It's not important," he said. "But I need you to look out for Layla while I'm gone."

"Look out for her?" Blaser said. "You mean keep her alive."

"Yeah. I can't take her with me. It's too risky. But I can't leave her here unprotected either. For all we know that's exactly what Ashcroft wanted by provoking this. If they're taking shots at Flick, then our women are in it. Serendipity and Layla, neither of them is safe."

"Our women," Blaser said, lightening the mood with half a smile. "I guess things went well last night."

"We'll talk about it later."

If he stopped for long enough to think about what had happened in the hotel, or what it had felt like to be with such a vivacious woman, he might want to ditch everyone and take her somewhere far away. Somewhere hot and tropical, where bikinis and mai-tais were the only concerns.

"It's okay to be into her," Blaser said, but he wasn't teasing. "It's okay to fall in love."

"You have to move back home," Ruger said, ignoring Blaser's comments.

"Excuse me? What?" Blaser asked, shifting his weight to his feet. "I have to what?"

"You have to stay at Mom and Dad's. It's the only way you can be sure Layla's okay," Ruger said. "I know it's difficult and you might not see much of Bri, but it's only a couple of days, three max."

"Which is it, Ruge? A couple or three? I'm not moving back to Mom's."

"It's not moving back, it's just like a weekend away," he said. Blaser's easy manner was a distant memory. Yeah, it wasn't ideal. He got that. He hadn't been wild about staying back at home himself, so he couldn't put up a credible fight against Blaser's objections. "You have to be near Layla to keep her safe, so you have to stay at Mom's with her. Unless you talk to Bri about moving in with you."

"It's too soon for that, we just found out… you know, and we need some time to process everything before we make big decisions."

"I know she's pregnant," Ivy said, pulling herself closer to her desk. "You don't have to talk in code."

"You do?" Ruger asked.

"Who do you think was there when she took the tests?" Ivy asked. Ivy and Bri were neighbors and had become close. Neither had another good friend, so the women confided in each other. "I agree with Blaser that it's too soon to rush Bri into moving. But if you're worried about Layla, she's better at the apartments than she would be at your parents' house."

"There's been no trouble at my mom's and Mom takes care of Layla. Out here there's… She doesn't know anyone and wouldn't know what to do. She might cause problems for herself."

"Problems?"

"He wants you to think he's worried about her," Blaser said. "What he's really worried about is her being hot around all the guys that live here. There are no guys around to move in on his turf at our mom's."

Now that Blaser put it like that… Was he concerned another guy might move in on Layla? Given the night they'd spent together, it had to be obvious they were starting something. Layla wasn't the type to have a bunch of guys on the go at the same time anyway.

"No one will make a play for her around here," Ivy said, swiveling to face them again. "No one hits on me."

"Everyone around here has met your husband," Ruger said.

Only a man with a death wish would think about trying to touch Dax Harrow's wife.

"Her husband is another good reason why Layla should stay here," Blaser said. "Dax knows what he's doing in a fight. He bailed Bri out, didn't he? If anyone tries to cause trouble for her—"

"Saying she would be safe here doesn't change the fact there's nowhere for her to sleep," Ruger said, more exasperated by Blaser's argument than opposed to it. "Are you going to sleep on the couch and give her your room? 'Cause she's not safe out front alone."

"I thought Suzette was staying in your apartment," Ivy said.

"She is," Ruger said. "Hence why I have nowhere for Layla to go."

"Is it that, or is it that you're afraid to have a girl in your house in case she never leaves?" Ivy asked, catching her pen in her teeth and raising her eyebrows at him.

"Yeah, it could be that, 'cause the last time I was a nice guy, I let Suzette move into my apartment and she's never planning on leaving."

"Kick her out," Ivy said.

"Like it's no big deal."

"Woman has a point," Blaser said.

Covering his eyes with a hand, Ruger exhaled. "Then you tell her to move, Blase."

"If kicking Suzette out is causing you trouble…" Ivy said, "I'll talk to her."

"No," both men said at the same time.

Suzette and Ivy were not the best of friends. Being neighbors, they'd had a few run-ins over noise levels.

"I would be perfectly nice about it," Ivy said. "The woman has no right to take up residence in your apartment, not when she's got a boyfriend." This caused both him and Blaser to peer at her. "Which I guess neither of you knew."

When Ivy tried to turn back to the desk, Ruger caught the back of the chair and pulled it out to spin her around to face them again. "Suzette has a boyfriend?"

"I thought everyone knew," Ivy said, but the innocent act was fooling no one. Given the women's fractious history, it was probably Ivy's intention to out Suzette's not-so-secret. "Bri knows and so does Lyssa."

Lyssa was Suzette's best friend; it was no leap that she knew about the mysterious man in Suzette's life. Lyssa and Bri were going to be family and Ivy was Bri's best friend, so word must have gotten around the female network.

"Bri knows?" Blaser asked.

Surprised that Bri hadn't confessed all to Blaser, Ruger continued the questioning. "Who is he?"

"If you're jealous then—"

Ruger caught the back of her chair and held it so that she couldn't sneak away again. Leaning over her, he was intent on getting answers.

"Oh no, you're not going to use that play. Every man who knows Suzette knows how… high maintenance she can be."

Suzette was a good-looking woman, but Ruger preferred his women to be a little less needy.

"Obviously some men are into that," Ivy said.

"Where did she meet him?" Blaser asked.

"How long has it been going on?" Ruger asked, wondering why Suzette hadn't asked this new boyfriend for kindness instead of relying on his. Then a thought struck him. "Have they been doing it in my place?"

In his bed was more what disturbed him, but he didn't want to go there.

"I'll say," Ivy said. "Sometimes I think she's trying to out-do Dax and me. But I don't think the guy likes that idea. They do it at his a lot too."

"How would you know how often they have sex at her boyfriend's place?"

"I think if you want to know about Suzette's love life," Ivy said, "you should ask her."

"You can't stand each other," Blaser said. "Don't pretend to protect her now, Ive, come on, tell us. You told Bri so—"

"Bri figured it out for herself," Ivy said. "She shares a wall with Suzette too."

Bri was in the first apartment on the upper floor of the building, Suzette was next door, and Ivy shared the third apartment along with her husband, Dax. If Ivy and Bri found out by overhearing what Suzette was up to in her apartment, Ruger's connect the dots of the flow of knowledge through the women hadn't been too accurate.

"She did?" Blaser asked.

"Yeah, she figured it out while Dax and I were away in California. She's probably known about it the longest. Though I guess Suzette probably told Lyssa before the rest of us knew."

"I don't have time for this," Ruger said and flipped around to look at Blaser. "I have to get on the road. Just look after Layla, okay? Talk to Bri and if she will give you up then I'd appreciate it if you'd stay over at Mom's just while I'm away."

"If something goes down over there, I can't look after Mom and Layla alone."

"Dad is still capable," Ruger said. "Once I get the story from Drew, I'll be in touch. If I think there's any real chance of danger coming your way, I'll clue you in."

Psyching himself up to head out on the road without Layla, Ruger spun around, but Ivy caught his arm. "Dax and I will watch Blaser's back. We'll keep her safe."

"Thanks," Ruger said and left the garage to get on with his to-do list.

He didn't know much about Ivy, other than she could be a vixen. Dax was capable, he'd saved Blaser's life at least once. Telling himself that Layla would be safe, he started to dial Lyssa because she was next on his list. He couldn't shake the discomfort at not being by Layla's side when she could need him but taking her with him was just too risky.

SIXTEEN

LAYLA HAD BEEN DRINKING tea on the back patio with Prudence and Lyssa when Lyssa's phone rang. She hadn't seen Ruger since he dropped her off there that morning. The phone call he'd got at breakfast played on her mind.

She should've got the full story. Under Ruger's advisement, she couldn't use any of the phones in the Warner house to call Drew for more information. That meant until Ruger reappeared, she couldn't get the full story. Trusting that he would come to her as soon as he could, she was surprised to learn he was calling Lyssa.

Lyssa left the table and walked to the back of the yard to talk to him. Once again, she was excluded. Danger could be closing in and no one was telling her a damn thing. Were Ruger and Drew keeping things from her? They might think they were protecting her, but she didn't feel protected, she felt like the pitied burden.

"Ruger is always going a thousand miles a minute," Pru said, topping off each of the glasses. "He's very dedicated."

Layla wouldn't ask Pru questions about what she thought Ruger did. The search for answers would only lead to more questions.

"He is," she said.

"Did you enjoy your night away?" Pru asked.

"Yes," Layla said, sitting forward to sip from her glass.

"He does go away a lot. Too much. But I think he's ready to settle down."

Pru made no secret of the smile that was asking if she was ready to settle down too. After only one night together, that was impossible to tell.

"He mentioned a change in his career path," Layla said, hoping she wasn't revealing any secrets.

"Ruger isn't afraid of change. He never has been. He adapts to whatever the situation calls for. You said you are between jobs at the moment?"

Mandy had left a voicemail advising that her employment was terminated. Duh. A handsome guy came and abducted her from the meeting, she couldn't blame Mandy for thinking she was flaky.

"I move around a lot," Layla said, having already told Pru she had traveled the country after her mother died. Pru was easy to talk to but had a clear agenda she was hesitant to encourage. "I think I'll spend some time with my brother soon."

If he would have her, she'd go see Drew and Serendipity once the Ashcroft case was over. Talking to Ruger about her past and about how her mother's death affected her, she was ready to discuss it with Drew and find out just how it had affected him. If they could both be honest, maybe facing those truths would bring them closer.

"He's in Atlantic City, is that right?"

"Yes," she said. "For now anyway."

"Family's important. I think you can see we value it here."

"Yes."

"Sorry to interrupt," Lyssa said, coming back to the table with a more solemn expression, clutching her cellphone to her chest. "Can I borrow Layla for a moment?"

"I'll leave you two alone to talk," Pru said, rising with her glass in hand and retrieving the pitcher of iced tea. "Come into the house when you're ready."

"Ruger is coming over," Lyssa said as Pru retreated toward the house. "But he won't be staying long."

"Okay," Pru said and disappeared into the building.

Lyssa came to Layla's side and sat down to take her hand. "You need to go upstairs and pack a bag. Do you have many things here?"

"Pack a bag, why?"

"You have to come and stay with Colt and me for a few days."

"Why?" Layla asked, snatching her hand back. "What's going on?"

"I don't know the details, but you don't have to worry, we have plenty of space. Blaser will be staying as well."

Layla didn't trust the doctor's expression of calm because she could see the quake of concern beneath. "Why would Blaser come and stay with you? What about Bri?"

"She and Blaser don't live together. She will probably visit him. But don't worry, it will just be for a couple of days."

And then what? Layla didn't like the mysterious behavior. She would be the first to admit she didn't know everyone in the Warner family well; she hadn't been around them for long. But she could tell when someone wasn't giving her the full story.

"You all know, don't you?" Layla asked.

Ruger hadn't told his mother the truth, so she assumed his brothers and their partners didn't know it all either. Turned out, she was the only one in the dark.

"Know?" Lyssa asked.

"About Drew, about what he's into?"

"No," Lyssa said, putting her cellphone onto the metal-framed table and dragging her chair closer. "All I know is Ruger has to go out of town for a couple of days and he's concerned for your safety."

"Why should I believe you?"

"Because what I do requires trust and I know trust is rooted in honesty," Lyssa said. "I do know that what he's doing is connected to what happened to Bri last year. I have been helping Bri work through some of her trauma. I can't break her confidentiality with the details. Colt hasn't told me everything about your connection. He's been working another case and we haven't seen much of each other this week. I will say that the brothers have had a bit of an... awakening recently. Honesty has become more crucial in their relationship. So the chances are Colt and Blaser know all the details."

That came across as honest. Lyssa didn't have to offer any more information beyond her initial statement, yet she had.

"There's no reason for you to be endangered because of my problems."

"Don't worry about that," Lyssa said, wearing an encouraging smile. "Colt won't let anything happen to you. He won't let anything happen to me. Ruger went to Blaser for help because he knows the debt they owe is shouldered by both of them."

So caught up in her flirtation with Ruger, she'd lost track of the debt he'd referred to. For a time, she'd almost forgotten about the trouble Drew was in too. Until then, it had seemed so far away, but it was creeping closer. Whatever Ruger was going to do, she wanted to be a part of it. She didn't want to run and hide, to leave the danger to Drew and Ruger.

"You said that Ruger's coming here?"

"Yes."

"I'll go and pack."

Letting the doctor believe it was her intention to pack and do as Ruger had ordered, Layla went upstairs to gather her possessions. Getting everything in her suitcase was a tight squeeze. As she was finishing up, she heard a vehicle pull into the driveway.

Peeking out of her bedroom window, she saw Ruger exit his truck and head down the path toward the back door, purpose in his stride. If he wanted to get on with whatever he had to do, he wouldn't linger long with his mother.

So she sat on the bed beside her packed suitcase, ready to go. Sure enough, she heard his approaching gait less than a minute later and then her bedroom door opened.

"Are you ready to leave?" he asked, not coming further into the room.

"Where are we going?"

"Lyssa said that she told you," he said, leaving the door to take another step toward her. "You have to go and stay with her and Colt this week."

"This week? I thought it was only going to take a couple of days."

"I don't know how long it will take. I hope it will only be two days, three at the most."

"What is going on?" she asked, getting to her feet. "I'm not a pinball you can just bounce from one relative to another whenever it suits you."

"Hey, I said Blaser should come and look after you here. It was Lyssa who suggested her place. I'm just trying to make sure you are comfortable and safe."

"Great, then take me with you."

"No." There wasn't any indication of wiggle room in that response. He didn't smile, he didn't err, and his expression came over all stony when he got closer. "I am not taking any risks. I told Jansen I would keep you alive and that is what I intend to do. His first condition was that I not bring you anywhere near him."

"You're going to see Drew?" The anger she'd been accumulating in preparation for releasing it in a torrent, instead bled away in the blaze of hope that she might see her brother. "Please let me come with you. I want to see him."

"No," he said again.

Rushing into his arms, she tried to will him to change his mind. "How would you feel if one of your brothers was in trouble, wouldn't you want to help?"

"You can't help," Ruger said. "And I'm only going to see him for long enough to get some information. I'm not hanging around there. I've got somewhere to be."

"Tell me what's going on, Ruger. I'm not going to let you walk away from me without any idea if you'll come back."

"What I'm going to do isn't dangerous," he said, but his exhale betrayed she'd wheedled her way into his psyche a little. "I'm going to do what I do. I'm going to collect goods and take them to a buyer, that's it."

"I thought your days as a fence were over," she said. "You told me that—"

"This isn't work… it's personal, okay?"

"What's the big secret? What is this debt that you owe Drew? I deserve to know."

"The debt doesn't matter."

"It does. It's what motivates you, and Lyssa seems to think Blaser is as invested in this as you are."

"He is," Ruger said then faltered. "He was."

"Was? What changed?"

"I started to fall for you, that's what," he said, pulling her near. "I told Drew I would look after you because I wanted to repay what he did for someone I care about."

"Care about… like a woman?"

"Yes, she's a woman, but not my woman. She's Blaser's woman."

"Bri?" He nodded. "What happened to her?"

"It's a long story, but Jansen pulled her out of a sticky spot. We owe her life to your brother."

"So now you want to repay that by saving mine?"

"I won't have to save yours, okay? No one will get near enough to jeopardize you. I want you to stay with Colt and Blaser because they're smart guys who know what it's like to care for a woman. They'll protect you with their lives."

"I thought I wasn't going to have to be saved," she said, resigning herself to the truth that this man was going to hold onto his secrets. "Will you tell Drew I love him?"

"I will," Ruger said. Pressing a hand to the back of her head, he forced her to rest her head on his chest. "I'm sorry I don't have time to tell you everything, and I promise I'll stop shuttling you around as soon as I get back."

"You can't promise that. Not until you have your own place."

"We'll figure something out. Last night won't be the only night we have."

The idea he might not come back, that something could happen to him before they had the chance to find out what was between them…

She squeezed her eyes closed. "You better come back to me, Ruge. If you're not back in three days I'm going to come and find you, and if you're dead—"

"I won't be dead," he said, laughing and sweeping her hair aside when she leaned back. "I'm just going to drop off some things to our friends. They're friends who have been there for us before, I won't leave them high and dry."

"You owe a lot of people favors, Ruger," she said. "Will you be repaying debts for the rest of your life?"

"No, this is it," he said, kissing her. "I promise once this whole mess with your brother is over, you'll have me all to yourself."

"All to myself… maybe by then I'll have been plucked off the street by another handsome stranger. One who would take me to a karaoke bar."

"If karaoke is what it takes to be with you, I guess I'll have to find it in my heart."

"You want to be with me?" she asked.

Rushing him on the language score that morning had seemed hasty in light of her own indecision. Now she feared they didn't have the time to mess around. If that did end up being the last time she saw him, she didn't want to always wonder how he felt.

"Yeah," he said. "Last night was just the beginning."

SEVENTEEN

LONG GOODBYES WEREN'T HIS STYLE. Ruger was used to being on the road and when it came time to leave his family behind, he liked to slip out quietly. Kissing Layla goodbye felt different. Walking away from the woman he'd spent the night with felt wrong.

The promises he'd made about their relationship just beginning were true. Layla wasn't like the women from his past. But getting involved with the person he was supposed to be protecting for a man he respected should be wrong.

Jansen hadn't been the one to meet him when he arrived in Atlantic City the previous night. Serendipity had answered her boyfriend's phone and had agreed to meet him in a diner. The brief meeting was enough to let him know Jansen was safe. For now. But close to something Ashcroft didn't want the world to know. Serendipity hadn't elaborated. Time was against them. She was due to meet Jansen.

The couple were running out of friends. The attractive woman who'd sat opposite him had dull brown hair that didn't appear to be natural but was as non-descript as her clothes and demeanor. This was a person trying to blend into the background. With her beauty, that was quite a difficult feat.

After passing on Layla's message to Serendipity, Ruger escorted her to her car and returned to his own. Choosing to drive for an hour before stopping, he found a motel and slept the night away with thoughts of Layla chasing him.

His first thought when he woke up in the motel was Layla. She remained in his thoughts through breakfast and the drive he embarked on after leaving the motel. It didn't seem to matter he'd seen her the previous day.

On the road, looking for his turn, he couldn't shake the image of her standing there in his childhood bedroom watching him go. She had been worried, actually concerned for his safety. There was no sass, no witty remarks or jokes for him to volley back. Pure love emanated from her as she stood there, hands clasped beneath her chin.

In the week and a half they'd known each other, there had been plenty of bonding time, plenty of time to talk and flirt and kiss. Perhaps they should've spent their time on more serious matters, but getting to know her, and her quirks, was too much fun.

When Jansen called, the danger she was in reared up. The bleak reminder shone through the prism of his mind's eye, and he didn't like the ominous possibilities. He should've taken more time to brief her on what was going on. It felt dishonest leaving her with only half a story.

Colt and Blaser would take good care of her. Lyssa would like having Layla around. The women were as feisty as each other. His brothers were no doubt enjoying a triumph of teasing in his absence.

The turn he was looking for apparently came out of nowhere. The road was long and straight, and despite the light in the sky, he couldn't see anything that looked like a break in the trees up ahead.

Just then, an opening appeared. Lost in the muck beneath and the trees above, it would be easily missed if a person wasn't looking for it. Slamming on the breaks, he backed up to turn onto the dirt road.

Lucky the truck could handle it, he trundled along bouncing in the divots caused by weather and other vehicles. The route was overgrown. Bushes crowded in on each side making the road so narrow he'd doubt it was passable if he hadn't been told otherwise by someone he trusted.

As quickly as the road popped up, a clearing opened. In front of him was a house, no more than a wooden shack really, an off-road vehicle parked beside it. This was the place.

Flashing his headlights four times, he warned those inside that he was there. If he omitted the signal, he was likely to have his head blown off by those he'd come to help.

The mud under his feet distracted him when he hopped out, but the creak of wood under foot up ahead grabbed his attention. Just as he'd expected, Rushe stood at the top of the shack stairs, a shotgun pointed straight at him.

"I come in peace," Ruger said, holding up his hands in surrender.

As soon as Rushe recognized him, he lowered the gun.

Flick was already in the doorway behind him. "Help him with the bags, Lover," she said, her hand curling around the doorframe.

"I'm not anyone's valet," Rushe grumbled at her over his shoulder.

"Ignore him, Ruger, he's in a bad mood," Flick called out, and stayed put as Rushe trudged down the stairs and through the mud.

Trying not to show fear, like a man would when faced with a ferocious dog, he attempted a smile without taking his eyes from Rushe who was getting closer by the second.

"Does he bite?" Ruger murmured.

Flick must've heard him because she replied. "Only when I ask nicely," she called out. "Lover, you're scaring him. Ruger is here to help us; it would be best if he didn't think you were going to kill him!"

"The meds?" Rushe asked, slamming the truck door, forcing him to stagger out of the way.

In its place, Rushe thrust out an open hand. Meds. Right. Going to the rear of his truck, he unhitched the tailgate and pulled out a holdall to retrieve a large paper bag from inside.

"Painkillers, antibiotics, everything you asked for," Ruger said, handing over the bag. "Birth control pills are in there too." His joke only made Rushe's glare turn into a growl. Snatching the bag, Rushe headed back to the house. "Pays to have a doctor in the family."

What would Rushe have done to him if he hadn't brought all the requested supplies? Probably best not to think about it.

"Come inside!" Flick called just as Rushe grabbed hold of her and pulled her into the cabin.

The truck was still loaded but refusing a request from the lady of the manor wouldn't be smart. Not that the manor was much to look at. In the mucky surroundings, there were trees and bugs, and not a whole lot else. The wooden building was so old and rickety, he doubted it was watertight.

Ascending the stairs, he grabbed for the banister only to find it shakier than the stairs beneath his feet. Getting up them fast, he crossed the porch and ran through the door into a large, T-shaped room with a kitchen running away from the living space that filled the breadth of the building. Two doors occupied each wall flanking the kitchen.

"There's a bathroom if you need it," Flick said.

Rushe was beside her on the plaid couch pulling something from her elevated arm that he held so tight grooves formed in her flesh.

Taking a step to the side, he saw Rushe peel a bandage from Flick's arm. The red streak on the white fabric could only be one thing.

"You were hit?" Ruger asked, now understanding Rushe's foul mood.

Hurrying over, he crouched in front of her while Rushe tossed aside the stained fabric and hoisted her arm higher to take a closer look.

"It's nothing. Barely a flesh wound," she said to Ruger while watching Rushe examine her.

Although the words were aimed at him, they were for Rushe as well.

In Ruger's own assessment, she was right. The bullet had just sliced her skin. It hadn't even gone so far as to damage the muscle. The round had just grazed her and no more.

Rushe washed the wound. While he wouldn't correct a guy like Rushe—especially when his woman was injured—he was far from gentle. Rushe made no apology for his actions even when Flick bit her lip against the sting of iodine. Tears came to her eyes when Rushe scrubbed dirt from the wound, but she didn't recoil. She didn't move an inch.

Flick was from a wealthy family and had been raised in privilege. That life was behind her now. Far behind her. To be with Rushe, she'd had to endure a lot of crass behavior and dangerous situations. Watching her sitting there, allowing her lover to do the necessary work, without whimpering or complaining, Ruger garnered new respect for her.

But it was too much to watch a woman in pain. "Do you want me to do that?" he asked.

Rushe kept working.

Flick shook her head. "He'll be done in a minute."

True enough, a score of seconds went by, then Rushe pressed gauze to the wound and taped it on. It had been tough to watch her suffer, but Rushe did everything right. The wound might not be deep, but it was still a wound. Next Rushe retrieved pills from the bottles in the paper bag and tipped some into his hand. Cradling Flick's head, he tossed them into her mouth. She picked up a glass of water from the floor to help swallow them down.

With the formalities out of the way, Flick relaxed. Rushe put a hand on her head and stroked her hair once before he got up and went out. Assuming Rushe was going to unload the truck, he intended to go help until Flick spoke.

"How is Bri?"

Letting Flick take the lead, he figured it was better to follow her than pursue her boyfriend. If help was needed, someone would ask. So he sat on the couch in the spot Rushe had vacated.

Reconsidering their proximity, he shuffled back a few inches. "She's good. Still with Blaser."

In his conversations with Flick over the phone while trying to get in touch with Jansen, he'd learned she was rational. A far easier person to deal with than her boyfriend.

"From what you told me, they're soulmates," Flick said, cradling the glass of water on her lap.

"I'm surprised you believe in that."

"You are?" she asked and smiled. Her vibrancy echoed against him. "If I didn't believe that Rushe was the only guy out there for me, I'd have run away a long time ago."

She was still smiling, so her statement didn't raise any concerns. "Actually, Bri's pregnant," he said.

It might be a secret back home, but he doubted that Flick would come in contact with any of his family members any time soon.

"Good for her," Flick said. "That's great."

"It's a secret, it's still early but—"

"I'll keep my fingers crossed and my lips sealed," Flick said, sitting up to put her glass on the floor again. "We'll need to send her something."

"Send who?" Ruger turned to see Rushe come in and dump the things from the truck in the middle of the floor. "What is half this stuff?"

"You didn't write the list, I did," Flick said, scurrying off the couch to go check out her spoils. "So shut up. You can complain when you write your own list."

She began to unpack the food items and put them in the kitchen cabinets with one hand. When Rushe saw her struggle, he crossed to her and took over the task, following where her finger pointed as to where things should go.

"Bri is pregnant," she said to Rushe. "Isn't that great?"

"Bri?"

"The woman I was locked in Victor's dungeon with, remember? The woman Jansen saved with me when he ran the van off the road." With her back to the unit, she propped her hands on it and leaned back to gaze up at Rushe. "The woman who is marrying Ruger's brother, the woman he's doing this for."

Blaser and Bri weren't actually engaged, not that he'd heard anyway. Now that she was pregnant, a wedding would make sense, except the couple didn't even live together yet.

"She's still working with Lyssa, you know, working through her issues."

"She went through a difficult time," Flick said. Leaving Rushe in the kitchen, she came over to stand behind the couch. "The man who touched her deserved to die; he was a sniveling bastard."

Rushe came up behind her and put his hands on her shoulders. "We're done talking about this," he said with a tone of warning when he looked at Ruger.

Jansen had saved Flick and Bri. Many men were thankful for that.

"Jansen said you picked up his sister, Layla, in Miami?" Flick asked, conceding to Rushe's command without acknowledging it.

"Yeah," Ruger said.

"What's she like?"

"A pain in the ass. She's a sassy handful, but she's smart enough to know Ashcroft could cause problems for her. So she's behaving."

"Interesting," Flick said. "Maybe I'll try that sometime."

From the way Rushe's eyes rolled, Ruger doubted that. Rushe went back to the supplies and began to sort through the weapons and survival gear.

"She's beautiful. She's got long dark hair and big bright eyes, and her body—" Stopping himself, he frowned, and noticed Rushe had stopped what he was doing to frown too. "I'm sleeping with her," Ruger confessed.

Rushe went back to his task.

Flick squealed and bounded around the couch to sit down and snatch his hands. "That's a leap," she said. "Does Drew know?"

"Who's Drew?" Rushe asked, unsheathing a knife, proving that even when the guy was busy, he was on alert and always paying attention.

"You know who Drew is. Jansen, Layla's brother. The guy who hangs around with Serendipity. Not everyone is known by just one name like you," Flick said and tsked. "You just keep working, thug, and I'll handle the gossip."

"There's really no gossip," Ruger said.

"Sure there is," Flick said. "So is it just sex or…"

"I don't know what it is. I think she's great and she can handle my family."

"That's a bonus."

"But she doesn't even have a fixed address and I'm supposed to be getting out of this game. I don't know where I'll end up."

"You're getting out of the game?"

"Now that Colt and Blaser know, it's only fair to them. I don't want anyone to get hurt. Anyone else. Bri did get hurt. If that happened again…"

"I understand," Flick said. "What do you want to do? Have you thought about it?"

"No. I've never been a 'future' kind of guy. I just do what needs to be done in the now."

"You'll have to think about it now. You'll have to earn money somehow."

"I've got enough to keep me going for a while. But you're right, it won't last forever."

When he had worked for Victor, he knew both Rushe and Jansen as criminals, formidable ones at that. Ruger had left before Flick got mixed up in the mess, so he hadn't met her until after the fact. But in the circles that he ran, he'd heard tales of the couple and the terror they could conjure. Since getting to know Flick personally, he was pleased, and surprised, to find that she was actually a sweetheart and not at all scary.

Though the power she wielded over Rushe, and the love she had for him, had caused death and destruction. Ruger could tell by looking at her that she wasn't at all ashamed or remorseful of that.

"You'll figure it out," Flick said, patting his hand. "You could figure it out with Layla. Maybe you could come up with something together."

That was an idea. One which relied on him opening up to Layla about the possibility of a future and Jansen had told him that idea made his sister run a mile. While Ashcroft and his men were a threat, Ruger couldn't take the risk of scaring her away.

"What do you know about the Ashcroft situation?" Ruger asked.

Serendipity had been cagey and hadn't revealed much. Ruger couldn't blame her. She didn't know him and was living under siege. For all she knew, he could've been an imposter and she'd said as much to his face.

"That all the stories are true and that he'll do whatever it takes to maintain his lifestyle. He's not a man afraid of authorities," Flick said. "He thinks he's all powerful and so he underestimated the threat Jansen and Serendipity represented."

"How long do you think this will go on?" Ruger asked. "I mean, what's the end game?"

"Serendipity is close. She's been shopping around for a while and has a potential buyer; a newspaper wants to break the story. Although she's only given them tasters, they're concerned for her safety. It's going to be bumpy."

"Like it isn't already," Ruger said. "For all of you."

"When Ashcroft heard Jansen's girlfriend was writing a story and that she was close to selling it, he must have panicked and sent his man in. The one who gave me this," she said, twisting her arm.

"He sent the guy in to take you out before the story could be told," Ruger said.

"Yeah," Flick said. "The guy demanded her notes, and her computer, he took everything he could get his hands on, Jansen's files and his photographs."

Which he would've gotten away with had he not started firing. The bullet that hit Flick sealed the shooter's fate and Rushe had snapped his neck. At least Serendipity and Jansen didn't lose any of their evidence.

"What did you do with the body?"

"I didn't deal with that," Flick said.

Made sense, she would have been too busy bleeding all over the floor.

Why did he ask that? Wasn't like he wanted to be an accessory to anything. Information like that made him a target. That was the last thing he wanted to be while protecting Layla. Maybe he'd asked them because Blaser asked him. His brother put the question in his head.

"Time for you to go," Rushe said and marched to the couch to haul him onto his feet.

"No need to get physical," Ruger said unsure what caused the change in the previously silent man.

"He knows where we are," Flick said, getting to her feet. "If he was a snitch, the cops would be all over this place."

A cop, or someone working for a cop, would ask the location of the body. Was that the red flag Rushe sensed? It just seemed like a logical question. Either that or his dumb adolescent brain was excited by the notion of such a violent thrill.

"I'm working for you guys," Ruger said. "I came here to help because we're all in this together. I have Layla at my brother's place, and I'll do whatever it takes to keep her safe. I left her there under the care of brothers I trust with my life, but it's driving me crazy not to be with her. If something happens to her while I'm not there—"

"What?" Rushe asked, grabbing his jacket, yanking him forward.

"Put him down," Flick said with a tinge of annoyance. "Think of what you've done to protect me in the past. You know how it felt to leave me open without you at my side. It didn't matter how many times I told you I was okay, or that I could take care of myself. You still didn't feel right about it."

"That's different," Rushe said, glaring again before releasing Ruger.

"Different?" Flick asked.

"I love you," Rushe said.

"Yeah, but how long did it take you to admit that to yourself or to me? Maybe Ruger doesn't know it yet, but it doesn't make it any less real."

"I'm not in love," Ruger said, considering what it would be like to care for a person so much.

Rushe and Flick might be an unconventional couple living in an unconventional way. But it worked. Rushe adored her and she was crazy for him. The most dramatic stories that circulated about them were always related to the couple fighting to save each other's lives or to be together.

Since leaving Layla, she had occupied his thoughts. His fear that something lethal could happen to her while he wasn't at her side tied him up in knots. Maybe it was love, or maybe it could be, but he would never be able to answer those questions until he got himself back to her side.

EIGHTEEN

LYSSA AND COLT'S TOWNHOUSE was amazing. Set over three floors, it also had a basement. Lyssa used the first floor of the house to see patients, but the other floors were for living in. Before its partial transformation, the bedroom allocated to Layla had been the main guest bedroom, but it now contained the various items needed to convert it into a nursery. That Colt hadn't put Blaser in the room, given its nursery accessories, was understandable. The sight of baby things could stress out the strip club owner or overwhelm him with the reality of expecting his own child.

The first night there had been great fun. The reality of the prospective danger to her life seemed like a distant threat when she was ensconced in the bosom of this family. After Lyssa helped her to settle in, they talked and cooked together, then the men came in to eat and she spent the evening listening to stories of Ruger.

If he'd been present, he would've hated every minute of the conversation. But she was so grateful to get to know him from the people who knew him the best. Bri hadn't come over to visit, so Blaser had spent portions of the night on the phone and texting, keeping in touch with his love.

That day, Layla woke up without purpose. She hated days like that. The men were busy with their trade and Lyssa had patients to see downstairs. She'd been left with instructions to stay in the townhouse, away from the windows. Colt even gave her a panic button to press if anything happened or danger found her.

Being caged made her uneasy. The idea that these thugs were getting away with penning her in really pissed her off. She'd spent some time internet window shopping, because she had no way to buy anything. She wasn't allowed to use her cards and had no delivery address. Her Miami address was her billing address, but it was unlikely she'd ever set foot in that apartment again.

Thinking about distractions like dinner and dancing and dating, she fell into old habits and looked up ads for the local area. Coming to a new town wasn't a unique experience. She followed the same routine on arriving somewhere new. Researching apartments and job vacancies, she sought something to excite her about starting over.

Not too long into her search, one ad caught her attention. Reading it maybe ten times, she was taking notes when she heard Lyssa coming up the stairs at lunchtime. Printing off the advert, she shut down the computer.

"What do you think of this?" Layla asked, striding into the kitchen and putting the printed advertisement beside Lyssa's salad plate on the kitchen table.

At first, the doctor didn't respond, she just read the advert and carried on eating. When she was finished, she looked up. "It's great. Are you considering it?"

Layla put her hands on the table and in a curved descent, she sat in the chair opposite the doctor. "It's premises and it has an apartment above."

"Yes, I see that," Lyssa said. "It's in the Warner neighborhood."

"Yeah, I noticed that," Layla said, reaching over to whoosh the advert across to her side of the table to read it again. "The owner died suddenly. There's a fully ready salon. It says the apartment's been vacant for a while, but I could fix it up."

"You said you were a cosmetologist. I think it's a great idea, if you think that you can take it on."

"Her son is renting it while he decides what to do with it, business and apartment. It's only a one-bedroom, but from the pictures online the place is huge." Her eyes scanned the words on the paper, and she could feel them glittering. This was a chance to build something for herself. She had always loved hairdressing and had only left it because of her relationship demise. On starting the course, the goal had been to have her own place, and she had a chance at achieving that ambition. "He might consider selling it to me if I can make it work."

"I guess this means you're hanging around."

That statement made Layla stop reading and plant her hand on top of the paper. "I hadn't thought about it like that."

"I think it's an excellent idea and I have faith you can pull it off. It's less than a mile from Pru's house, and she'll certainly send business your way. She has a lot of influence in the community."

"I couldn't ask her to do that."

"You wouldn't have to," Lyssa said. "That's the kind of thing she does for family."

"I'm not family."

"Not yet. But you are seeing Ruger."

"Do you think this will freak him out?" Layla asked.

Most men were commitment-phobes, but she wore that badge too. Taking the salon on was a sign she was sticking around. Ruger might take that to mean she was cozying up to him and expecting their flirtation to become something more serious.

"Ruger is smart," Lyssa said, finishing her lunch and taking her plate to the sink to wash it. "You have to make a decision based on what you want and that doesn't have to include Ruger. Yes, we all think you're great and it's obvious Ruger adores you, but you shouldn't pass up a chance at something you want to make a go of because you think a man might take exception to it."

Lyssa had a terrific way of cutting through the bullshit and getting right to the point. An opportunity like this was rare. The price was low because the owner wanted to rent the place quickly. She could take over the business and have somewhere to stay so she wouldn't be sponging off the Warner family anymore.

"I don't know," Layla said. "I don't want him to think I'm making assumptions. How terrible would it be if I signed on for this and then we broke up next week?"

"People who live in the same cities and neighborhoods the world over get together and break up. Who cares if you have an ex in the town? You're not going to be the only ex of Ruger's around here."

Oh, not a nice thought, but Lyssa had a point. If things didn't work out with Ruger, she would have her own sanctuary that wasn't reliant on him or his family. She had lost her job in Miami and had pretty much decided that the climate down there wasn't for her anyway.

Just because she broke up with a man didn't mean she had to leave the state. Though that was her usual MO, she was sure that Ruger wouldn't make things awkward or difficult.

There was always the chance things would work out with Ruger. If they did, this was her foothold in the community, her chance to make money, and a home for herself with him. Atlantic City was around five hundred miles away. Being closer to Drew than she had been in a while was a plus. Close enough that they could get to each other by car in a day in case of emergency, but far enough away that she wouldn't have her big brother breathing down her neck.

"Can I borrow your car?"

"I don't have a car," Lyssa said. "But I can call Colt and he can take you over."

"Isn't he working?" Layla asked.

"He had work to do this morning but called to say he would be back in an hour or so. Why don't you call the number on that advert, and you can check out the place? Colt and I were going to Pru's for dinner tonight anyway. If you could make the appointment before that, we could all go over together, what do you think? I'd be honored to come and see the place with you."

Another female perspective would be useful. It was unlikely Colt would know much about hair salons. Taking the advice, she used Lyssa's phone to call the number on the advert for an appointment.

Trying not to get her hopes up too high in case it didn't work out, she was thrilled to set the meet when Colt would be home and Lyssa would be free. For now, she had no way to get in touch with Ruger. She didn't want to harass him while he was dealing with such a precarious situation anyway. But when he got back, he could be in for a real surprise.

THE PLACE WAS PERFECT. The shop was set in a row of others with the apartment access at the back. The other stores would mean she had passing traffic and there were no other salons so no direct competition. Colt talked to the son of the woman who'd owned the shop and found out their mothers had known each other. Ted, the deceased woman's son, and Colt had gone to the same high school, though Colt was five or so years younger than Ted.

The only thing that concerned Layla was the size. The actual salon was much bigger than she had realized. There were ten stations. As a one woman show, she wouldn't be able to handle that many clients at the same time. Ted reassured her there were a couple of younger local women training who could come in and help out. Although they weren't fully qualified and were still at college, it would be good to have support.

Upstairs, the one bed apartment had a separate kitchen and bathroom with several closets. A couple of which had the potential to be knocked together to make another bedroom. A point of interest if she did decide to stick around and maybe buy later. At the moment, Ted was renting month-to-month while he sorted out the paperwork, but he did have a view to sell in the near future.

His mother had rented out the apartment a few times. The previous tenant left a few months ago. The place needed a good clean, but it was fully furnished, and Ted was leaving it that way.

"This feels too easy," Layla said when she was alone with Lyssa in the living room of the upstairs apartment looking down on the happy, clean street below.

"Maybe it's just meant to be," Lyssa said. "If you don't feel comfortable, or you don't want to do this, we can walk away. Ted won't cause any trouble."

Trouble wasn't what Layla felt there. It felt like home, and she had the help of Lyssa and Colt, one of the nicest couples she'd ever known.

"It feels right."

"Then sign on the dotted line," Lyssa said, joining Layla at the window. "It can be undone if you change your mind. I'm sure Ted will be reasonable. If you can afford the deposit, there's no problem. Ted has shown us the books and the salon certainly generates enough revenue. His mother worked it alone with the help of the younger ones. You can do it too. I don't see any reason why not. The client base is already there and Pru will help you. She'll be over the moon when she hears about this."

They were supposed to have dinner at the Warner house that night. Colt and Lyssa were supposed to at any rate, Layla was just tagging along. If she signed up, she could make the announcement at dinner. It wasn't something that could be kept a secret, even if ideally it would wait until Ruger returned.

For one thing, she had no idea when he would be back. For another, it was a small community. As soon as the locals heard the salon was occupied again, there would be plenty of faces pressed to the glass, desperate to discover the identity of the stranger in their town.

"Okay," she said turning around and widening her smile. "Let's do it."

"Ted said you could move into the apartment right away. Colt and I can help you bring over your things. Ruger wants you to be safe though, so it would probably be best if you stay with us until he's back."

"I want to stay here," Layla said. "If I'm honest, I need some space. Who would think to look for me here? If it's that big a deal, Colt or Blaser can stay in the bedroom, and I'll sleep on the couch."

"Uh, no," Lyssa said, putting an arm around her. "You can sleep in the bedroom, and they'll take the couch. But before we make decisions about moving in, let's deal with the paperwork."

Lyssa was insightful but practical too. She hoped they'd find a way to maintain a friendship even after she and Ruger broke up.

Going down the stairs, they discussed the formalities with Ted and Colt in the back shop, where the salon supplies were kept. The coffee machine and small refrigerator signaled it doubled as a breakroom.

After everything was signed, she tugged out her checkbook and leaned on the counter with the intention of writing, but Colt's hand caught the pen before it reached the paper.

"What?" Layla asked, peering at him from her bent position. "What's the problem?"

"You can't write a check, Layla."

Her ties to the Warner family made her a promising prospect for Ted. One thing they hadn't told him about was the hitmen on her tail.

"I can," she said and straightened up. "If I don't, I'll lose out on this opportunity."

Lyssa searched in her purse and produced a checkbook which she handed to Colt. "We'll take care of it," she said.

Colt plucked Layla's pen from her hand and began to fill out a check.

"I can't ask you to do that," Layla said, watching Colt as he wrote.

"You can pay us back when everything's straightened out," Lyssa said, giving Layla's hand a squeeze.

Drawing in a long breath, Layla couldn't argue with the sense of what the couple were saying. But she had to give voice to the niggling suspicion that kept cropping up in her mind every time she thought about breakfast at the hotel.

"Thank you," Layla said. "Though I'm not sure that it makes a difference how careful we are. They already know I'm here."

Colt stopped writing and slowly turned until his eyes met hers. Layla anticipated a response. Except Colt said nothing to the revelation, so Lyssa filled the silence.

"Uh, Ted, could you give us just a minute please?" Lyssa asked.

"Sure," the lanky redhead said and departed the back shop.

"What do you mean they already know that you're here?" Lyssa asked, coming around her to stand next to Colt. "Why would you think that?"

"I saw them at the hotel, yesterday morning," Layla said, leaning against the counter where the two checkbooks were laid out. "I wasn't sure at first. It was just an odd car that caught my attention for a couple of fleeting seconds. I tried to shrug it off. But the more I think about it, I don't know, it's just instinct, I guess."

"Instinct," Colt said, giving away nothing of his reaction to the news.

"I guess maybe I'm being stupid, maybe it wasn't them at all. It was just a car in a busy street, there were dozens of them."

"In my experience, nothing outranks instinct," Lyssa said. "And Colt would agree if he wasn't working up such a lather."

"I'm not mad," he said. "Why didn't you tell Ruger?"

"Maybe she did, and he dismissed her," Lyssa said. "Did you?"

"No," Layla said, shrinking under the scrutiny. "Ruger was on the phone with Drew when I noticed the car then he whisked me out of the hotel and dumped me at your mother's. There was no time. Everything after happened quickly. He seemed to be on this important mission. I didn't have the time to—"

"When your life is in danger, you make the goddamn time," Colt said, his severe tone caused Lyssa to take his hand.

"Calm down," Lyssa said. "It's okay. We're here with her. Nothing is going to happen."

Snapping around to look at his fiancée, Layla was forgotten. "Ruger will go nuts when he hears about this and I'm the one who has to call and tell him."

"You don't have to tell him," Layla said, but the couple ignored her.

"I have never seen Ruger irrevocably angry," Lyssa said. "He'll make a joke and you'll talk him down."

"Not about this," Colt said. "You have never seen what he's like with a woman he cares about. He's protective of his girlfriends and after what happened with Bri… he already feels responsible for one woman being traumatized, if it happens again… I don't know how he'll turn out."

"You're his brother," Lyssa said, stepping in to rub his arm. "You know how to help him. You and Blaser are here, nothing is going to happen to Layla."

"Not until these bastards want it to," he said and exhaled. Pushing Lyssa out of the way, he stalked to the loveseat and then turned to examine both women. "We better get over to Mom's. I don't want to be late. We'll call Ruger from there. I'll just have to hope he doesn't drive off the road in his hurry to get back here."

"He trusts you," Lyssa said, traversing to him and taking his hand. "He knows you'll look after Layla, just like you trusted him to look after me."

"That was different. I needed someone to cover the front while I was around the back. I was right there the whole time. It would've been tough for him to screw up."

"Are you saying that he wouldn't have done whatever was necessary to protect me?"

"He would have, of course he would have."

"Just like you'll do anything for Layla."

The couple shared their intimate moment. While Colt kissed his fiancée, Layla ripped out the deposit check Colt had written and took it to Ted on the sidewalk outside with the building, keys in his hand.

"Thank you," he said. "When would you like to move in and open up?"

It was on the tip of her tongue to say as soon as possible, but Colt came out with Lyssa tucked under his arm.

"All done?" Colt asked, more relaxed than he had been inside.

"We were just talking about a moving in date," Ted said.

"It will be a couple of days at least," Colt said.

"We can pick up the keys tomorrow if that suits everyone," Lyssa said, checking each expression. "That will give us a chance to clean up and get the place ready for Layla before she opens up."

"But she won't be moving in right away," Colt said.

Layla was speechless that the couple was taking such a leading role in the decisions about her life. With no opportunity to assert herself, she listened to the men confirm a time the next evening and then Ted was in his car driving away.

Glaring at Colt and at Lyssa too, Layla wasn't going to let them get away with such heavy-handed behavior. "What was that?" she asked. "What did you think you—"

"You're under my protection while Ruger's out of town," Colt said. "I'm not protecting you here. When Ruger gets back into town, you can take up this fight with him. But until then, you do as I say."

"Or what?" she asked.

"Or you'll find all your liberties taken away," Colt said. "If what you said is right, and the car outside the hotel was Ashcroft's men that means the danger is here. While you're in danger and in my house, you're endangering people I care about."

"Colt," Lyssa murmured.

"I'm sorry, Layla, but that's the way it is," Colt said. "I won't let Lyssa be hurt by this and Bri's been hurt enough already."

"It sounds odd hearing you come to Bri's defense after the way you treated her when she and Blaser got back together," Lyssa said.

"We've been through a lot since then and figured a lot of stuff out as a family. She's one of us now."

"And how do you know that Layla isn't?" Lyssa asked. "Have you spoken to Ruger about how he feels?"

"Why would I have done that?"

"Because if in six months they walk down the aisle, you'll be telling everyone that she's one of us too."

"When Ruger tells me she's his, I'll change my tune," Colt said. "Come on."

Loosening his arm from Lyssa's shoulders, he took her hand and turned to lead her to the car. Lyssa was wearing an expression of apology, but Layla couldn't argue with what Colt had said. Neither she nor Ruger knew how they felt about each other yet, and she didn't want to hurt people who had been kind to her.

Lyssa was Colt's future, as Bri was for Blaser. At the moment, she was no more than a distraction for the youngest Warner. In due time they'd figure out how they felt about each other, but that didn't affect the danger she was in now.

The only conclusion she could reach was that Ashcroft's men were watching her. Without evidence to the contrary it seemed sensible to assume that was the case. Since she knew they were out there, she was more alert, though if they knew she was aware of them, they would probably skulk back into the shadows.

The more imminent concern was for Ruger and if he would be upset or angry when Colt revealed her suspicions.

DINNER AT THE WARNER house went without a hitch. Colt showed no signs of his earlier annoyance and Layla was surprised to hear there was an engagement party happening that weekend, there at the Warner home. The couple had set a date for the wedding, just twelve weeks away. Would she be around to witness the event, or would Ruger be done with her by then?

While they were in the living room drinking coffee, Colt slipped away. At first, she thought nothing of it, but when ten minutes passed and he still wasn't back, she figured he was talking to Ruger.

Sure enough, less than five minutes after that, Colt came back into the living room, cellphone in hand.

"Phone," Colt said to her as he came back to join the family.

From his glare, it was obvious Ruger hadn't taken the news well. She didn't want to be berated by her one-time lover over the phone but putting up a fight in front of Mr. and Mrs. Warner would be disrespectful.

"Thanks," she said, rising and taking the phone. She excused herself and went outside to the back patio before lifting the phone to her ear. "Hi, honey, miss me?"

"Oh, honey, is it?" he asked. "You weren't thinking that when you started keeping secrets."

"I didn't keep a secret," she said, frustrated he felt the need to be dramatic. "What did Colt tell you?"

"The truth. Something you should've done."

"Look, it was just a creepy feeling," she said. "I didn't know for sure. No one jumped out of the vehicle wearing an Ashcroft button."

"A creepy feeling is enough; a creepy feeling could've changed things. When there are crazy, violent people out after you, creepy means a whole helluva lot."

Surprised by the potency of his reaction, she pulled out one of the patio chairs and sat down. "I'm sorry, Ruger, I... I didn't think it was a big deal. I really just tried to shrug it off."

"Well don't next time, okay?"

"Okay."

"Now I'm worried about you, see? I'm driving faster than I should because I want to be there. I have to get to you. Like I wasn't already in knots about being away from you, now I have to deal with this?"

"You were in knots?" she asked, a sappy spiral of flattery zipped through her.

"Yeah. You better be ready for some action when I get back there."

"Sex," she whispered, caught between the buzz of intimacy and the regret of eagerness.

Perhaps if Ruger was only enticed by sex, there would be no future for them after all.

"What other kind of action is there? You think I'm going to come in there and start beating on you? I might be pissed, but I've never raised my hands to a woman yet."

"I just thought maybe, you know, you missed me."

"I do, I just said that, didn't I? Now listen to me, Colt and I have figured it out. You're going to stay at his place tonight and then tomorrow he'll take you to Blaser. You can help out at the garage or at Risqué. Wherever Blaser is, you stay with him, okay? I'm going to be back tomorrow. I've only been back on the road for an hour, I'll drive for as long as I can, but I'm going to need to stop and sleep eventually."

"Drive safely," she said. "Don't worry about me. I'll do what Colt says."

Much as it pained her to take orders from anyone, if it appeased Ruger, then she would comply. She'd never forgive herself if Ruger drove himself off the road through tiredness.

"I didn't expect you to give in so easily. Have you fallen and hit your head? Been replaced by a doppelganger? What?"

"You might not care about me beyond sexual satisfaction, but I care about you. Your family love you and they need you."

"Oh, I screwed up," he said, losing some of his anger to contrition. "I do miss you, Legs. Do you think we jumped into the sack too soon? You regret it?"

"No," she said and sighed, fixing her sights on the clear table in front of her. "Did Colt tell you what I did today?"

"No."

"Oh," she said, taken aback by Colt's omission. He hadn't been as honest as Ruger thought. "What did you do today?

"I got a job," she said. It wasn't the whole truth, but this wasn't the time to have "*the talk.*"

"A job? You better not be working at Risqué. I will kill Blaser if he—"

"No, it's not at Risqué. It's at a salon, near your mom's."

"That's good. It will keep you busy. But you can't start until this Ashcroft crap is dealt with. If you're out in public like that, the guys could take a shot at you and anyone standing beside you—"

"I know, Colt has already given me the 'endangering people he cares about,' bit."

"I care about you, Lay," Ruger said, his voice becoming softer and more gracious. "We're going to get through this, you and me. I'm going to be at your side until all the danger is taken care of."

And afterwards? Drew had to hurry up and do whatever he had to do. She wanted Serendipity to get the story out there and to hear that all the guilty parties had been brought to justice.

But when all of that was done and the danger was gone, would her appeal to Ruger remain? No one had mentioned any commitments he'd made to women in the past. If he liked to bed and bolt, she'd made a terrible decision to spend the night with him.

She didn't want to be anyone's temporary distraction, but if Drew hadn't sent Ruger to her, they never would've met. Could Ruger be a distraction for her too? She couldn't think like that. She wasn't the type to fall into bed with someone just because they were there.

The intensity of their bond could come from the danger. When that was gone, what would be left for them to share?

NINETEEN

RISQUÉ WAS IN FULL SWING by the time he arrived seeking Layla who Colt had confirmed was there. Cranky, tired and frustrated by traffic holding him up, all he wanted to do was get his girl, and get the hell out again without answering too many questions.

The guys on the door didn't acknowledge him. They were dealing with a gang of idiots shouting about a bachelor party. Some of them were already too drunk to stand on their own two feet. More delays. He passed the throng of men and headed for the family corner.

Before he could get there, however, he spied Layla standing at the center of the bar with three men laughing at whatever she'd said. Smiling, she took her drink from the bar and tongued her straw into her mouth. The action had the men transfixed; he knew exactly what they were thinking because he'd been witness to that act too.

Without any thought for tact, he marched over, shoved one guy aside and got hold of her arm. "What the hell are you doing?" he demanded.

"Celebrating," she said, hollowing her cheeks to suck the alcohol from the glass.

Her glittering eyes and glossed lips were very pleased with themselves. Shame he couldn't reciprocate.

"So you thought you'd get drunk with a bunch of strangers?"

The men weren't backing off, in fact one of them moved in closer with an air of propriety. "I don't know who you think you are, man, but the lady is having a good time."

"The lady is wanted by a hitman," Ruger said. "And she's not going home with you, so back off."

"Who says she isn't?" the guy piped up.

Most men didn't even try to stand up to him. With his superior height, he intimidated most people. He could tell from the way the guy puffed himself up and the distinct scent of liquor that he thought more of himself than the rest of the world saw.

"I say she isn't, and she says it too," Ruger said. If he started a fight, Layla would be left alone and open to attack. Glancing to his right, he saw Dax, a Risqué security guard, approach and they made eye contact. If something was going to go down, Ruger had back up on hand. "Cut your losses and go home."

"Who do you think you are?" one of the guys hollered, but he wasn't paying attention to Layla's gaggle anymore.

Layla was watching something. When he followed her line of sight, he saw a guy by the entrance, just inside.

"Who is that?" Ruger asked her.

"I don't know." Without sparkle or charm, he saw the sheen fall from her mask. "He looks like…"

"The guy you saw in the car?" Ruger finished her sentence and their eyes met. She didn't have to confirm it. Tearing his eyes away, he sought out Crystal, who happened to be behind the bar with Blaser. "Crystal! Come here."

Keeping his eyes on the guy by the door so as not to lose him, Ruger tried to be discreet in his scrutiny. Dax was moving closer to the person of interest. Good, he'd seen it too. His ally was being discreet and keeping busy, so as not to alert anyone to their suspicions. Had he got a bad feeling from the guy? Made sense. The perp was standing at the door taking in his surroundings, without admiring the view. Definitely suspicious.

Crystal came up at his side. "What's the problem, Ruge?" she asked. "Layla's just having some fun, nothing wrong with that."

Reminded of the letches around his girl, he grabbed Crystal's hand and put it in Layla's. "Take her to Colt's office."

"What's going on?" Destiny asked, sauntering over.

"Ruger's in a snit about Layla flirting with these hotties."

"Oh, baby, don't pout," Destiny said, arranging her body around his.

His sense of humor abandoned him. Snatching hold of Destiny, he shoved her back and then glared at Crystal. "I don't have time for this shit, Cryst, get her upstairs, now."

It was so unlike him to snap that Crystal jumped to action, dragging Layla away from the bar. Destiny trotted on behind the women, no doubt in search of the gossip. He would apologize and deal with them later.

Whirling around, he advanced on the suspicious guy. The perp noticed—which wasn't difficult given his height—and began beating a path out of the club. But Dax was on him. The two disappeared into the corridor leading to the main entrance. With Dax and Risqué security on the job, the dirty work would be done by the time he caught up.

Turning into the poorly lit corridor, his supposition was confirmed. Security men from outside crowded around Dax, who had someone pinned to the wall. Slowing his pace, Ruger wanted the stranger to know he wasn't in Kansas here. With power like Ashcroft behind him, the stalker probably believed himself invincible. But there in Risqué, Warner word was law.

"Keep your mouth shut," Dax said, slamming the guy to the wall and searching his person for weapons.

Good call. Dax found a gun, which he handed off to one of the security guys.

"Get rid of it," Ruger said when he got there, and the bouncer toddled off.

With Colt's connections to the cops, it was easy for them to make an anonymous weapon donation to the precinct. Disarming men who abused their power was fine by his conscience. He didn't like that the guy had so easily brought a weapon into a place filled with people he cared about.

Staying behind Dax, who still pinned the guy in place, Ruger scrutinized the stranger from head to foot. "Ashcroft likes them young I see," he said. "Inexperienced."

"I got all the experience I need," the guy said, trying to wriggle free of Dax's hold without success.

"Not from the picture you're in now," Ruger said. "My man here can snap you and nobody here will speak to witnessing a thing."

"I'm not the killer here, you are."

"Your buddy shot at an innocent woman," Ruger said, assuming that he was talking about the guy Rushe killed. "What's your name?"

"Suck my dick."

Pursing his lips in a smile, Ruger tilted his head before he shook it. "That's not a service we offer here at Risqué, but I guess now we know how you spend your Saturday nights. What's your name?"

"Answer him," Dax growled, increasing his pressure on his captive's chest.

"Padget."

"Padget, I'm glad you came to visit us," Ruger said. "Saves me the trouble of tracking you and your colleagues down."

"It's not gonna work," Padget spat out, glaring at both Dax and Ruger. "You'll never be able to protect her."

"We're doing okay so far," Ruger said, giving up his humor.

"Yeah, only 'cause he hasn't given the word yet."

"So why are you here? Sightseeing?"

"I'm here to watch her, to figure out what's going on. It wasn't tough to track her down. Just got hold of Potter, he was the last guy to see her in Miami."

Potter. The guy from Miami. The one Layla had been in a meeting with when Ruger approached. Damn, he'd made the rookie mistake of using his name. Ashcroft now knew everything about him and his family.

"You've got a lot of pretty girls around here," Padget said. "It will be a shame to see them all out of work when we shut this place down."

"Many have tried," Ruger said, finding humor in his aggression again. "You're not the only one who has friends in high places."

Though to be honest, his contacts didn't quite reach beyond a governor. Bluffing wasn't beyond him. If they could slow Ashcroft down, make him think twice before hurting Layla, that might buy Jansen and Serendipity enough time to make their case to the public.

"Not high enough," Padget said. "We know you, know your family, you can't take a shit without us knowing about it."

"They do say knowledge is power," Ruger said. "But I don't think that's what they meant. If you're here to take her out, what's stopping you?"

"I'm not here for that. I report back and when it's time to make the move, I'll get word. You and your girl won't stand a chance."

"As you can see, I have plenty of back-up," Ruger said, nodding at Dax. "Run back and tell your boss that, then tell him my associate who snapped your buddy's neck isn't done yet. You make sure he knows who he's messed with, because my associate won't stop until your ranks are decimated. He'll go straight to the top; anyone who messes with his girl is on borrowed time."

"You don't scare me," Padget said.

Dax grabbed his hair and smacked his head off the wall behind him. "We don't care if you're scared," he said. "Deliver your message like a good little errand boy and when you're ready for the fight, you know where to find us."

"It takes some kind of coward to hide behind the likes of you, Padget," Ruger said. "Ashcroft isn't fooling anyone. If he had the balls to face up to guys like me and my friends, he wouldn't need grunts like you."

Dragging him away from the wall, Dax threw Padget toward the exit. "Consider yourself barred."

Regaining his footing, Padget glared and wiped his hands down his clothes where Dax had touched him, but he had no chance of finding composure or making a dignified exit. Security from the door came up behind him to seize his shoulders and he was carted out like any other common miscreant.

"Thanks," Ruger said.

"No worries," Dax responded. "Is your girl okay?"

Layla was his girl now. That being the case, he was peeved she'd been flirting at the bar. Hurt pride wasn't top of the conversation list, however. He had to catch up and find out what she'd been up to since he'd been out of town.

"Think so," Ruger said. "I'm going to check."

"If there's gonna be a brawl…"

"You'll be the first to know," Ruger said and turned on his heels to stalk through the club and up to Colt's office.

Dax was a fighter. At the illegal fight night there at Risqué, Dax had wiped the floor with his opponent. He hadn't been present that night, but it was fast becoming legend. With the current situation, it helped that Dax was married. He understood the primal need to protect his woman, something new to him that hit hard when he saw Padget in the doorway.

In Colt's office, the women were seated in the sofa and loveseat by the door.

Layla did not look like she was having a good time. "What happened?" she asked, springing to her feet before he was fully in the room.

"Can you guys give us a minute?" Ruger said. Crystal rose and had to grab Destiny to force the tiny woman to leave too. "I'm sorry that I was short downstairs."

Destiny didn't respond to his apology. Crystal patted his chest and departed, shutting the office door behind them.

"Will you just tell me?" Layla demanded. "Was that him? Was that one of Ashcroft's men?"

"Yeah, it was. Maybe now you'll listen to me."

"Listen to you about what? I did everything I was told."

"Yeah, and it still could've gotten you killed," he said, navigating the furniture to get to her. "What were you doing flirting with those guys?"

"I was with Blaser. He was looking after me. One of the guys offered me a drink and it's not like that was going to kill me, not here, in this place owned by your family. I know there are no drugs allowed in here, so they couldn't spike my drink."

"You can never be a hundred percent sure."

"I think if I fell down and had to be carried from the building Blaser or security would've noticed," she said, returning his glower. "I was safe."

"And if one of them had a knife or followed you to the restroom?"

"I use the restroom in the employee locker room. Blaser said I could, and customers aren't allowed back here," she said, bringing her hands to her hips. "Why don't you just say what you're really thinking instead of making up these excuses?"

"What am I really thinking?" he asked.

He liked being taller than people and right then it served his purpose. He might be incapable of intimidating her, but him having a superior position irked her, and he wanted her pissed off just like him.

"You're jealous," she said, resting her hands on his chest. "I wasn't going home with them. I wasn't interested in them. I was having a drink and a laugh at the bar, and they came over. Nothing physical happened. We were just talking."

"Talking to guys like that encourages them. If we're a thing then you're going to have to get used to—"

"What? What will I have to get used to?" she asked, her laser focus narrowed on him.

She was all about this fight and oblivious to everything else.

"Not flirting with other men."

"Like you flirt with Destiny? She was up here talking to me about you, asking questions about us."

"So what? We're friends. It's no big deal."

"No big deal to you maybe," she said. "But you didn't tell me I was getting in the middle of something. Are you using me to upset her? Your family think there's something between the two of you."

"This is nuts," he said. Losing his gusto, he backed off and dropped down onto the couch. "I'm not messing around with Destiny, and I know there was nothing between you and those guys."

Forcing himself to lean forward, he doubled, and caught his face in his hands.

"What's wrong?"

Her voice was soft, and her knees came into view when she sat beside him. Then her fingers lost themselves in his hair and he relaxed. Going at each other wasn't going to solve anything but it did prove one thing, she was the girl for him.

He didn't have the time to explain anything. Truth was, he wasn't sure he could put words to what was going on inside him. Sitting back, he took his hand to her hip, but neither of them spoke. From the look on her face, he'd guess she was waiting for him to start the conversation.

The office door opened, and Blaser came in, relieving the pressure of confessing his turmoil.

"I called Colt," Blaser said, closing the office door. "He's getting in touch with Rushe."

"He'll have a tough job," Ruger said. "I just came from where Rushe and Flick are holed up. It's not in a cell service area."

"Which is why I'm here," Blaser said. "Colt needs the sat-phone number."

"I can give him the details," Ruger said, leaving the couch and Layla. "But I don't know if it will connect. They're in an overgrown area."

"Rushe has resources. He can get serious guys here to cover Layla's ass. You know that Colt and I will pull our weight, but if it's not enough—"

"What about Dax?" Ruger asked, approaching his brother. "He seems like the kind of guy who would have useful contacts."

"He is," Blaser said. "But how much do you want to tell him? He's not really a guy who operates on blind faith."

"He did with you. He trusted you when it came to the fight night. You could've set him up."

"I was desperate, and he knew it. I also gave him and his wife jobs and a place to live."

"I think I'll be able to convince him," Ruger said, putting a hand to Blaser's shoulder, then patting the other one. "Stay here for a minute. I'll be back."

On leaving Colt's office, Ruger didn't look back. Layla would have an opinion she'd be itching to share. But there wasn't the time to take a vote. Keeping her safe was all he cared about.

TWENTY

LAYLA COULD'VE LEAPED to her feet and demanded the brothers hear her, but she didn't. Remaining on the couch in Colt's office, where Ruger had left her, she watched him go, then made eye contact with Blaser.

"Your brother's a difficult guy to read," she said.

"You think?" Blaser asked, sauntering to the fridge in the corner. "I'd say he's pretty straightforward."

"No offense, but from what I understand, none of you knew what Ruger did for a living until very recently. He's obviously good at keeping secrets."

"I'll give you that," Blaser said, opening two beer bottles, then coming over to join her on the couch. "But I think it's obvious how he feels about you. No chance of him keeping that secret."

"Oh really? Then could you clue me in?" she asked, taking the proffered bottle.

"You're not serious," he said, positioning himself in the corner of the couch.

"We had sex. It's really not a big deal."

"So you're worried that Ruge is getting himself too attached to you? When do you plan to bolt?"

"Me?" she asked, twisting to glare at him. "Your brother hotfooted it out of the state barely an hour after we fell out of bed."

Blaser shrugged and took a long swig from his bottle while keeping his eyes on her. "Maybe the sex sucked."

He wanted a reaction, and she hated working herself into a flap, thus giving him one. "The sex did not suck. The sex was incredible, amazing, probably the best sex I ever had."

"Maybe it wasn't as memorable for him."

"If that's true, why does he keep talking about doing it again?"

Triumphant, she smiled and enjoyed the cool slick liquid of her drink as it slid down her throat.

"If the sex isn't the problem, I'd guess he's protecting himself."

"Protecting himself from what?"

"From you," Blaser said. "You don't hang around. You take what you want from a guy then you disappear. Isn't that what I've heard about you?"

"Who told you that?" she asked, the wind lost from her sails.

"Women talk," Blaser said.

Ruger had told Lyssa, Suzette, and his mother about her aversion to proposals. It wasn't outside the realm of possibility that Bri heard the story from them. With a baby on the way and a life in upheaval, shouldn't Bri have better things to talk about than her relationship MO?

Opening her mouth wide to retort, her thoughts were in such disarray that she wasn't sure what to say. Ruger might be holding some of himself back because he didn't want to get too invested. And so long as she felt he wasn't completely invested, she would hold a part of herself back too. It was a vicious cycle.

"I get what it's like," Blaser said, shifting to the front edge of the couch. "I know it's tough to put your faith in another person."

"I thought you and Bri had been together forever."

"It's not that simple, nothing really is. I've always loved Bri, but I have a tendency to… act in her best interest."

"What's wrong with that?" Layla asked.

"I don't always ask her opinion on what that might be before I act," he said. "There were tensions between our families too and I spent some time in prison, which kept us apart."

"But you're together now."

"Yeah, we are, but getting here wasn't easy. We only made it because… in the end we were honest, with ourselves, with each other, with our families and with the law. Either one of us could've given up… if we hadn't been willing to give each other our all, we never would've made it."

"Seems to me like you're making an argument in favor of protecting yourself."

"Then you're not paying attention," he said. "Why do you run away when a guy proposes? Why are you so afraid to take a chance?"

"It's not about taking a chance."

"Seems to me it is," he said, leaning away as her frustration grew. "Life is nothing but a game of risk. We weigh up options, make decisions, and we hope they pay off. Sometimes we're rewarded and sometimes we're punished. At the end of the day, if you're not willing to take risks then nothing incredible will ever happen."

"Nothing tragic either," she said, pushing her beer onto the coffee table. "We lose everyone in our lives eventually, why set ourselves up for that pain when we can protect ourselves from it?"

"I don't know how much you know about Bri's past." Layla glanced over her shoulder to see him examining the label on his bottle. "She took a risk reconnecting with me and went through a lot of pain. That didn't stop her coming back to me. From trying again and taking another risk."

"Maybe she's stronger than I am," Layla said, twisting to rest her shoulder against the back of the couch. "I was sheltered from life growing up. We didn't have a dad, but my mom gave my brother and me everything she could. We were happy and then she got sick and… Watching her suffer was difficult. I thought I learned a lot from the fight, she just wouldn't let her illness beat her. But the cancer was stronger and when she did leave us… it was so sudden. I wasn't ready… I wasn't prepared… I went from proud and optimistic to devastation that I… I promised myself I would never be that helpless again, that I wouldn't let any tragedy take me by surprise, that I would always be prepared."

His eyes fell to his lap. Did her words resonate with him, or did he think she was full of crap? The Warner boys were lucky. They had their parents, who were still together, happy, and healthy. Unless he had lost someone close to him, it would be difficult for him to understand her position.

After he pondered her words, he rolled the base of his bottle against his thigh and made eye contact with her again.

"It's impossible to always be prepared," he said, softer than before but still matter of fact. "Shit happens in life and a lot of it is unfair. Your mom getting sick… she lost the lottery; that could happen to any of us on any day. There's no way to prepare yourself for that."

"Sure there is," she said, bouncing closer. "All we have to do is stop ourselves from getting too close. If I don't have a partner and a family, they can't be taken from me."

"You have a brother," Blaser said. "And you do care about people. You're polite and respectful of my parents. You're friendly with Lyssa. If you don't let yourself care, if you don't let yourself love, maybe you can limit the hurt… but you're never going to experience the happiness either. You're depriving yourself of something I'm damn sure your mother would want you to have. Would she be proud of you for shutting yourself off?"

"My mother would be proud I'm making smart choices."

"Smart? Not settling down, bouncing from city to city, never building a life for yourself? I think you should talk to Lyssa about this."

"You're suggesting that I need therapy?"

"Grief counselling isn't exactly her thing," Blaser said. "But putting up barriers to commitment and intimacy—"

The office door opened. Ruger came in with Colt. Thank God Blaser didn't continue, she had no desire to share her damage with everyone. Not that she considered herself damaged, or at least she hadn't, not until the conversation with Blaser.

"You two were talking about me," Ruger said, casting a suspicious eye over them.

"Nothing wrong with your ego, is there?" Layla asked.

"Nothing wrong with any part of me. I'm in full working order."

She remembered.

"You're in a better mood," Blaser said. "I guess your conversation with Dax worked out?"

"Talking to him gave me an idea," Ruger said. "As for if there's trouble? He'll be around if we need him."

"What about you?" Blaser asked, nodding at Colt. "Did you get hold of Rushe?"

"Not yet, but I'll keep trying," Colt said. "He'll want in on this after what Ashcroft's men did to Flick. It doesn't hurt to have a guy on our side whose specialty is payback."

"Who is this Rushe guy?" Layla asked all the men. "Does Drew know him?"

"Who's Drew?" Blaser asked.

"My brother," she said before turning back to Ruger. "What does Rushe do?"

"First and foremost, he protects Flick," Ruger said. "His girlfriend. He's crazy in love with her, like obsessively. They're like Bonnie and Clyde only with a specialty in implements of torture."

That didn't sound pleasant, so she chose not to ask any more questions. "I'm sorry I asked."

"Come on," Ruger said. "I should get you home. You shouldn't be out in public; you should be safe."

"Are you going back to my place?" Colt asked.

"Or Mom's?" Blaser asked.

Layla didn't miss how both brothers fixated on her as she got up and began to head for the door. "Neither," she said. "I think I'll let Ruger in on my secret tonight."

Colt and Blaser laughed, but Ruger remained perplexed. "What secret?"

"You'll see," Layla said, linking her fingers with his and dragging him out of the office.

TWENTY-ONE

"YOU BOUGHT THIS PLACE?" Ruger asked, turning in a slow circle to examine the living room of her apartment.

"I didn't buy it," Layla said. "I'm renting. But if it works out, Ted says I can buy it."

"Works out?" Ruger asked, coming to a stop when he faced her again. "With the business?"

"What else?" she asked, leaving her perch against the windowsill. He wanted to know if she meant with him, he had to, because she had considered the possibility herself. If they broke up and she lived so close to his mother, it would be inevitable that their paths could cross.

"I'm happy that you're planning to stick around, even after this business with Ashcroft is through."

"I wouldn't go that far," she said, a prickle of anxiety made her wince. "It's not unlike me to pick up and start afresh somewhere. Doing this, it's sort of just a continuation of the theme."

"Okay," he said with the slightest nod. Raising his elbows to her shoulders when she got to him, he let his arms rest outstretched behind her. "I'm not going to say anything about that."

"Though clearly you have something you want to say," she said.

The tinge of attitude in her tone suggested she wanted to provoke a fight. Did she?

"I might," he said. "But I am not going to say anything to scare you off. I don't want you to run away. I want you to stay."

"You do?"

Such a revelation should be reassuring, but the churn of retreat set her insides on edge. Closing her eyes, she chastised herself. Ruger wasn't trying to scare her. Nothing he'd said proposed a commitment between them. He was merely being supportive. Yet even that was enough to set off alarm bells.

Renting the place had been an exciting achievement but being there with a man she'd been intimate with, the whole situation seemed oppressive.

"Yeah, whether we're together or not," he said. "I think it's about time you stopped running."

"I'm not running." Her petulant response was juvenile even to her own ears. "I'm sorry," she said and sighed. "Your brother made me feel like an idiot tonight."

"What did he—"

"It's not his fault, I am an idiot," she said, taking his hand to guide them both over and onto the couch.

"Okay, I don't know what—"

"My mother's death caught me off-guard," she said. Never having spoken about her feelings regarding the loss of her mother, it was a difficult conversation. Cutting through the bullshit was easier with Ruger, which was odd given him being a joker. Even though he tried to hide behind his humor, she read the depth of his character that lay beyond it. Maybe it was easier to see what others didn't because she herself was so good at concealing truth behind wit. "I was devastated when it happened because I'd been so optimistic about the future. I was so young and... I was still naïve enough to believe that if you believed in something, you had the power to make it come true. But it's not true. We can't will our own destiny to turn out how we want it to."

"No, we can't," he said, stroking her hand. "I can't imagine how terrible it must have been for you. My family is close and… I don't know what I'd do if I lost any of them."

"The worst part is the lack of control. I wanted to feel that if I'd done something differently, if we'd taken a different approach, then it would've made a difference. Eventually you realize that with something like cancer, you don't have that choice, you don't have any choice. All of us, me, my mom, and Drew, we had no influence over the outcome. The disease is vicious and indiscriminate. I got so angry when I fixated on that idea of helplessness. I promised myself that I would never get into that position again."

"So you don't let anyone get close."

"I guess I don't."

"And you don't let yourself rely on your brother, which is why you always live far away from him."

Releasing some of the tension that came with discussing such a sensitive subject, she exhaled on a shrug, trying to slow her words and her thinking down. "I suppose I'm not as complicated as you thought."

"Listen," he said, snagging her wrist to pull her body into his. "We're all simple creatures and it's natural to worry about being hurt when you've gone through pain like you have."

"But life is a game of risk. If we don't take a chance, how can we expect a reward?" she mumbled, using Blaser's sentiment.

"There are different kinds of risk," he said. "Getting close to people, trusting people, yeah that's risky, but the rewards are worth it."

Shifting out of his arms, she wanted to read the nuance of his expression when asking her next question. "Why did you hide your profession from your brothers for so long?"

Maintaining eye contact as he considered his response, she appreciated that he wanted to get his words right. From her experience that night, answers didn't come easily. "Fear of judgment at first, I guess," he said. "I started in college. It was just dabbling for cash. But I connect with people, they could approach me. I was good at matching people with merchandise. I'm good with faces and names."

"There must have been chances for you to be honest," she said. "Throughout all the years since college, you could've told them."

"Blaser went through a rough phase. Until he went to prison, he was involved with some shady characters who got him into a lot of trouble. That caused friction in his relationship with Colt, who was a cop at the time."

"You didn't want that same friction?"

"I thought I was doing them both a favor. Colt needed someone to vent to and Blaser didn't need any excuse to get deeper. The last thing I wanted to do was fall in with the criminal element of our family. We have cousins who are pretty deep in organized crime."

"Weren't you pretty deep?"

"I guess, but I justified it to myself. I told myself it wasn't as bad, that I wasn't really doing anything wrong," Ruger said. "If we try hard enough, we can convince ourselves of anything."

"Yeah, I guess we can."

It had been easy for her to dismiss her fears about the man watching her. That had come back to bite them. In every relationship, she assumed it was doomed, even when it was going well.

"Convincing yourself to buy this place though, that's a decision I approve of."

Relaxing into a smile, she didn't correct his assumption that she would go from leasing to owning the property. "Good."

Losing his mouth in her hair, he asked, "Does my mom know about this place?"

"Yes," Layla said. "Colt, Lyssa, Blaser, Bri, Suzette, everyone knows."

"I'm so proud of you for doing this. My mom will have clients banging down your door to get an appointment."

"So now that my future is in the bag," she said, not ready to commit either way to anything in her future just yet. "What about yours?"

His chest expanded then shrank when he exhaled a long breath. "I was up in my warehouse while I was away, picking up a few things."

"You have a warehouse?"

"Yeah," he said. "I had to keep the merchandise somewhere."

"Did being there make you nostalgic?"

"The opposite, to be honest. I feel ready to close that chapter and move on, I'm just not quite sure how to do that, or how I'll make it happen."

"When the chance presents itself, you'll know what to do."

"It might have already."

Tipping her head back, she noted his curious expression. "Are you going to expand on that?"

"Not yet, I have to talk to a guy first. If it works out, I'll clue you in."

She couldn't exactly object. Hadn't she done the same with her decision to rent the apartment and salon? If they were going to be together, they'd have to work on making joint decisions rather than working alone.

"So can we stay here?" she asked, making an effort to include him in decision-making, though she would argue if he didn't give her the response she wanted.

"Ashcroft's men are closing in," Ruger said. "If Colt gets hold of Rushe then we can—"

"We don't need Rushe," she said, soothing and stroking his cheek. "We can handle this."

"In any other situation I'd appreciate your optimism," he said, frowning when she flinched at his use of the last word. "I don't want to take any chances with your safety. If anything happened to you, Jansen would never forgive me."

"Are you still doing this because you owe my brother a favor?"

When his palm cradled her hand, he smiled. "No."

"Didn't think so," she said. Slapping her hands onto his chest, she balanced her weight and bounced over to straddle his lap. "Did you tell him about us?"

"It didn't exactly come up in conversation," Ruger said.

With a smile, she shook her head. "Are you afraid of my brother?"

"In my defense, I didn't actually see your brother. I met with Serendipity."

"Do you think he's okay?" she asked.

It was unlike Drew to delegate dangerous tasks to his girlfriend. Either her brother was wounded, or he trusted Ruger more than she'd realized.

"I think he's fine," Ruger said. "They have more dangerous threats in their neighborhood than me. Me, Rushe, and your brother have faced down some pretty nasty characters."

"You're a very honorable man, Ruger."

"It's a rare quality for men in my line of work."

"Former line of work," she said, pressing closer. "Now you have to start thinking about your future."

"I'm thinking to about ten minutes in the future," he said.

The lazy movement of his presumptuous smile made her take hold of his face. "Oh, yeah, and what do you see?"

"There's a bedroom through that wall, right? I see you, me, nakedness, there's lots of panting and rutting."

"Ten minutes, huh? Plan to spoil me with foreplay, do you?"

"We can watch the previews after the movie," he said, throwing his arms around her.

"That kind of defeats the point," she said, clambering to catch hold of him when he propelled up onto his feet.

"This is going to be at least a double feature," he said, carrying her through to the bedroom.

"Only if I enjoy the first showing."

"You'll enjoy it," he said, kicking the bedroom door out of the way. "This performance will be tailored for your pleasure."

His promises of pleasure guaranteed oblivion. That's what she needed, to be a woman with a man, lost in the haze of the night. Lovers lost in the dream of forever without uttering words of confirmation.

The bed had yet to be tested, but when he collapsed down onto the mattress, it held. That spoke nothing to how it would hold up when a guy the size of Ruger pushed it to its limit. His lack of concern about the furniture—and every other drama in their lives—bled into her until she was loose, pliant and up for just about anything.

Kissing her neck, he linked their fingers and raised them to each side of her head to give himself a lever point. When he pushed his weight away from her, she looped her legs around him trying to tempt him into bringing it back.

"Let's take our time," he whispered into her ear and went back to pampering her with his mouth.

She didn't feel like taking things slow. The passion was an outlet for the worry she'd held for him while he was out of her sight and the concern she still had for her brother.

"This was a great idea," he said, splaying his hands on her hips and skimming them upward under her top to slip it up over her head.

"The apartment or the sex?"

His smile descended to her mouth, and he answered her by teasing her tongue. Letting his slick, rough muscle dive into her mouth, the speed of his kiss increased. While matching his pace, her own smile grew.

"You want me," she teased, sucking his tongue as she pulled back from their oral union.

"You need me to draw you a diagram?" he asked, brushing her hair away from her forehead and matching her cocky expression. With a quick kiss, he pounced off the bed and shirked his top then his jeans. When he was naked, he opened his hands at his sides, putting himself on display for her. "Does this help, or do you need a flowchart?"

Sitting up, she grabbed his wrist in one hand and his dick in the other to pull him down on top of her. "You're a bastard," she said, laughing.

Seizing his mouth, she warmed him back to his fervent pace and managed to finagle her way out of her clothes while he was distracted by her mouth. Returning her hand to his engorged member, she rolled her thumb around and over his head and began to hum.

Licking her lip, Ruger kissed her chin then took his mouth to her ear. "The next part is where it gets really interesting."

Still with a smile on her face, she turned her head to find his mouth and kissed him before she spoke. "Show me," she murmured, meeting his eye.

Parting her legs, she tilted her hips, and he let her guide him inside. He was teasing her yet allowing her to take control of their bodies.

Adjusting to his size wouldn't take her long but adjusting to how her heart swelled at the sight of this man's smile would take a lot longer. Ruger wasn't like any man she had ever known but trusting him could only come after she learned how to trust herself.

TWENTY-TWO

RUGER PUT LAYLA into Colt's office in Risqué for the second night in a row. He had to give her credit for not complaining. Bringing her to Risqué was necessary. All the players he had to talk to were there. He didn't like that Ashcroft's men knew about the club, not only because of its connection to Layla, but its connection to his brothers, his family.

Blaser wasn't at the bar. Crystal informed Ruger that his older brother was upstairs in his office. So after settling Layla in Colt's office, Ruger went to the next room, and walked in on Blaser and Dax in the middle of a game of pool.

Blaser's office was the largest, which made sense as he ran the place. To the left of his office, behind a now open curtain was a pool table, one the brothers frequently used to break the intensity of awkward conversation. Ruger assumed these guys were using the game for the same purpose.

"Am I interrupting?" Ruger asked though he went into the office and closed the door without intention of backing out.

He had to talk to Dax and didn't mind Blaser being present to hear his offer.

"Could be," Blaser said. "What do you need?"

"I'll leave you guys to it," Dax said, propping his pool cue on the wall.

"Actually, it's you I have to talk to," Ruger said, much to Dax and Blaser's intrigue.

"Really?" Dax asked. Widening his stance, he folded his arms. "Ain't I feeling the brotherly love tonight, what is it?"

"I'm warning you now, Ruge," Blaser said, leaning over the table to take his shot. "Dax charges a fortune if you want him to beat the crap out of someone."

"No, I have an offer that will lead to him paying me," Ruger said.

Dax's expression didn't flinch.

Blaser stood, and with an outstretched arm, he leaned on his cue. "Really?" he asked. "Now I'm intrigued. There's no chance of me giving you guys' privacy."

"You hear about what I did up in Jersey?" Ruger asked. Dax nodded once. "I have a warehouse, just outside Atlantic City."

"Yeah," Dax said in monotone.

"I need it empty," Ruger said. "There's a fortune in there."

"What's that to me?" Dax asked. "I'm no fence."

"No, but you've got connections in this part of the world. I figure you'd know some people who might be interested in taking that merchandise off our hands."

"Our hands?" Dax asked.

"I'll give you twenty percent of whatever you make."

"Twenty percent?" Dax asked, one corner of his mouth quirked. "I could make more than that in a night doing something I'm a lot better at than playing salesman."

"You sold drugs, right?" Ruger asked. All good humor left the room. "You dealt with some shady guys and sold a far riskier product to men more inclined to screw you over."

"What do you know about it?"

"I made some calls today," Ruger said. "And it's no secret Suzette has issues with your wife. She repeats pretty much everything she hears."

With pursed lips, Dax inhaled, but Ruger wasn't concerned for Suzette's safety. Ivy and Suzette might not get along, but after checking on the Harrow couple, Ruger was confident Dax wasn't the type to hurt women.

"What the hell you doing checking up on him?" Blaser asked, crossing past Dax to face off with his brother. "If you need information about my friends, you come to me. You don't go nosing around in their business."

"I know people who can find out things," Ruger said. "People I trust."

"Why not ask them to do your dirty work?" Dax asked.

"I didn't do anything you wouldn't have done when it comes to protecting your interests," Ruger said. "And I offered full disclosure to show you trust, to develop trust. You would've thought less of me if I ran in blind, wouldn't you?" When Dax relaxed, Ruger was assured he was right. "I don't want anyone knowing I'm getting out of the game until I'm gone. You know how it is."

"If you need help, you come to family," Blaser said to Ruger, but got no reply.

"How much are we talking?" Dax asked.

Ruger would never ask Blaser to get involved and was glad Dax was of the same mind, as was confirmed by both men completely ignoring Blaser's comment.

"Close to half a million maybe," Ruger said. Dax's brows arched. "Depends on who you know and how much they're willing to pay. I can give you my book and tell you who might want what."

"Why the hurry to get rid of everything?" Dax asked.

Ruger had to give the guy credit for being wary. They weren't close and Dax probably hadn't done any homework on him... yet.

"I'm ready to move on," Ruger said. "And as you might have noticed, I'm dealing with family matters at the moment."

"Let me look into it before I commit to anything," Dax said. "I'll need to do some checking of my own."

"I understand," Ruger said. "The offer is there. When you've made a decision, give me a call."

Most of the criminals Ruger dealt with were mid to low level crooks. Dax wasn't in that sphere, at least he hadn't been. When Ruger had started asking around about Dax, he was shocked to hear just how deep in the criminal underworld he had once been. Blaser was a stickler for his tenants and employees abiding by the law and while Dax might fit that bill now, it hadn't always been the case.

Dax put his cue back in the rack on the wall. "I'm going downstairs to check in."

Ruger didn't need to hang around now that he'd put his plan to Dax. "I'm going to head off," Ruger said to Blaser. "I stashed Lay in Colt's office. I think she's getting sick of the sight of the décor in there."

"Hold up a sec," Blaser said.

Dax glanced back at his boss and then left the office.

"What's up?" Ruger asked.

Blaser wasn't the type to make a scene for no reason and he could cut to the chase with the best of them, so Ruger wasn't left wondering about his brother's motives for long.

"I want you to take over here," Blaser said.

"Take over what?" Ruger asked, not following his brother's implication.

Blaser bent over the table to take another shot and since Dax had departed mid-game, Ruger went across to retrieve a cue. If he was going to be there anyway then he might as well make the most of it.

"Risqué."

His assessment of the table would have to wait because as Blaser rose, so did Ruger's attention. "Excuse me?"

"I'm going to be a dad," Blaser said. "I can't run a strip club."

"You love this place. This place is your baby."

"Except now I'm going to have an actual baby," Blaser said. "I can't work all hours under the sun anymore. I don't want to. Now that I have Bri, I have an actual life and finding out she's pregnant puts everything into perspective. I can't explain it, but… the old shit isn't as important anymore."

"Blaser Warner, Family Man," Ruger said, trying with no success to suppress his amusement. But Blaser didn't seem to mind the jibe. In fact he stood taller, as though he wore the title with pride. "Who'd have thought it, huh?"

"Certainly not me," Blaser said. "Take your shot."

"What does Bri say to you giving up Risqué?" Ruger asked, lining up a shot.

"We talked about it… I don't know. She'll appreciate me being home nights, I know that."

"Are you moving in together? Have you decided?"

"We're looking for a place closer to Mom."

Ruger's bark of laughter preceded a grin that made his eyes water. "I never saw you running home to Mom. Oh, this is gold."

"Laugh it up, brother," Blaser said. "Let's see how you react when you knock Layla up… won't be so funny then, will it?"

"She's like… sand, you know, I can fill my hands with her, but when I try to take her with me… she slips away."

"Poetic," Blaser said, moving around the table to examine the pool balls. "You want her?"

"I don't know what I want," he said. "The idea of the future… commitment… it doesn't feel like it fits, you know? But living without her, watching her walk away… I'm not sure I'll be able to."

"Trying to put all the pieces together this early on is impossible. All you've got to do is think about her moving on with another guy… I can't imagine waking up without Bri. There are times it's daunting, woman, kids, home, business… but think of the alternative. Is it really worth letting her go just so you can sit around your apartment alone scratching your balls without her bitching at you?"

"Fatherhood is going to suit you," Ruger said. "I can tell already… do you know if it's a boy or a girl?"

"Bri wants it to be a surprise," Blaser said and supported himself on his cue again. "So are you going to accept my offer or what?"

"This place?" Ruger asked. "I don't know if I see myself in a management position."

"Would you rather be someone's subordinate?" That made Ruger bob his head as he considered it. "Dax has agreed to take on some of the responsibility, but I'd rather it stayed in the family, you know?"

"So you have something to pass onto Junior?" Ruger asked, finding his grin again.

"It's a good earner. Dax will buy me out and I need the capital. We're going to open a second garage, somewhere close to Mom's, since that's where we'll be living."

"You have this all thought out."

"Colt will sell to you, if you want it. I've already discussed the whole plan with him."

"If you're moving, that means you won't be managing the apartments anymore either. How does Mattie feel about that?"

"Mattie will be the last one to know," Blaser said, in reference to their cousin who actually owned the apartment building. "I won't tell him until we're set up somewhere else."

"You know that Mattie has ears everywhere. He'll figure it out when he finds out about Bri's condition."

"Which is why we're not telling people about the baby yet," Blaser said.

"Word spreads around here, fast," Ruger said, sinking a ball. "Mattie would buy this place, if you just want it in the family."

"And what would Mattie do with it?" Blaser asked. "I might be walking away for the good of my child, but I'm not throwing Risqué to the dogs."

"Have you talked to Dax about that? He's a fighter and—"

"Ivy keeps him in check," Blaser said. "And Dax is a guy who knows the value of not shitting on your own doorstep."

"You really trust the guy."

"Without him things might not have worked out in my favor with Bri… You've done your checking; you trust him enough to let him deal with your business."

"I considered your silent endorsement too, but yeah, he seems like a good guy… all things considered."

"It's easier to trust him when you've seen him and Ivy together. She's got him wrapped around her little finger. It's funny to see such a capable guy jump for a woman."

"You think that's funny? You should see what you're like with Bri."

"I won't deny it," Blaser said, managing to pot two balls with one shot. "Maybe that's why Colt and me want to see you settle down too."

"Don't push it, and don't talk like that in front of Layla. She's dealing with enough shit."

"Starting a business and trying to duck assassins, yeah, I guess she's distracted… might make it easier for you to slip in under the wire though. She cares about you. Anyone can see that."

"You're singing her praises now, you might not be when you hear how she feels about strip clubs," Ruger said. "Your offer is interesting, but if I'm with Lay, she won't be happy about the arrangement."

"Interesting," Blaser said. "Your woman or the family business… I guess Dax will be on his own."

TWENTY-THREE

RUGER HAD BEEN APOLOGETIC when he put her in Colt's office for a second night running. Layla wasn't concerned. The environment didn't matter. She had to finish her plans to open the salon as soon as possible. Her to-do list was stretching longer and longer. Disposable cash was a problem, though that might be an advantage given she was renting. Making drastic changes could be expensive. Doing anything structural might increase the property's market value, but that return wouldn't land in her pocket unless she bought the unit and that wasn't a sure thing.

Still, she wanted to put her own stamp on the business and needed to get some supplies. A lick of paint wouldn't cost too much. Such a small alteration shouldn't upset Ted, providing she didn't choose anything garish.

The apartment upstairs needed some love too. When she'd spoken to Ruger about re-upholstering the furniture, he'd reined her in. With her lover's encouragement and confidence, she could be ready to open up as soon as next week.

She was tapping her pen on her chin when the office door opened. Colt came in with Lyssa.

"Hey! How are you doing?" Lyssa asked.

"If you guys want to be alone, I can go," Layla said, gathering up her notebook and pen.

"No, don't be silly," Lyssa said, seating herself on the couch. Colt continued deeper into the space, but with her back to the room, she didn't see exactly where he went. "What are you up to?"

"Making plans," Layla said, waving her notebook in the air.

"It seems to be going around," Lyssa said. "Blaser and Ruger are discussing the future too."

"We don't know that," Colt said, appearing in the periphery to hand Lyssa a bottle. "Do you want a drink, Layla?"

She shook her head and Colt walked off again.

"You've caught the family in a real transition phase," Lyssa said. "It's exciting that you're taking on your own ventures too. I suppose that means you're part of the transition."

"Transition?" Layla asked.

"I'm going next door," Colt said, passing them and departing.

"This is like the ladies waiting room," Lyssa said. "We get planted in here while the men make plans in Blaser's office."

"And you're okay with that?"

"I'm only kidding," Lyssa said. "If I thought Colt was keeping me out of the decision making, or expecting me to defer to him, I would put him in his place. The brothers need to work things through with each other. Given the bumps in their relationships, it's important they use this bonding time. Bri and I try not to get in the way of their man time."

"That's considerate of you."

"You're doing it too, just by letting Ruger leave you here."

"It's not the same," Layla said, slipping her notebook and pen back onto the table. "I'm not... you know. You and Bri are family, I'm just..."

"What are you, Layla?" Lyssa asked, lowering her chin.

The doctor's tone had taken on a curious edge, was she being analyzed? "I'm a distraction."

"Do you want to be a part of Ruger's future?"

"The future," Layla said. Taking a deep breath, she rubbed her cheeks. "Everyone is obsessed with the future. I don't know what tomorrow is going to bring, I can't think about where I'll be in three months or three years."

"Like I said, the family is in a transition phase. I suppose we're all looking to the future at the moment. Now that Blaser is going to be a father, he's giving up Risqué and moving to a family home near his parents… as soon as they find it."

"That's sensible, he and Bri have a future. They have a child to think about."

"He's offering Ruger the position."

"The position?"

"Taking over management of Risqué," Lyssa said. Layla had to laugh. "That's funny?"

"I passed judgment on Bri when I heard what Blaser did. I couldn't imagine any woman being comfortable with her man managing a club full of naked women. I said something like that to Ruger."

"And now you feel vindicated?"

"No, oh, no," Layla said, sorry her words had been misconstrued. "I don't think Bri has forced Blaser out, their circumstances have changed. I laughed because now I'm the woman seeing a man who manages a strip club."

"There's no guarantee that Ruger will accept," Lyssa said. "If he knows you have a problem with it, he may refuse. Blaser has other options. One of his security men, Dax, he has the ability and the capital to get involved. I know that one of the head dancers, Crystal, has taken on a lot of management with regards to the dancers. So don't worry, if you're uncomfortable with Ruger taking over, he won't take it."

"Family is important to him," Layla said. "And he should take the position. He would be ideal. He's personable, comfortable with the women, and it will give him direction, which I know he's struggled with since giving up his other vocation."

"You're important to him, Layla. Don't underestimate that. Blaser and Colt know how to prioritize the women in their lives. Ruger may well follow their lead, and his brothers will understand."

"You can't live your life for another person and make your decision based on their wishes."

"No, but you can live your life *with* another person and make decisions together. You have to consider how you feel about Ruger managing Risqué and assess what your real objections would be. If it's an insecurity in your relationship, well… I can help you with that, both of you."

Layla relaxed into her smile. "Ruger would love me for that, if I told him we were going to land on your couch."

"I've been trying to get Ruger onto my couch for a long time."

"You think he's screwed up?"

"No," Lyssa said. "Sometimes people need help and there's no shame in that. I have skills that can help people, and when I see people I care about suffering, I want to alleviate that."

"Do you ever use your skills on Colt in the bedroom?" Layla asked, widening her smile.

Lyssa reciprocated. "I've taught him a few things," she said, wearing a sly look.

"I bet you have."

"He's more open-minded now."

"In bed?"

"Oh, no, he's always been happy to try anything there," Lyssa said wearing her own smirk. "But when it came to people, he could be a bit judgmental. He took issue with Bri and Blaser in the beginning, and when he found out about Ruger and what he did to earn his money… being understanding wasn't his default position. But I helped him work through it and now he's more accepting."

"But Ruger is giving up that aspect of his life, he's going straight."

"Yes, he is, and I know he's taking that very seriously. He wants a clean break. His reason for going next door wasn't to hear Blaser's offer, it was to make an offer of his own."

"An offer?"

"To Dax, the man who stepped in last night when Padget showed up," Lyssa said. "Dax has a past and connections. Ruger wants him to clear out the warehouse for a percentage."

"You know everything. How do you know this?"

"Colt and Ruger are close; they always have been. Ruger kept what he did a secret and I think it's something he regrets. He feels like there is ground to gain in recovering Colt's trust… While Colt feels guilty his baby brother felt the need to keep the secret in the first place. Yet, Colt knows he would have been too judgmental to accept it before…"

"Before you?"

"Not to blow my own trumpet," Lyssa said, pulling her feet up onto the couch. "I could sit here and pull apart their motivations all night. Needless to say, we're all moving forward. Ruger wants to get rid of the items in the warehouse holding his merchandise. Blaser wants to pass on the mantle of this club to free himself for fatherhood and to give Ruger purpose."

"And Colt?"

"Colt wants his brothers settled. He's always been the responsible one. He was a cop, married, and believed he had the respectable life, but he lost it all."

"Then he found you."

"It's amazing what love can do for you, Layla, if you're open to it."

"Blaser is learning that too, now that he has Bri and a baby on the way," Layla said, not wanting to face the doctor's knowing expression. "He told me being together wasn't a foregone conclusion for him and Bri."

"They have a complicated past and have overcome obstacles, but it's made their relationship stronger."

"And how do you feel about the baby and all?"

Displaying no resentment, Lyssa inhaled and lifted her shoulders before she let them fall. "It's no secret that Colt and I have been trying to get pregnant," she said, smiling. "But I don't resent Bri and Blaser's happiness. They deserve it, and it won't lessen our joy when we are expecting."

Layla believed her. Finding out someone else had reached her goal must have had some impact on Lyssa's confidence. Yet, she didn't show it. The goodwill was genuine.

Because she didn't want to poke a sore spot, Layla moved the conversation on. "What about the apartments?" she asked. "Doesn't Blaser manage the apartment complex he lives in?"

"At the moment, he does," Lyssa said. "But the apartments belong to Mattie Warner, a cousin Blaser hasn't had the best luck with. He won't be sorry to say goodbye to that job."

"So he's going to leave his cousin high and dry?"

Even if the men didn't get along, it seemed spiteful to walk out without warning.

"No! Mattie's brother Gus lives there. He'll take over the management full time along with Suzette. She lives there too."

"In Ruger's apartment. She's your best friend, isn't she? What does she have to do with it?"

"Well…" Lyssa said, her eyes slunk left and right, then she settled her saucy smile on Layla. "If you can keep a secret?"

It seemed like no one could keep a secret around there. The brothers told each other everything and they shared it with their women. Except Lyssa was a doctor and knew when discretion was required.

Leaning over the table, Layla nodded. "I can keep a secret."

"Suzette and Gus are seeing each other," Lyssa whispered. Layla opened her mouth in an "*Ah-ha*!" Lyssa clasped her hands, slid her feet from the couch, and bowed to lean closer. "Suzette hasn't had the best luck with men. Gus is easy going and I don't think he'd have the energy to treat her wrong."

"How did that happen and why is it a secret?"

"It started a while ago. They were sleeping together, she told me about it at the time. Neither of us were sure if it would stick or not. Suzette wanted to keep the dalliance a secret in case it fell apart."

"I guess it stuck."

"It started when Gus took Suze back to her apartment after a fight she had with her neighbors, Dax and Ivy."

"I heard Suzette doesn't get along with Ivy."

"She's a lot more relaxed now that she's getting some too," Lyssa said. "Gus is a good guy. He took her in to calm her down and I guess the sparks flew. Suzette shrugged it off as just sex at first, but now they're seeing each other almost every night."

Everyone was pairing off. Layla had seen this before. She'd stayed in so many states and had so many friends, yet it was the same story over and over. Friends coupled up and settled down. Some bought houses and had kids, others went off to see the world. Sometimes she wanted to know what it was like to have security like that, to have someone watching your back and be there by your side no matter what.

Settling down came with getting older, when people slowed down and assessed where their life was headed.

Ashamed that she hadn't managed to establish so much as a fixed abode let alone a romantic partnership, she began to see how life couldn't go on the same way forever. She had to stop, to grow up and take ownership of her destiny.

"Your mind is wandering," Lyssa said. "Anything you want to share?"

"I think Ruger should take over from Blaser." He was at the same sort of life crossroads and taking over the business could be exactly what he needed to give himself purpose. "The role would suit him."

"Is that what you were thinking about?"

"I was thinking that I want to make a go of the salon. I hadn't realized how important it was until now. I have wasted every opportunity I've had in my life so far and don't want history to repeat itself."

"Why do you think you did that? Why did you waste those opportunities?"

"Fear," Layla admitted, confronting emotions she'd tried for years to bury. "I thought I was protecting myself. But I've just been juvenile. If I'm not careful, I'll end up alone with nothing to show for myself."

Lyssa was easy to talk to. Layla hadn't meant to open up, yet there she was starting her own impromptu therapy session.

"And that made you think about your work at the salon and the potential it has?"

For maybe the first time in her life, making plans wasn't such a terrifying idea. "It made me think about the future."

"And do you see Ruger in that future?"

"His family… all of you… you've made me feel like I'm a part of something, and for the first time, I find family appealing."

"But?" Lyssa asked.

The doctor was good at what she did. "There are so many things that I don't know about him, like this debt he has to repay to my brother. How can I be with him when I don't understand how we ended up together?"

Lyssa came closer to take her hands. "Why did your brother leave the police?"

The doctor was just being polite and probably already knew the answer.

"He was suspended pending an investigation into alleged misconduct," Layla said. "He resigned."

"Do you know what the misconduct was related to?"

"Yes," Layla said. "He was undercover working for a man named Victor. When Victor found out Drew was a cop, he kidnapped Serendipity. Drew did what Victor asked him to because he was trying to protect Serendipity."

"Bri was kidnapped by Victor's gang, just like Serendipity, and he did it because Ruger refused to work for him."

"Oh my God," Layla said, twisting closer. "That's why Bri is working with you, because of what they put her through?"

Lyssa nodded. The doctor's specialty implied Bri had suffered true horror at the hands of those criminals.

"Ruger didn't know about it at the time," Lyssa said. "But when Bri told me and the truth came out, Ruger promised to make it right. He promised it to himself and to Blaser and Bri… Your brother is the one who saved her life. The one who got Bri away from Victor."

So that was the debt owed. As much as she berated her brother for taking risks, she got a sudden understanding of just how those risks could pay off. Guilty tears came to her eyes. How many times had she complained about his risks? But if he didn't take them, good people might end up dead. Knowing her brother accomplished such a feat made her so proud he was willing to do what others were unable to.

A tear rolled down her cheek. "If Bri is your patient…" Layla whispered.

Lyssa smiled and squeezed both of her hands. "She and I spoke about it. I'm not breaking any confidence. She will share the details with you in her own good time, but we agreed that it was time you knew the truth. You're part of the family now. Ruger and his brothers, they find it harder to talk about Bri's ordeal and Ruger would never want to betray her, as he may feel he was doing if he told you everything. So I'm taking that dilemma off his hands."

With greater knowledge, so many things made better sense. Bolstering herself, she wouldn't ask for consolation. The situation had turned out well for everyone… in the end. Now she could be proud of her brother and proud of Ruger too.

Walking away from a person as evil as Victor was absolutely the right thing to do. He couldn't have known what the consequences would be. But he was a good man. The guilt probably consumed him. Making herself smile, she resolved herself to lightening his load for him as best she could.

TWENTY-FOUR

"I THINK YOU SHOULD DO IT," Layla said.

Ruger had retrieved her from Colt's office, and they were in the car on the way back to her salon, her apartment, her bed.

He had been quiet and hadn't filled her in on the men's discussion. That didn't matter because Lyssa had clued her in. The process of sharing in the family was divided down gender lines.

The Warner men talked to each other, brooded, and then when it came time to make a decision, they consulted their women. The women did their best to keep the wheels turning and used their feminine alliance to ensure decisions were made with full and accurate details, rather than the perhaps biased view of their partners.

"You said you couldn't be with a guy who managed a strip joint."

Ruger understood the way it was too and didn't insult her by playing dumb. The unspoken understanding that family was always fully informed and protected to the death—even when they wanted to bang each other's heads together—

emphasized just how this family had accepted her as theirs, she was a cog in the wheel now.

"I said that before I'd been to Risqué, and I'll admit that I was prejudice against strip clubs. I don't think I like the idea of you ogling naked women all night, but I get now that Blaser doesn't do that."

"After a while it becomes passé," he said, leaning toward her.

Exhaling a smile, Layla folded her arms. "So you won't be interested in my naked form later?"

"The women in Risqué aren't the same thing, they're employees and a lot of them have been there for a long time. They're like cousins or sisters or something and they're completely off-limits. I'm the type of guy who doesn't like flashy women, and you don't get much flashier than a stripper."

"And so my naked form is…?"

"Private and high on my list of priorities."

She laughed. "That's good to know."

Ruger pulled into a parking space at the front of the building. As they were making their way inside, his cellphone beeped. Thinking that it could be Drew with an update, she paused to watch him retrieve his phone from his pocket and read the message.

"It's Dax, he's on the road north and wants the address of my warehouse. He's going to check it out. I offered him a cut for selling off the goods still on my books," he said, thumbing in a response to the message. "I guess he finished vetting me or Blaser talked him into it."

When he was finished, he rested a hand between her shoulder blades to direct her inside. Jumping into bed would come, but neither was in a rush. They got rid of shoes and jackets, then Ruger went to retrieve a bottle of wine from the fridge. Only when they were together on the couch, did the conversation continue.

"So you would be open to it?" he asked, pouring the wine. "To me taking over Risqué?"

"I think the question is whether or not you're open to it. I didn't ask you before I signed the lease on this place, did I? You have to do what feels right for you."

"Cards on the table," he said, sitting up to hand over her wine. "Being with you feels right."

"That's a good place to start." The corners of her mouth began to rise. "I think it might be interesting to maybe…"

Lacing their fingers together, she toyed with his digits.

"What?" he asked, raising their joined hands to his face. "Maybe what?"

"Hang around and see where this goes."

"Yeah?"

"I can't keep running forever, can I?"

"No, you can't," he said and dipped his head to tempt her mouth, but she kept them apart.

"Lyssa told me," she said, putting her glass on the table. "She told me about the debt, about Bri… about how you met Drew through Victor."

For a moment, he leaned back, and his furrowed brow made her hold her breath in anticipation of how he might react.

He exhaled and his expression relaxed into a smile. "Thank God," he said. "I didn't want to keep anything from you, but I wasn't sure… I didn't want Bri to think that I'd—"

"I understand," she said, touching his lips. "We don't have to talk about it. I just wanted you to know that I knew."

Bowing to her, he brought up her chin to find her mouth. Ruger had put his life on the line for her, he was working to protect her brother to repay a debt. Honor was important to him and a man with such integrity wouldn't stray.

Except to an outsider Ruger's honorable nature wouldn't be obvious. Not in that moment. With a certain move, he scooped her legs up off the floor and got her onto her back on the couch.

Getting comfortable between her thighs, he picked up the hem of her top and nibbled her jaw as his hand went upwards to seek out her breast. His squeeze was enough to wring a whimper from her. They'd had the day together, but he'd helped her out in the salon. She'd been strict about them working during the day light hours.

If Ruger was going to start managing Risqué, he would probably be out all night and she would have to make exceptions when their schedules allowed precious time alone. Did these thoughts really belong to her? She was actually considering mundane day-to-day life in a nine to five while dating a guy she could actually have a future with.

Laughing, she pushed his torso up to meet his eye. "Something crazy happened the day I met you," she said. "I don't know what it was but… this feels sort of cosmic, doesn't it? If you hadn't gotten involved with that maniac, Victor, you never would've met my brother. You'd never owe him a favor and you'd never have come for me."

"Cosmic is good," he said.

Though he maintained eye contact to imply he was listening and interested, he was also fumbling behind her trying to elevate her weight to give him a shot at her bra clasp.

"A long chain of events brought us to this moment. That can't be an accident, can it?"

Fate wasn't something she'd spent a long time considering, but it was hard to argue against. If they'd come across each other in the course of life, they'd never have got together, he was too casual, too much of a joker.

She'd have dismissed him as a guy after one thing. He didn't show the responsible side of himself to many people. Their situation forced him to show that side, and in the course of that, she'd been drawn into the bosom of the Warner clan. They were all there to look after not only themselves, but those in the exclusive club.

"I should know better than to try talking to you when your hand is in my bra," she said.

"I'm listening," he said, nodding. "But can I respond after… you know."

"Oh, honey," she said, crunching up, she gave him the access to unclasp her bra.

As it released his face lit with joy.

Consuming each other in a kiss again, his weight relaxed over her. Her top was still in the way, but he seemed to enjoy teasing her mouth, trailing his mouth to her neck, up to her ear to whisper words of his pleasure into her before returning to her mouth.

His teasing tongue didn't only enjoy using words to torment her, he also used it to tantalize her flesh. Wriggling, she couldn't stop herself moving against him, using him to stimulate herself. A twist of dynamic bliss curled and sparred within her, urging her to move faster and whimper louder.

He held her shoulders, pinning her down, and when their eyes converged, his intensity drenched her.

With ideas of intimacy and being lost to their raging hormones, she barely heard the shatter of glass or the explosion of sound before it. A shower of plaster was her first real clue. The crumbled material was rough against her skin and crowded her eyelashes.

Ruger was on his feet, giving her space to sit up and bend to shake the dry dust from her face. "Are you okay?" he asked, crouching beside her to get a better look.

"Yes, I'm okay. What was that?" The window had a large, jagged hole in it with cracks emanating to the frame. Twisting in her seat, she sought out the burst plaster and noticed something embedded in her wall. "What was that?"

Ruger pounced up, examined the hole in the wall for two seconds, then went to the window. "Gunshot," he said. "Wait here."

"No, but—"

He was already past her and running down the stairs. If someone was shooting in her window, that person could still be outside. She didn't want Ruger to face such a dangerous person alone. Making a target of herself by going to the window wouldn't be smart, so she stayed on the couch and lunged across it to grab the phone that had just been installed that day.

She dialed nine-one-one but could already hear distant sirens. Someone else must have called in the shot. She was still on the phone when Ruger came back up the stairs, gun in his hand.

"Where did you get that?" she asked, fearing he'd gotten hold of the perpetrator and possibly done him damage.

"My truck," Ruger said. Distracted, he went back to the window to observe the street below. "The fucker is gone."

"Good," she said. He spun around. "What were you thinking running down there like that? You could've gotten yourself killed!"

"That was a risk I was willing to take. They know where you live, which isn't a leap given they're watching you. That was a warning shot. They meant to miss. Next time we won't be as lucky. I have to call Jansen."

Storming over, he snatched the phone out of her hand and hung it up.

"What are you doing?" she asked, leaping to her feet. "I was waiting for the operator."

"The cops are already on their way," he said.

She snatched the phone back and hung up before Ruger finished dialing Drew's number. "If they know where we are, they could be listening, remember? You told me that. You said they had the means to listen in to phone conversations."

"It's not as difficult as it used to be. But you just had this phone put in, I doubt they'll have bugged it already."

"That's not a risk I'm willing to take," she argued, standing up to him though he towered over her. "If they can listen, they might be able to trace, and I will not let you endanger my brother."

The sirens wailed into the street. She reached past him to put the phone on the hook.

"What are we going to tell them?" Ruger asked.

"The truth," she said. "We were making out when someone shot through our window."

"They'll want to know about enemies. They won't assume this was a skilled assassin, they'll assume that the shooter meant to kill you."

Trying to take his hand reminded her of the gun, and she stepped back. "Unless that thing is registered, you better put it away."

"It's registered," he said. "I have the paperwork. They won't give me a hard time about it."

"They might."

"We have cop relatives and Colt has contacts from his time working there. Don't be surprised if they treat you well and believe what you say."

"My brother used to be a cop too, you forget," she said. Someone started hammering on the door. "And I'll bet Colt's already on his way over."

"That's usually the way it works. This is a good neighborhood, and we're close to my mom's." He headed for the stairs. "We better let them in before they damage your property."

"I guess having connections works sometimes," she said, joining him as they descended the stairs. "Wait…" She paused to hook her bra again. "Don't forget how things turned out for Drew. The cops are great when they're on your side, but if they turn on you."

"They had good reason to turn on your brother," Ruger said, continuing down the stairs. "He screwed them over."

Ruger opened the door, but she stayed still. Did he honestly believe her brother hadn't been justified in what he'd done to protect Serendipity? They hadn't discussed details of the past, about how he got involved with Victor, or how Drew had gotten out of the peril he and Serendipity were in, saving Bri in the process. Before building big plans to hitch herself to the Warners, they'd have to talk. She'd thought it wasn't necessary. Apparently, she was wrong.

TWENTY-FIVE

TEN MINUTES AFTER the cops showed up, Colt arrived. Ruger had noticed his brother on the perimeter of the property talking to various cops and neighbors. Both he and Layla were kept away from others while they gave their official statements. Some of the neighbors gave statements as well.

As perplexed as the local cops were by the random shooting in an affluent neighborhood, they did their due diligence and asked all the appropriate questions. Someone was going to look into this incident further.

He'd have to get in touch with Jansen to find out how things were going at his end and if the chase was heating up.

After the cop taking his statement wandered away, Colt was soon in his place. "How close did they get?" his brother asked, probably trying to lighten the mood in this tense scenario.

"Too close," Ruger said. "Thank God I was on top."

"You weren't…"

"Almost," Ruger said.

"That could've been embarrassing."

"Or traumatizing."

"Don't think you'd have been put off sex for life," Colt said. "My lady will work through your issues."

"You should start carrying her business card," Ruger said, finally managing to relax.

Layla was safe. For now. His concern for her grew. Although he'd done his best to keep her in his eyeline, he was so much more aware of those in her periphery.

Anyone could be a threat, ready to sneak up on them. He hadn't done his best work protecting her; he'd been too busy trying to get her naked.

"Don't beat yourself up," Colt said, squeezing his brother's shoulder. Colt had always been perceptive and had been in a similar position himself with Lyssa. "Caring about the girl isn't a failing. It just means you're likely to do whatever it takes to keep her safe."

"I don't know how to keep her safe," Ruger muttered, watching Layla's hand gestures as she spoke to cops. "These guys could come from anywhere at any time. How do you prepare for that? How can you protect her from an enemy you can't see?"

"You could hole yourself up somewhere if you want to," Colt said. "Like Rushe has done with Flick. I'm sure they could recommend a good hiding place."

"Layla is just through telling me how she wants to make a go of this place. We were talking about… being together."

"That's great."

"It won't last long if this continues," Ruger said. "I have to talk to Jansen, get him to back off."

"You would tell him to sacrifice the truth to protect your girlfriend?"

"Who is also his sister," Ruger snapped, taking his focus from Layla to glare at his brother. "Who cares about some dumb story? It's not worth losing her for. Who the hell does Jansen think he is?"

"You forget that it was his woman who started this. And it's about more than just the story. What Ashcroft is doing is wrong and if you think his crimes are victimless, you're either naïve or just plain stupid.

"Jansen and Serendipity are doing what needs to be done and they're putting their lives on the line to do it. And I'm warning you now, if Layla hears you talking shit about her brother, there won't be much of a future for you."

"I can't play nice and pretend I'm on the same crusade as them," Ruger said. "I can understand their position and what you're saying. But any practical argument goes out the window when I look at Lay and try to imagine what my life would be like if I fucked this up and she got hurt because of me."

"None of this is because of you and we're all doing our best to keep Layla safe," Colt said. "You can come and stay with Lys and I if you want."

"No," Ruger said, shaking his head. "I'm not putting you both in danger too. These people have proved they can track us down no matter where we go. I just don't like us being sitting targets."

"What's the alternative?" Colt asked. "Do you want to take the fight to them?"

That thought stopped Ruger cold. Flick had gotten hurt because Ashcroft's men had blindsided them. If Jansen knew where Ashcroft's men holed up, where their sanctuary was, where they felt safe, maybe they could use that information to their advantage.

"Taking the fight to them sounds like exactly what we should do," Ruger said. "I bet Rushe could recruit a few guys to help me out."

"You think Blase and I can't handle it?"

"I think I don't want you and Blase near it. You've got Lys and he's going to be a father. Your days of playing with fire are over. Soon as Lys is pregnant, you won't be able to come out on these kinds of calls either. Get your priorities straight."

"I don't need you to worry about my priorities. You went out there on your own for years, now you have back up."

"I won't let you do it," Ruger said. Digging his hands in his pockets, he stepped back. "You and Blase have paid your dues, sit back and enjoy it."

"Soon as Layla is safe, we will. Do you think Lys or Bri would be with guys who would sit back and let an innocent woman be harmed? Both of them have faced shit in their lives. They wouldn't want Layla isolated."

"I've got to talk to Jansen," Ruger said.

"My thought exactly," Layla said, approaching from behind Colt. "I have to talk to my brother. Can I use your phone, please?"

Icy words and a lack of eye contact. Was she pissed off? About the shooting? Had to be, he hadn't done anything wrong.

"He'll go crazy when he hears what happened," Ruger said, taking his phone from his pocket.

"I know how to handle my brother," she said, holding out a hand in expectation of him handing over his cellphone, which he did.

"I need to talk to him too, so…" Layla was walking away and dialing, so he didn't bother to finish his sentence.

"That's the cold shoulder if ever I saw it," Colt said, closing in at his side to rest an arm around his shoulders. "Are you sure you were getting busy when the shot went off?"

"That's where it was headed," Ruger said. Layla was further along the sidewalk, with her back to the group of neighbors still trying to nosy in on what was going on.

"Maybe next time, let her know," Colt said, giving him a pat on the back then retreating.

He couldn't see her expression but could tell from the way her body moved that Jansen wasn't taking the news of this development well. Just as he thought.

TWENTY-SIX

"WOULD YOU STOP TALKING?" Layla said, trying to cut Drew off, but he kept ranting.

"You just couldn't keep your head down, could you?" Drew said through the phone. "I told you not to piss anyone off. I should've known that was beyond your capability. How did you draw attention to yourself this time?"

"I did not draw attention to myself," she said, fixating on the strip of exposed brick in front of her. "You're the one up there causing all this trouble and I'm the one who got shot at! A little sympathy here, brother."

"Okay, you're right, okay, I'm sorry. Tell me again what happened?"

"We were shot at," Layla said.

"How many shooters?"

"We didn't see the shooters," she said. "They were gone by the time Ruger got down the stairs."

"Okay, how many shots?"

"Just one, Ruger thinks it was a warning shot, a kind of 'we're watching' sort of thing."

Scuffing her foot on the sidewalk, she admitted to herself it was reassuring to hear Drew's voice. She really wished he was there to play big brother.

"How close did this warning shot come to you guys?"

"I don't know," she said. "We were lying on the couch, neither of us saw it. The bullet stuck in the drywall above us. If we'd been sitting up, it would've been close."

For a minute, he didn't say anything. She pressed her hand to the cool brick and closed her eyes. Having him there would be a comfort, he probably wished he could be there to look after her too. It couldn't be easy for him to be torn between the woman he loved and his sister. Drew wanted them to be safe but couldn't cover all the bases alone. Hence why he needed Ruger.

"Why were you lying on the couch together?" Drew asked. His tone lost some of its angry panic and took on a curious, shrewd hue that stifled her words. "Layla?"

"Uh… we were… uh…"

Being with Ruger was public knowledge there. Drew had no way to know about their association unless he was told… which she had just taken care of.

"Goddamnit, Layla," Drew chastised, erasing the need for her to finish the sentence. "You're sleeping with him, aren't you?"

"Maybe," she said. At least that served as a distraction from the possibility of death looming over them. "Why do you care? It's my business, not yours."

"Because you don't know enough about him. You don't know who he really is. I sent him to you, and it wasn't as some sordid screw-a-gram."

"Drew! It's not like that it's—"

"What? It's special? You care about each other," he said. She didn't appreciate his mocking. "I sent him down there to take care of your safety not your sexual needs. I'm going to fucking kill him."

"No, you're not," she said, taking the risk of glancing over her shoulder to check Ruger and Colt's position. They were where she'd left them except Ruger was scrutinizing her. "I've been with loads of guys, in loads of relationships, and you've never cared about how any of them have treated me. Believe me, in comparison to some of my exes, Ruger is a saint."

"I didn't set you up with any of your exes," Drew said. "And Ruger is involved with criminals, Lay. I don't want you being party to any—"

"He's getting out—" Drew began to laugh. A growl of anger tensed her until her fingers curled. "He made that decision before he and I got together. Not that that's any of your business either."

The call was supposed to console her. Make her feel better after Ruger's disappointing comment about Drew and his history with the police. Instead, she found her brother mocking her boyfriend. Neither of them seemed to respect each other and the last place she wanted to be was caught in between them.

"It's my business if he's going to mess around with my sister."

"If he was such a crook, why did you trust him with my safety? Was it your idea to off both of us so you wouldn't have to worry about taking care of your inconvenient sister?"

"Hey!" he said, now he wasn't mocking or laughing. "I take your safety very seriously. There are plenty of guys I would trust to take a bullet for you. That doesn't mean I want them sleeping with you. If he hurts you and this all goes to shit, as your relationships always do, you'll blame me for getting the two of you involved with each other."

"I will not," she said, understanding where Drew's aversion to the relationship came from. "I can take care of myself."

"I wish that were true, Lay. I hate you being out there alone. Serendipity and I have been through some shit, yeah, but it means something to have someone to come home to. It makes you fight harder. All I've ever wanted is for you to have that kind of security."

As she drew in a breath, she turned to lean on the wall. "How do you think it feels from my point of view? You're up there, taking care of business, and I'm down here, never knowing if you're alive or dead. I can't help you. I can't come for you. I can't be there for you."

"You don't have to worry about that."

"I do worry about that," she said. "Telling me not to worry won't change the fact that I do, and I should… we're family."

"No, I mean, you don't have to worry. Dipity has a buyer. The paper wants to verify some facts before they run the story, but it will be out in the next few days if everything checks out. And I know it will 'cause I gathered most of the facts. Once their lawyers sign off, it will be printed."

"That's great," she said. The rush of pride eradicated all previous emotions. "This could all be over in a day or two?"

"Once it's out there, Ashcroft can't come after us. If he tries it, he makes it a bigger story. We'll have full protection, and we'll make sure you're included under that promise."

"Does Ashcroft know? Could that be why he sent his shooter today?"

"It could be," Drew said. "But if you want to come up here, you can come now."

"I can?" she asked.

Her initial elation waned when she noticed Ruger on a path to her.

"I was going to call you about it tomorrow. I hoped we'd have a concrete print date by then."

Since hearing what he was into, she'd wanted to be with her brother. If she left now, protection was guaranteed. But it meant leaving Ruger. Would he assume she didn't trust him to protect her? She wanted to be with her brother. If she left now, would Ruger still be there for her to come back to when everything died down?

TWENTY-SEVEN

"I DON'T LIKE IT, LEGS," Ruger said.

He was patching the broken window with cardboard. Luckily, it was a dry night, but they wanted to keep the breeze and the bugs out.

"I didn't think you would," she said, using a cordless vacuum to clean up the drywall powder spread on the couch and floor.

He'd come to her outside and had his own conversation with Drew, a somewhat contrite conversation, until Drew told him about the deal with the newspaper. Ruger's demeanor changed in an instant, and his apologies went out the window.

Their conversation continued after the cops left. Colt got the neighbors back to their houses and then left her and Ruger alone. This was the first chance she and Ruger had to address what was going on in Atlantic City.

"Jansen thinks he can take care of you now, but this is when the situation is at its most dangerous," he said, using his task as a distraction to balance his mood. While talking to her brother, Ruger's face had set itself in a frown and although she could only see his profile, that frown was still there.

"Ashcroft is a rabid dog trapped in a corner. When the story breaks, there won't be any need for him to maintain his mask."

"The idea will be that when the media start digging, the DA will have to as well, or face suspicion himself," she said, lifting the cushions to vacuum those and the upholstery underneath. "It won't take the press long to put the governor and DA together, so the DA will want to distance himself quickly. I would assume Ashcroft is going to fight the charges. He's not going to roll over and admit the truth. He'll have a story, an explanation of some kind that he'll want to feed to the public."

"That's a lot of assumptions and I don't like those. It's going to be a circus," he said. She returned the vacuum to its charging point and went over to flop onto the couch. "The media will be all over Ashcroft, sure, but they'll want to know about the woman who broke the story too. They'll want to know where she got her facts. Drew and Serendipity are going to be a focal point. Do you want to be a part of that?"

"I want to be with my brother," she said, rolling onto her side and propping her fist on her temple. "This is going to be difficult for him. He doesn't like the limelight. Serendipity won't give up her sources, so Drew probably won't be caught up in the madness."

"Except he's not going to walk away from Serendipity, is he? They've been together for a long time. He'll be a part of it as her boyfriend if nothing else."

Finishing his task, he put the tools on a nearby table and turned to look at her.

"Is that why you're objecting?" she asked. "You think Drew will lose sight of my safety when he's lost in the craziness of the press?"

"No, I just—"

"The newspaper will take good care of them. I believe that, and Ashcroft won't go after them because if he does then he's only proving their case, isn't he?"

"He can call them liars. He can smear them in the press. Jansen has a checkered past. Don't forget that. As soon as the papers get a whiff of him leaving the department while on suspension, they'll want to know every detail of what went on."

The irritation of earlier flourished again. "Which we both know you fault him for," she said.

"Excuse me?"

"Your comment earlier, about Drew screwing over the cops."

He threw up his hands. "So that's what had you in a snit…?" He shook his head. "I don't fault him. I think the cops treated your brother like crap. I meant that's why they did it and they believed they had good reason to shut him out. But if I was Drew and someone had my girlfriend? I would have done exactly the same thing. He faced some terrifying odds, but he kept on going, because he knew he had to get her back."

"Oh," she said, glad he didn't condemn Drew's previous behavior, though that made little difference to their current situation. "Shouldn't I be with him despite the odds we're facing?" Determined, she sat up straight. "Doesn't it reflect negatively on my integrity if I'm not? He doesn't have to be alone on this one. I can be with him; I can support him."

"Calling it a circus doesn't come close to what it will really be like, Legs."

"Being with my family when they need me, that's what I'm supposed to do," she said, grabbing a cushion to hug in her lap. "But I will be sorry to leave you."

"Hey," he soothed, coming over to sit at her side and take her hand. "You've seen how close I am to my family. I understand why you want to be there for Drew and if it was me, I'd want to be with my brothers too."

"So why are you trying to talk me out of it?"

"Because I don't want to see you get hurt and I don't want the media to attack your character either. If you're front and center with Drew and Serendipity, Ashcroft will come for you as well."

"And they might link you and me," she muttered, considering for the first time what would happen if the media, or the cops, began to look too deeply into Ruger or his brothers.

Blaser had done time inside, and Colt had left the police department in the midst of a scandal just like Drew. Intense scrutiny could reveal secrets and tear the family apart.

"They will," Ruger said. "Because if you're going, I'm coming with you."

"You can't," she said, pulling his hand away from hers and shifting down the couch. "You have to stay here, and I have to go be with Drew."

"Why?"

"Because if the media start investigating you and your brothers… all that you've built, your family, they could face public scrutiny too."

"They could, but we'd deal with it."

"No, I couldn't do that to you," she said, tossing the pillow aside and leaving the couch. "What about your mom and dad? They don't know about your former occupation." Dax had travelled up to New Jersey the previous night to check out Ruger's warehouse with a view to deciding if he wanted to clear it out. Getting rid of the goods was supposed to signal Ruger's new start. If the media descended on the still full building, Ruger and Dax could end up in hot water. "They're going to do everything they can to discredit everyone we care about. Ashcroft will make it happen. I'm sure he has his own contacts in the media. That's probably how he held them off for so long and why Serendipity had such trouble finding a buyer for her story."

"It could get messy," he said, rising to follow her path. "But I'm not going to abandon you, none of us are. You belong to our family now. You're one of us."

"I appreciate you saying that," she said, pleased when he took her into his arms. "But that doesn't mean I can turn my back on my old family. Drew is all I have. I can't let him face this alone."

"He has Serendipity, and he has contacts up there who will look out for him, Legs. Let's sleep on it and discuss it again in the morning. This has been a long night."

When he led her through to the bedroom, she followed on, no clearer on her intentions. Everything he said made sense, but it still felt right to be with her brother, and she couldn't drag Ruger and his family through the mud, not after all they'd been through.

Guiding her onto the bed, Ruger crouched before her to slip off her shoes. As he stood up, he took the hem of her top and drew it up over her head.

"No teasing?" she asked when he approached from above to urge her onto her back.

"No teasing."

Shuffling back, she rested on the pillows and lifted her arms up around him to welcome a kiss. Just over an hour ago they were in the living room talking about being together and now she was talking about leaving him. Sometimes it seemed fate didn't want her to find any peace.

Yet as his mouth explored her neck, she closed her eyes, content he was a man who wouldn't let her get away if he truly wanted her. Ruger was thorough and he was dedicated, she might not have the strength to commit to their relationship, but if Ruger decided being together was what he wanted, he would pursue her. She was sure of it.

Working her fingers down the buttons of his shirt, she peeled it back from his torso. As she tugged at the cuffs to free him, her fingers danced across the ridges of his chest. Crunching up, her mouth took over for her fingers, which went to work on his jeans.

It was late and tomorrow would bring decisions she didn't want to face. Flouting responsibility was one of her specialties. In that moment, that felt like a good thing. Holding her head in both hands, Ruger took her from his body and brought their mouths together again. If they hadn't been interrupted before they'd have been in bed already and she wouldn't be famished for the release.

"There better be no bullets this time," she murmured, curving her body upwards to move against the solid security of his.

"No bullets, but I guarantee explosions that will make your ears ring."

"Cocky, aren't you?"

"Practiced," he said, kneeling up to force her jeans down her legs. When he stood to pull them from her ankles, he kicked off his own clothes too. Collapsing over her, he braced on one arm to let the other slip down her body over the swell of her breast to the curve of her waist and down to the slight protrusion of her hip.

Distracting her with a kiss, he parted her legs and dipped his fingers into her. Circling a fingertip inside to test her resistance, all he found was a juicy, welcoming home. When he realized that, he retreated an inch to kiss the tip of her nose.

"Still warm," he muttered and edged his finger deeper, then withdrew to slide up to her clit.

He circled and repeated the action in lazy maneuvers meant to make her wriggle and whimper. No teasing? His actions were a tease in themselves.

"I'm ready," she muttered, biting into her lip to stop more words of urgency from escaping.

"Around me you always are."

More of that arrogance, yet it didn't deter her. She raised her hips into the caress of his hand and when the spasm of orgasm made her scream, he sprang into action. Positioning himself against her sweet spot, the head of his cock slid through her juices and invaded her. Moving in time with her panting, she gasped in oxygen and breathed out his name.

Languishing in the haze of endorphins, the buzz in her gut increased until the pressure between her thighs sent her into a tense spasm.

"Yeah, Lay, that's it, baby," he hissed out through his teeth. "You like that, Legs?"

"Ruger!"

Her eyes burst open, matching with his. That connection of their souls met the connection of their bodies. Gritting his teeth, he pumped into her again, and when he hit deep, his face contorted in time with his own climax.

Falling to the side, he pulled her close, his harsh, huffing breaths humid in her hair. She didn't care they were sticky, that they were really too hot to snuggle. Closing her eyes, she didn't say another thing. The fraught night fell away in time with the ebb of their bliss. Tomorrow, they would have to decide what the future held for them.

TWENTY-EIGHT

THE BATTERING ON THE BACK DOOR was alarming, but with it being broad daylight outside, it was unlikely her early morning visitor was sinister. Ashcroft's men didn't announce themselves either, so she was sure opening the door wouldn't lead to her murder.

Tying her robe tighter, Layla got to the door, opened it, and came up short when Drew was standing there filling the frame.

"Uh… Drew, hi."

Ruger was busy in her shower, washing off their morning in bed, and could possibly come out of her shower buck naked. That wouldn't leave much chance of easing her brother into accepting their relationship.

"Hi?" he asked. "That's all you have to say?"

"Oh, don't be dramatic," she said, stepping aside when he came marching in.

"Do you know how easy it was to find you?" he asked. "You've rented property, are you crazy? You're making yourself a cozy little life here while there are maniacs after you?"

"And whose fault is that?" she asked, going up the stairs because she had no reason to keep Drew in the salon when her apartment was up the stairs.

Being in a robe, she didn't want to be on show through the large salon windows to the neighbors especially with a strange man. The community didn't know this was her brother. All they'd know was that she went to bed with Ruger and woke up with a second man.

Going into the kitchen, Layla began to brew coffee while Drew wandered around the living room to check out the apartment. After he was satisfied he'd learned all he could about the layout, Drew went to the window and pulled off the cardboard covering the bullet hole.

"Hey!" she chided.

"You're going to get someone in to fix the window today, aren't you?" he asked, touching the jagged edge of the glass then turning to see the hole in the wall. "One shot?"

"Yes," she said. "Colt Warner might be able to get you a copy of the police report."

"That would be helpful," Drew said. "But we know who shot at you."

"That doesn't make me feel better," she said. "Ruger saying they didn't mean to shoot me didn't make me feel better either."

Going to the couch, Drew crouched, his attention went back and forth between the bullet hole and the window a couple of times, then he began to aim with an imaginary gun toward the window from his crouched position.

"What are you doing?" she asked, coming over with two cups of coffee and seating herself on the couch.

"The shooter must have been on the roof across the street," he said. "The shot couldn't have come from the street, or the bullet would've hit the ceiling, but it came in on a descending trajectory. Where did Ruger check for the shooter?"

"I don't know," she said. "You can ask him yourself when he comes out of the shower." Drew glared his disapproval, but that only made her widen her smile. "I'm glad you know the truth. Now we can all get along with the truth out in the open."

"The truth might be out in the open, but that doesn't mean I'll be getting along with anyone."

"Where's Serendipity?" she asked.

"Rushe came and picked her up. I don't know where they are now."

"And you're comfortable with that?" she asked.

Teasing her brother came second to her concern for her future sister-in-law.

Drew shifted position to slide up and sit beside her. Taking his coffee off the table, he took a drink before he spoke. "Rushe is the only guy I'd trust."

"Rushe and Ruger," she said, but he glared again.

"I trusted Ruger more before I found out about the two of you. What were you thinking, Lay? The guy is supposed to be protecting you, why did you seduce him?"

"You think I'm the temptress?" she asked. "I'm offended."

"No, you're not," Drew said. "And it doesn't matter who did the seducing, you had to approve, or it wouldn't have happened. I know how stubborn you can be."

"Because you're just as stubborn?"

"Because I lived with you for long enough," he said. "When Ruger's ready, I'll get him to take me across the street."

"If Ashcroft's men are watching me, they'll see you here. Shouldn't you be laying low? I don't like you wandering around in the open."

"It's what you've been doing and you're still here. There's no reason to off me now. The evidence has been gathered and it's in appropriate hands. They could kill me for spite, but that would just make the story juicier and more scandalous."

"You put a lot of faith in these maniacs being smart and rational. Shooting at women seems to be their MO, first Flick and then me. I hope Serendipity is really safe, wherever she is."

"Dipity is safe," Drew said. "Until you meet Rushe you won't understand how I can be so confident about that."

"Until I meet him? I have no interest in meeting the guy. He sounds like a meathead."

"Careful what you say when he's around. Flick is never far behind Rushe, and she takes exception to anyone ridiculing her lover."

The couple did seem intriguing, would she be able to hold up under that kind of scrutiny? Drew had a reputation with these astute, calculating people. Layla had a habit of saying inappropriate things that embarrassed people.

"So where is Ruger?"

"He's in the shower," she said, leaning forward to put her coffee down. "Do you want me to go and get him?"

"No," Drew said. "I'm not sending you into the bathroom with him. You might never come out and I do not want to listen to a play-by-play of you with your new boyfriend."

"I doubt he'd want to mess around with you in the next room. He knows what you're capable of."

"Just so long as he remembers that for as long as he's with you," Drew said, slurping his coffee. "Renting this place, shacking up with Ruger, are you planning to stick around here?"

"Actually, Ruge and I were going to talk about that this morning," she said, curling her legs under herself while being careful to keep her robe over her thighs. "We were talking about making a go of it and then last night happened. I was going to come up to Jersey to be with you and Dipity when the story broke."

"What sense is there in that?" he asked. "Before, fine. After? Dipity and I plan to disappear for a while after the story breaks. We're not interested in the limelight."

"The press will be all over you. Ruger said you two could be slandered, and I wanted to be by your side to show my support."

"It's guaranteed Ashcroft will try to discredit us, which is why we wanted to give the newspaper running the story a chance to verify some of the case facts themselves first. If they know the story is legit, they can run with it, no matter what Ashcroft says about Dipity and me."

"You think martyring yourself will make the story more credible?"

"Don't take everything so personally," he said, taking her hand. "Dipity and I will be fine. We'll just go off and take a vacation before we look for the next story."

"Oh, great, so we'll go through all this again?"

"Next time we'll avoid political officials."

"Great plan," she muttered.

The bathroom door opened. Ruger came out in a plume of steam, thankfully holding a towel around his hips.

"Jansen," he said, his attention flicking between them on the couch.

"Go put some clothes on, we have work to do," Jansen said, drawing his scowl away from Ruger and planting it on her again.

Layla lunged over to pinch her brother's arm, but Ruger shuffled off into the bedroom to get changed.

"Give him a break," Layla said. "He's doing what he promised you. I'm still here, aren't I?"

"Yeah, but you're a little too rosy-cheeked for my liking."

Rolling her eyes at her brother's disapproval, she didn't let on just how much she enjoyed their sibling banter. It had been so long since they'd been together, she had almost forgotten what it felt like to be under Drew's wing.

"I want you to meet his family, to see just how good these people are. I think once you do, you'll change your tune."

"You're not dating his family, you're dating him."

"Colt is an ex-cop just like you," she said, hoping to summon some points in Ruger's favor.

"Yeah, and Blaser is an ex-con. You're crazy if you think I didn't do my due diligence before handing my only sister over to this guy."

"See, you do care," she said widening her cheesy grin and leaning closer. "I don't give you a hard time about Dipity."

"I'd like to see you try. Dip and I have been together for so long, I'd be surprised if you can remember a time she wasn't in your life. If Ruger was one guy of a few, I'd be more relaxed about it, but I know you. He'll start to get heavy, and you'll panic, then you'll run."

"Everyone has such faith in me," she grumbled, slouching around her coffee mug. "I'm not a slut, you know, and I don't see you rushing to get married either."

"I haven't married Dipity 'cause of you," he said. "I'm terrified if I ask her, she'll run, just like you do every time a guy produces a ring."

Astounded, she was on pause when Ruger came out of the bedroom and Drew got up to talk to him. They went to examine the window. Drew went through the same routine he had when he first came up the stairs, but she was immobilized. Drew held her neurosis as an example of how women reacted to commitment?

Completely by accident, she had managed to screw up her brother's life. She didn't act in a normal or rational way, but without their mother to guide him, she had been his go-to person for examples of the behavior of the opposite sex.

"We're going outside," Ruger said. He had to duck down and force her chin up with a finger to get her attention. "Legs?"

"Okay, yes," she said.

"Get dressed and we'll go out for breakfast when we're through."

"It will have to be a quick breakfast," she said.

"Why?" Ruger and Drew asked.

"Because I have plans later," she said, pinning Ruger under her stare. "So do you."

"I do?"

"The engagement party is tonight," Layla said. "You're supposed to be going with Colt to pick up supplies."

"Shit, that's tonight?"

"Yes, which makes dragging him out last night all the more terrible. The poor guy has enough on his plate."

"My mom and Lyssa will have taken care of everything," Ruger said to her, then switched his focus onto Drew. "You can come if you want."

"A party?" Drew asked. "I'm not really in the mood."

"Get in the mood," Layla said.

Her brother's foul attitude might be justified given what he'd been through recently. And he might not like Ruger very much at that moment. But the Warner family had been kind to her, and she wasn't going to let Drew ruin a special event in their lives.

"We'll talk about it at breakfast," Ruger said. "We don't have to be at my mom's until lunchtime, right?"

"Yes," Layla said and accepted Ruger's kiss.

Kissing her reinforced the sincerity of their relationship in front of Drew. She liked that Ruger wasn't afraid of her brother freaking out on him. It had been their plan to leave the salon and eat lunch at the Warner house where Pru would lay out the itinerary. So far all they knew was the men were supposed to pick up the gazebo and the food for the grill, while the women stayed home to decorate and arrange the flowers.

Being included meant a lot to Layla, although she did feel like a fraud. If she was going to walk out on Ruger, should she be ingratiating herself with the family? Except with Drew there, she didn't need to leave… the future had become even less clear.

TWENTY-NINE

ALREADY THE WARNER HOUSE looked beautiful. When Ruger called his mom to say they wouldn't be there for lunch, she was very understanding. Pru had dozens of questions about the previous night and Ruger did a good job of answering them without lying directly. That the distinction had to be made broke her heart.

After leaving Drew at her apartment, they hurried over to Ruger's parents', but lunch was thoroughly over by the time they arrived. They were both put to work without delay and hadn't seen much of each other since.

At the kitchen island with Bri, Lyssa and Suzette, the women were allocated the task of folding linen napkins into fancy shapes. A new table had been set up beyond the back door where the napkins would be displayed behind the food.

Ruger worked with his brothers, moving furniture from the living room and putting down floor coverings to protect the carpet. Lyssa was patient as Layla screwed up the napkins time and again. Her head just wasn't in the game.

"I'm sorry," Layla said, giving up on her latest napkin effort.

"It's okay," Lyssa said. "Keep practicing."

"We heard about what happened last night," Suzette said, keeping her volume low as Pru Warner was flitting in and out issuing instructions to the men and making lists.

Being a part of the group reminded her of the first night Ruger brought her into the Warner house. The women had been around this island, and the clique had been intimidating. Since then, it had become normal to be included in the gaggle.

Lyssa would be patient and urge her to talk using leading questions. Bri would be quiet, but listen keenly, and she would speak up if someone said something out of turn. Suzette would just be loud and direct, showing no hesitation if she wanted a certain piece of information. Had Suzette always been so outgoing or had her relationship with Gus brought her out of her shell?

"I'm sorry we dragged Colt out last night," Layla said to Lyssa, flattening the napkin to try the folding again.

"You didn't drag him out," Lyssa said. "He has family in the police department. Whenever the Warner name pops onto the police radio, you can be sure someone in the family will get a call."

"And that's always Colt?"

"It's whoever's most closely related to the Warner involved," Lyssa said. "So if it's Ruger or Blaser, Colt gets called."

"Blaser and I have dragged him out a time or two," Bri said. "Colt's great. He's very understanding."

These days. Bri and Lyssa made eye contact then smiled. Colt was understanding these days with Lyssa keeping him straight, the doctor told her that wasn't always the case.

"I don't understand why Ruger's name would have come up over the police radio. We weren't the ones who called the cops, I mean I tried to, but they were already on their way."

"This is a close-knit neighborhood. Everyone knows Ruger's girlfriend bought the salon. Pru is conjuring up business for you already," Lyssa said. "It wouldn't surprise me if that was exactly what the police were told when the neighbor called in."

"Not much business going on at the moment," Layla said. "I had hoped to open next week, but after last night… a shooting isn't exactly good for business."

"Are you kidding? That won't deter people around here," Suzette said, completing another napkin to perfection. "Now everyone will want to know what happened and what you're involved in. They like to think they're nice and respectable, but they're nosy gossip hounds just like women the world over."

"Speak for yourself," Lyssa said with a smile.

"You get to pry into people's private, secret business for a living," Suzette said. "You can afford to appear aloof elsewhere."

The women laughed.

Pru came over, sticking herself in between Layla and Lyssa. "How is it going?"

"Great," Lyssa said.

"We still have to prepare the canapés, the salads, and the condiments. Why did Colt insist on this being a barbeque?"

"Because he's a guy," Suzette said. "He's lost all privileges when it comes to planning the actual wedding. Lys and I got away with so much just because we gave him carte blanche with the engagement party."

"Wise, I suppose," Pru said. "We're going to put gifts in the dining room and the bar in the living room. Blaser has chairs at his club, which the boys are going to pick up when they go for the gazebo. Ruger is talking about a music system. Do we plan to disturb the neighbors?"

"We don't need a music system," Lyssa said. "But it's nice of him to offer."

"Thank goodness for that," Pru said. "I'll let him know."

The woman disappeared.

Lyssa folded a final napkin. "Pinch can get anything," she said. "But his place of business is quite a drive away."

"Pinch?" Layla asked.

"One of Ruger's contacts," Lyssa said and left her stool to begin moving the napkins from the island to the table.

"Most of the neighbors are coming to this party. Colt's known them for years, so I don't think there will be anyone to bother with the noise."

"It's not a frat party," Suzette said, getting up to join her friend. "And you did offer to do it in the middle of the day."

"Early evening is the middle of the day as far as Colt and Blaser are concerned," Bri said, taking her share of napkins over to the table.

Layla might not have been great at the folding, but she could carry with the best of them, so she gave up with the cloth and took the last of the napkins to the table where Lyssa was arranging them in neat groups.

"That's true," Lyssa said. "The pair of them work at night."

"Who is looking after Risqué tonight?" Layla asked.

"Dax, Ivy and Crystal," Bri said, examining the spread on the table.

"I thought Dax was in Atlantic City," Layla said.

"He is, but he'll be back tonight. Crystal will be in charge until then," Bri said. "He's already driving, so he'll be back as early as possible."

"Oh, great," Suzette sneered. "At least I won't have to be around to hear Ivy welcoming him home."

Bri and Lyssa just laughed, so Layla figured the teasing was good-natured. She wasn't sure who knew what, or who was supposed to know what, so she kept her questions to herself. Lyssa helped to answer some of those questions with her next statement.

Leaning in closer to the huddle of women, she fixed on her best friend. "When you move downstairs into Gus' place, that won't be a problem for you anymore, will it?"

Bri laughed and Suzette hissed at her friend to quiet down.

Layla asked, "Why are you keeping your relationship with him a secret?"

"Because he's an oaf," Suzette said.

"Yes, but he's your oaf," Lyssa said and looped her arm through Suzette's. "You'll have to give in to it eventually.

Don't let your experience with Pete put you off commitment. Sometimes you have to take a risk."

"I know that," Suzette said with a long fed-up sigh. "You've worked with me so much since then, I'm not nearly as meek and jumpy as I used to be."

"Hard to imagine you like that," Bri said, a warm smile bloomed on her face. "Hanging around in Risqué so much has changed you."

"Gus has changed her," Lyssa said. "He's given her new purpose and a reason to stop drinking so much."

"Pete was the reason I drank so much," Suzette said. "I had to after the humiliation he put me through."

"Who's Pete?" Layla asked.

"My psycho ex-fiancé who stalked Lyssa," Suzette said. "And I'm not holding back because of Pete. I… Gus hasn't promised me the world or anything, I'm not getting ahead of myself."

"You know what Gus is like," Bri said. "He asked you to move into his place, didn't he? For him that's like a marriage proposal. He makes other men's nonchalance look like mayhem. He just doesn't understand urgency at all."

"There's no urgency," Suzette said. "I'm happy to see where it goes."

"You're desperate to be married and don't even deny it," Lyssa said, going to the fridge as the rest of the women returned to their places at the kitchen island to unpack the food the doctor was retrieving.

"I don't see Gus getting down on one knee," Bri said. "If you want it to happen, you have to make it happen."

"I don't see a ring on your finger," Suzette said, leaning back to glance at Bri's hand.

"That's not because Blaser hasn't asked me," Bri said, holding up her hand to examine the vacant spot. "I keep telling him to slow down."

"And Lys says I have issues?" Suzette said, leaving her seat to retrieve the kitchen utensils required for the food prep.

"We all have issues," Lyssa said, handing out the vegetables. "Even I'm not perfect."

"Oh my God," Suzette said, stalling and holding up both hands. "Did everyone hear that? Quick, someone write down the date and time."

"Bri will get there when she's ready," Lyssa said, handing out chopping boards.

"Except there is a looming deadline," Suzette said.

Layla joined in looking at Bri because she was curious about the woman's reaction.

"Maybe that's why I don't want to do it," Bri said. "I don't want to rush such an important decision."

"But you know you're always going to be with Blaser," Suzette said.

"She sure is," Blaser said, drawing the attention of the women.

The three brothers, along with their father, were negotiating a large tabletop and its separate legs out of the living room through the kitchen to take it into the backyard. As they were doing that, the women watched while dealing with the vegetables. None of them said anything else about the sensitive topic while there were listening ears in the vicinity.

Pru zipped across the kitchen in the wake of the men. Only after she disappeared outside—presumably to tell the men how to put the table back together in the place she wanted it—did the girls in the kitchen carry on their conversation.

"We're looking for somewhere new to live," Bri said. "Once we do that, we'll need our cash to get setup for the baby. Blaser is talking about starting a second garage closer to home. It's a busy time for us and our finances are tied up. I'm not going to be happy hurrying a wedding while I've got a baby bump. There's no rush, that's what I keep telling him, but he keeps on pushing."

"Because he loves you," Lyssa said. "We can talk about that if you bring him along to your next session."

"You know he'll say he doesn't have time," Bri said.

"When you tell him it's important to you, he comes," Lyssa said. "And you can promise him that we won't talk about his dick at all."

"Typical conversation for my fiancée," Colt said, sauntering into the kitchen and coming up behind Lyssa to watch what she was doing. "What are you girls talking about?"

"Blaser's penis," Lyssa said and carried on with her task.

Layla might have expected Colt to be shocked or upset, instead he smiled and kissed the top of his fiancée's head. "I really need to learn to stop asking."

"We're actually not talking about it," Bri said, "which is sort of the point."

"What are you not talking about?"

This time it was Blaser coming through the back door. He too went to his girlfriend. Wrapping an arm around her shoulders, he stole a raw carrot stick from Bri's board.

"Your dick," Colt said.

Blaser grumbled, which made everyone laugh.

"We're really not," Bri said, trying to turn and see him.

"It's okay, Doll, I'm getting used to it," Blaser said, massaging her shoulders as he munched on the carrot.

"Where's Ruger?" Layla asked.

"Making a phone call," Colt said. "My parents are arguing about the yard layout. We thought we'd leave them to it."

"Who is he calling?" Layla asked, unsure if she was more uncomfortable asking or not knowing.

"Your brother far as I can tell," Colt said. "Ruge said that Jansen showed up this morning at your place."

"After I spoke to him last night, I thought I was going to him," Layla said. "I didn't expect him to show up."

"You were going to leave?" Lyssa asked.

Each of the faces in the room were trained on her. Everyone knew the full situation, even if she hadn't been the one to tell them.

With a sigh, she relented the truth. "The story is going to break soon. Drew is expecting an answer on the print date today."

"You think Ashcroft is going to step up his game?" Colt asked.

"I think my brother shouldn't face being discredited alone," Layla said. "I want to be with him, to show my support."

"That's incredibly stupid," Blaser said. "Your brother is vulnerable already because he has Serendipity with him. Having you too… he can't watch you both at once, that's how Ruger got involved in this in the first place, remember?"

She didn't need to be reminded and especially didn't appreciate being reminded in such a condescending way, but Blaser was right.

"I know that, but once the story is out there, the danger goes away, doesn't it?"

"Maybe, maybe not," Colt said. "What's Jansen's plan?"

"He said he plans to lay low, maybe get out of the state with Serendipity for a while until the circus dies down."

"Smart," Colt said. "Once the story is out there, the rest of the media will take over the digging. The DA will have to investigate. He can't be seen to be complicit in Ashcroft's games."

"That's what Ruger said," Layla admitted.

"Never thought my baby brother was that smart," Blaser said.

Ruger came in, but he didn't come over to the island, he went to the living room door. "Lay, can I have a sec?"

She didn't like his solemn expression. Ruger wasn't known for being so grave.

"What is it?" she asked, sliding off her stool. "Is it Drew?"

Ruger trusted everyone there, but he still took the time to look at them all before he came over to her and took her hands. "The story is going out tomorrow."

"Tomorrow? That's sudden."

"Everyone reads the Sunday papers," Colt said.

Layla kept her attention on Ruger, who gave her a squeeze. "I guess they got the confirmation they needed. This is going to get serious very quickly."

"Where's Drew?"

"On his way back to Serendipity. He wants to get back there as fast as he can, and he asked me to look after you."

So either Drew didn't want her there or he still had concerns about keeping her safe while protecting Serendipity.

"Okay," Layla said, trying to process as quickly as possible. "Okay."

Withdrawing her hands from Ruger's, she went back to her job peeling vegetables.

"You don't have to be here," Lyssa said. "Both of you, if there's somewhere you need to be or—"

"No," Layla said. "Nothing needs to be done. We just have to carry on. The party is going to be great." Forcing a smile, those around her began to relax.

"Okay, you heard the woman," Ruger said, clapping his hands. "Let's get into the party mood. Who wants some music?"

THIRTY

THEY TALKED RUGER OUT of music in favor of getting the work done quickly. The women were still organizing food, and the men were in their trucks, preparing to pick up the items needed for that night. Pru was outside on the driveway handing out final lists to the men of what tasks had to be completed and when they should be home for.

"Pru really knows what she's doing," Suzette said. "She's a real godsend."

"She's been wrangling those males for years," Lyssa said. "She is well-practiced."

"Something you'll be in a couple of years," Layla said to her.

"Oh, Lyssa already knows how to push all of their buttons," Bri said. "Reading people is something she does well."

"It's in the job description," Lyssa said, taking the trays of completed canapés over to the counter to be covered before refrigeration.

"How long has Pru been out there though? It must be half an hour at least," Bri said. "Do you think we should worry?"

"I'm here. I'm here," Pru said. "Sorry, I got talking to one of your guests who arrived early, but he's not shy and says he'll help us out, isn't that generous? I didn't realize your well of friends ran so deep, Lyssa."

This statement intrigued them all to stop what they were doing and turn to see who was going to come in behind Pru as she came further into the room. An audible gasp circled the room when Governor Ashcroft walked into the Warner kitchen.

"Call the cops," Lyssa said.

"Now don't do that," Ashcroft said, holding up both hands in surrender. "I just came here to have a conversation. You wouldn't begrudge me that, would you? Not when you're about to take a man's life."

"What's going on?" Pru asked, a tremor in her voice suggesting she recognized her misstep.

"Don't worry," Bri said. "We can call Blaser and—"

"Is that your man?" Ashcroft asked, putting a hand on the back of Pru's neck to bring her closer to the group. "I watched this nice lady pull weeds for a clear ten minutes before I approached, and we talked for another ten after that. Your men are gone, ladies."

"It's me you want," Layla said, pulling off her kitchen gloves and hopping off her stool. "Leave these kind people out of it."

"I want to have a conversation with you, Layla, see if I can't make you see sense," Ashcroft said, giving Pru a nudge forward so she hit the center island. He unbuttoned his jacket and pulled half aside to show a gun in his belt. "And if these kind people like you, they'll let us have the conversation in peace and not do anything stupid."

Ensuring they all saw the gun; he examined every face then dropped the flap of his jacket to take Layla's arm and urge her into the living room.

"What's this about?" Layla asked, pulling her arm out of his hand and folding her arms. "You're insane to show up trying to intimidate me. It only makes your case worse."

"I'm not a monster," he said, holding open his arms. "I'm a patriot. I love my country and my state. Everything I've done, I've only done to make sure that Jersey gets what it deserves."

"You're going to get what you deserve when the media takes you apart. What you've done is selfishly line your own pockets. Since you've been found out, you've sent men to threaten and intimidate. Do you feel proud of hurting defenseless women?"

"I came here to show you I am not an evil man. I don't want to hurt you or your friends. All of this has gone much further than I thought it would. I'm not a murderer, and that's why I'm here," Ashcroft said, beseeching her with clasped hands and an open expression. She wasn't going to be taken in and remained defiant. "Some of my men are sure the only way to silence your brother and his woman is to take one of you out. I'm not sure I could live with that on my conscience. Taking bribes is one thing, but murder, that's on another level I'm not comfortable with quite frankly."

"And that's supposed to prove you're a redeemed man?" she asked, taking careful steps back toward the picture window.

"To best serve my state, I had to make sure my personal life was taken care of, you understand? That meant I couldn't have mundane worries like money and such."

"Don't you receive a salary for what you do? Somewhere to live, perks? I've seen the mansion. It's palatial. Are you telling me what you receive for doing your job isn't enough?"

"You can't understand the pressure I'm under," he said, skirting the couch to come toward her.

"You signed up for it. More than that, you campaigned, begging to be put in office. This is what you wanted."

"And that justifies what your family is doing to me?" he asked, lunging over to grab her upper arms. "I don't want to hurt any of you. Stop the story. Call up your brother and tell him to let it go."

"He won't do that," Layla said. "This is too important… and he shouldn't do it either. The public deserve to know what you are."

Throwing her from his grip, Ashcroft turned his back. "You're really going to make me do this."

"You can still do the right thing," she said, worried about the way his voice faded. "You can go to the press yourself, make a statement. Explain it to them like you explained it to me."

She didn't think anyone would buy all the, "*I did it for my country*" bullshit, but if it would get him out of there without hurting anyone…

"You're appeasing me," he said. "It won't work." Spinning to face her, his expression was severe. "Your brother and that piece of shit girlfriend of his, they're not going to know what hit them. I'm going to tear them apart. My advisors will—"

"They're prepared for that," she said, taking on his anger and throwing it right back. "The only person at fault in this situation is you. You can throw all the mud you like, and yeah, some of it might stick. But that won't change the fact you acted illegally."

"You can't prove it. You can't prove anything."

"The newspaper wouldn't be running with the story if they weren't sure there was truth to it. And your connection to the DA is going to create such a shitstorm for him that I guarantee he'll be throwing you to the wolves to protect his own ass. There is no honor among thieves these days, is there?"

"Ask your brother, he knows enough of them."

Ashcroft thought he could bully and intimidate her. Maybe he'd picked her believing she was the weakest link. Appeasing him hadn't worked and she wouldn't play it feeble and let this guy think he'd won. He was in all sorts of trouble. Her pride in Drew only grew when she saw how pathetic Ashcroft was.

"Do you think that's a fault? My brother used to be a cop—"

"And he resigned in a scandal," Ashcroft spat. "Don't think I don't know everything about him."

"He's not the only cop I know," she said, leaning closer, thinking of Colt and the Warner connections. "Getting information from official channels isn't as hard as you might think, even for those who don't pay or accept bribes. We know everything about you."

The specifics of Serendipity's story weren't even required. Witnessing Ashcroft unspooling betrayed his guilt and despair over the idea of losing his easy life. Pressing his buttons would ensure he acted more erratically. The bigger mess he was tomorrow, the less credibility he'd have to discredit Drew and Serendipity.

Just to look at the initially bold man, the tarnish was beginning to fade. His eyes were shifty and sweat formed on his high forehead.

"As you've pointed out…" she carried on. The paranoid creature in front of her wasn't the polished politician groomed by advisors to spit out sound bites. He was a man on the precipice, about to lose everything. "We have contacts in the underworld too."

Okay, so she didn't really have contacts, and the word, "*underworld*" made her sound like some kind of vampire sorceress, but the statement worked.

"Are you threatening me?" he asked.

"I'm not the one who showed up here flashing my gun," she said. "I'm telling you that information can be obtained from all sources. We're connected too. If you think you can discredit my brother and his girlfriend, and we'll just roll over then you're wrong. A man like you doesn't need to take bribe money unless he's fueling a vice. What is it, Governor Ashcroft? What's your vice? Are you a drinker or maybe it's a little powder pick-me-up you need to get you through the day?"

"Drugs? No! I do not take drugs."

"It doesn't matter. We can find that out," she said, strolling around him. "Maybe it's gambling, or is it the ladies you like… maybe it's the boys?" He whirled around, his wide eyes speaking for him. "I guess that's it. Would your wife like to know about that? Drew hasn't told me everything. I was happy to read the story in the paper with the rest of the country. You don't strike me as a party animal, but I guess the best of them never do."

"You don't know what you're talking about."

"I do," Layla said. "You're chasing your own personal high, like the power and influence you had wasn't enough. You wanted to show off. Your own greed got you into this and now there's no way out. The lucky part for you is that you have a smidge of time. If I was you, I'd make sure my family knew what was about to hit the headlines. Talk to your advisors and decide if you have a future in your party. Over the next few days, you're going to find out who your real friends are, and I'd bargain there aren't too many of them."

"You're enjoying this. You're a sick, twisted, vile—"

"I'm not enjoying it," she said, removing all smugness to glare at this tyrant. "I resent the fact you enjoyed what you did. That taking money from people to fuel your own misdeeds came at the expense of what was best for the people. You were elected to take care of your constituents and instead you abused them. Do what you will to my family, but I hope you rot in hell for what you've done to the credibility of this country."

Finished with him and this conversation, she headed for the kitchen, ready to tell him to leave or she herself would call the cops. What she didn't expect was for him to pounce upon her and grab a handful of her hair to force her down to her knees.

"You cost me all I love," he said. The barrel of his gun dug into her crown. "Now I'm going to make you pay for what you've done to me."

THIRTY-ONE

RUGER HAD BEEN IN his truck with Blaser when the phone rang. Before Colt finished relaying Lyssa's story, he'd turned the vehicle around to head for his parents' house again.

With the story so close to print and with Layla in a group, he'd believed she was safe. Cursing himself for leaving her unprotected, Blaser tried to soothe him by pointing out no one expected Ashcroft himself to show up. If a strange thug like Padget had appeared, their mom would've called the cops for sure.

"What's going on?" Ruger asked, as he leaped out of his truck and ran toward Colt on the perimeter of a police barricade setup around their mother's house.

"He's in there with them," Colt said.

With his arms folded across his chest, Colt watched the house. He showed so little emotion that Ruger got a chill.

"I'm sorry, man, I…"

"It's not your fault," Colt said.

Blaser was beside him with his fingers linked on his head. He slid them down to rub his face then squeezed his hands into fists.

"We can't just stand here," Blaser said and tried to walk forward, but Ruger held him back.

A dozen police vehicles were strewn across the street at various angles and SWAT had to be somewhere around too. A group of plainclothes men stood in a huddle in the center of the mess. The one with the bullhorn hanging loose at his side was in charge.

"Is that…?" Ruger asked, squinting at the man.

"The Chief," Colt said. "Yeah… I guess when politics are involved, it goes all the way to the top. I can't even get over there. No one will tell me anything."

"This is…" Blaser was pacing. "We can't just do nothing."

"What else can we do?" Colt asked, still fixated on the house. "They're all in there, Mom, Lys, Bri, Lay… your unborn child, Blase… We could lose it all. This guy… This one guy could take away everything."

That was a chilling and undeniable truth. Blaser paced, Colt stared. Off to the side, their father battled with a uniformed cop for information. The kid looked no older than nineteen. The rookie wouldn't know anything, but their dad had to feel like he was doing something.

"Has he made demands?" Blaser asked.

"No," Colt said. "Lys called the cops after she called me. Her line to the operator died when a bunch of Ashcroft's men stormed the house and rushed them. Ashcroft must have given them instructions to enter if he wasn't out within a certain timeframe, I don't know."

So Ashcroft and his men were holed up with all the women they cared about and there wasn't a damn thing they could do about it. Layla. He was terrified of losing her before getting the chance to say everything he wanted to say to her. Worse than that, what was happening was his responsibility. His fault. Not only might he lose the woman he loved, but his father and brothers could lose their women too.

This standoff had to be bringing back memories for Colt. Not long ago, they'd stood outside Lyssa's house as she was trapped inside with a mad man. That conflict had been over quickly, and they knew what the stalker wanted. This was different. Ashcroft wanted something none of them could give.

"Do you think we can get in from the backyard?" Ruger asked, leaning back trying to see what he could of the houses parallel to the back of his parents' home.

"They've shut down three blocks," Colt said. "We're lucky to be this close. There's a governor in there for crissakes, they're probably ready to call the National Guard. The FBI will be scrambling as we speak."

"Maybe Marine One will drop by to help," Ruger said. Humor helped him process, but his brothers didn't appreciate it. "Don't they want to keep this quiet? It's embarrassing for the establishment, isn't it?"

"Except they probably think he's the target not the perpetrator," Colt said.

"Where is his security?" Blaser asked.

"Got me," Colt said. "Those who were complicit are probably in there. If he wanted to have a private conversation with Layla, he'd have left anyone not in on the deal at home."

"I have to call Jansen," Ruger said, retrieving his phone from his pocket.

He'd put it off long enough. If Jansen was anywhere near a radio or TV, he probably knew what was happening already. Media vans were pulling up at a further perimeter being manned by more uniformed cops who poured out of a squad of vans.

"Someone should call Gus," Colt said, finally taking his eyes away from the house, he faced his brothers.

"Gus?" Ruger asked. "Why?"

"He and Suzette are seeing each other," Blaser said, pulling his own phone out. "I'll do it. But Mattie is not welcome at this party."

Mattie was Gus' brother and a crime boss in the area.

Ruger shook his head. "With this many cops around, I don't think Mattie will want to be a part of this."

None of them wanted to be a part of this. Ruger and Blaser were dialing, so Colt went over to console their father, still trying to talk sense into the cop. With a hand on his shoulder, the most responsible of the brothers reassured their patriarch. The whole situation was out of control. He couldn't picture the end game.

Ashcroft had to know this wouldn't end well for him. Not now he was being watched by people across the world. With bated breath, they braced for his next move.

THIRTY-TWO

"I AM SO SORRY ABOUT THIS," Layla said.

She had been apologizing ever since Ashcroft's men poured through the back door, taking the women in the kitchen by surprise. They had guns. Big, scary looking machine guns, that they held in what looked like military poses. These were professional thugs.

The women had been lined up on their knees with her, guarded by a man with a gun while the others rearranged the environment to accommodate their plans. By the way the place looked, there wouldn't be a happy ending.

They had closed drapes, duct-taped the edges and the center then piled furniture in front of the entrances. As for their hostages, they'd taped chairs together in a circle, facing outward, and then taped the women one at a time to the seats. All five of them had their hands taped together and forced over the backs of the chairs in an awkward, uncomfortable position. But at least they rubbed arms, that offered some comfort.

"This isn't your fault," Bri said. "The man is crazy."

Ashcroft wasn't in the living room anymore. He'd gone into the dining room to talk to some of his men but left them under guard. Being left trussed up was awful, but she felt worse these wonderful women had to endure the humiliation as well.

"My boys will think of something," Pru said. "We don't have anything to fear."

Each of the women had faith in the Warner men. Ruger would do everything in his power to help her, except there wasn't much he could do. The sirens outside had come thick and fast and were quickly intermingled and replaced with a buzz of constant activity outside the house.

The phone rang. Each of the women tensed and shifted, but none of the guards flinched. "Isn't someone going to answer that?" Suzette asked in a louder than necessary voice. "Hello! Governor!"

"Aggravating him isn't going to help," Bri said.

"Neither is him ignoring the phone," Suzette said. "We can't stay in here forever."

No, they couldn't. Ashcroft came persuade Jansen and Serendipity to hold the story, except now there was a whole new story. The old one would still be of interest because Ashcroft was current. Maybe that was his plan. But as the bad guy, he couldn't expect much sympathy.

Ashcroft strolled in from the dining room and picked up the phone only to drop it back into its cradle. His attention remained on the women as he sauntered closer.

"This was caused by you and your family," he said to Layla. "Are you proud of what you've done?"

"I'm not the one holding the gun," Layla said. "You can let them go. My brother won't care about their safety. If you want to persuade him to drop the story, the only person you need is me."

"The story just got bigger, didn't it?" Ashcroft asked. "Look at this situation. Do you think anyone will care about a couple of bribes with the sensational material they have now? The world's media is outside, reporting live. I bet if we turned on the TV, we would see it play out ourselves. Would you like to do that?"

"There's nothing wrong with my ego," Layla said. "I don't need to see squat."

"You do have a temper, don't you?"

"When someone threatens people I care about, yes, I do."

"I have an idea," Ashcroft said, coming closer still. If her legs weren't taped to the legs of the chair, she would lash out to kick him. No matter how much she squirmed, she couldn't get free.

"Your ideas haven't worked out very well for you today," Layla said. "Do you still think coming here was a good idea? Intimidating me didn't work and now you're in hotter water than you were before."

"Let's call your brother," Ashcroft said, snapping his fingers at one of his goons. He pointed at the phone for the thug to retrieve it and hand it over, which he did. "We'll call your brother, and he can bring his lady friend here. Do you think they would cover this story?"

If the situation was all over the news, her brother and Serendipity would already be on their way.

As to when they'd arrive was anyone's guess.

"Is that what you want? To take more innocent people down? Drew and Serendipity won't walk in here unless you let these other women go."

"And when they're here, we might consider that," Ashcroft said. "Now what's his phone number?"

"I don't have it," Layla said. She knew her brother's phone number but wouldn't call him up and lure him there when it would mean certain death. "Is this about revenge? Why do you want him here?"

"He tried to tear my life apart. I want him to witness his own demise."

"You can kill him, you can kill me, you can kill all of us. It won't make a difference. The story is still out there."

"Politicians aren't the only professionals who can be bought. Newspaper editors are partial to a pay-off too."

"Even if you've already done that, you can't erase this."

"I wouldn't want to… Once your brother is here, you'll see just how this can work in my favor. I won't be villainized. I am going to be the hero."

Layla couldn't envision how he would make that happen until the sound of feedback heralded a voice from outside. "Governor Ashcroft, are you safe? We need to negotiate with your captors. Please, ask them to pick up the phone."

The phone in Ashcroft's hand began to ring again and he smiled at her. "You see? They do not see me as the aggressor. I am in peril, I am a victim, and this is going to be my greatest hour."

THIRTY-THREE

"THEY THINK HE'S THE VICTIM?" Ruger said to his brothers, huddled together on the sidewalk, still by the barricade. Their father had regained some of his composure. Although the senior Warner's hands shook, he did his duty consoling neighbors. "That's not going to fly."

"What are you going to do about it?" Blaser asked.

Ruger was speed-dialing Jansen again. "I'm going to make sure the media get wind of the truth before the cops fuck this up." Lifting the phone to his ear, he listened to it ring and looked to Colt. "If you can think of anyone you can call to get the story straight, start dialing."

And his brother did just that as Jansen answered the phone.

"What?" Jansen asked.

Was that anger or concern saturating his voice? No doubt there was an element of both.

"You need to get on the phone with this editor who's printing your story. This is happening fast. The media are running with the cops' line that Ashcroft is the victim."

"How can he be the victim?" Jansen demanded. "He had no reason to be there. No reason to be in your parents' house threatening my sister."

"Maybe not, but the media haven't done their checking yet. It's all misinformation and assumption now. You have to get the truth out there before the cops start shooting at the wrong people."

"Okay. Okay," Jansen said. "Serendipity is calling now… If Ashcroft wants to come out of this as a hero…"

"Then he'll have to kill everyone in that house," Ruger said, pinning his own sights on the house.

He could understand the numbness that had overcome Colt earlier.

"He could be setting up one of his own men as a patsy."

"It will never work out," Ruger said. "You have the story. You've sold it to the newspaper and there's us. We would never let him win. If he takes out the women in that house, the rest of us have nothing to lose."

"I'm sorry about this, Warner. I got you in way deeper than you signed up for."

"Falling in love with your sister's done that to me. I'm not going to lose her to this maniac's delusions."

"You're right the story probably wouldn't fly. There are too many holes in it. He'd get away with it for a few days, maybe a week or two, then the media would lose their sympathy and start to do their checking. That's when his world would implode."

"That's not much of a consolation to us, because our women would still be dead."

"I'm on my way, Ruger. Whatever it takes, we'll get them out of there."

Optimism was appreciated but misplaced. There was nothing any of them could do. The cops wouldn't let them near the house. Just as he hung up, a gang of police officers came to herd them further away. The Warners and neighbors protested, but one of the wooden barriers was moved aside and a fleet of black vehicles poured into the already manic space. The FBI had arrived.

THIRTY-FOUR

"YOU NEED TO ANSWER the phone," Layla said, sick of the sound of it ringing. They had been restrained for over an hour and Ashcroft wasn't making any further moves.

"Once your brother arrives, we will."

"My brother isn't coming," Layla said.

"He's coming," Ashcroft said, full of confidence.

The canapés meant for the engagement party were being consumed by Ashcroft and his men. The prepped food would last them for a week. Lyssa and Suzette had had their mouths taped, one for trying to analyze the governor and the other for being too annoying. The only person Ashcroft seemed interested in was her. He dismissed the others but was open to discussion with her.

"I can get his phone number," Layla said. "Let me phone a mutual friend, he'll be able to give me it."

Ashcroft popped another canapé in his mouth and used the napkin tucked in his pocket to wipe his fingers. "You didn't want to phone him when I asked."

"No, but now I want to warn him to stay the hell away from here."

"That doesn't serve my interest."

"None of this serves your interest. They're going to find out the truth and when they do, the media will take you down." Layla had chastised Ruger for the opinion people could be vilified in the court of public opinion, now it was going to be her greatest ally. "They've had some time. Turn on the TV. I'll bet they're not reporting your heroism right now. The news will be asking why you were here and what business you had in this house. When they figure out that you have no connection to anyone here except your connection to Drew and Serendipity, they are going to put the pieces together. What will you do then?"

Padget had been wandering in and out of the various occupied rooms. He seemed to hold some kind of authority among the men and was keeping them in line as Ashcroft did his own thing.

"Turn on the TV," Ashcroft demanded when Padget came in.

The television was wall mounted and hadn't been removed with the other furniture. Unfortunately, it was on the wall behind her. She wouldn't be able to see what was going on outside where the media were filming. If Ashcroft saw she was right, he would have to reconsider his plan. That couldn't include hurting anyone. That possibility was too horrendous to consider.

Padget found the remote and turned on the TV.

A female newscaster's voice filled the room. "As yet unconfirmed reports of corruption in Governor Ashcroft's office seem to be the catalyst for this event. We're still piecing together how the governor ended up here when no known associates can be found in the area—" Ashcroft snatched the remote control from Padget and stabbed a button, either to mute the offending screen or turn it off.

"As yet unconfirmed," Layla said. "How long will it take them to confirm? I bet your DA buddy is already starting to sweat."

"How did you do this?" Ashcroft demanded.

"I didn't do anything. Your own greed got us here," she said. The phone began to ring again. "Maybe now would be a good time to answer that."

"The FBI are here," Bri said. "They're all over the TV. The cops must have been biding their time until the FBI got up to speed. I'd bet they won't be patient in moving forward now."

"If they blast in here and see this setup…" Layla said, trailing off to let the sentence finish itself in his mind. His face was glowing red, and his strides got longer as he paced the width of the room and back. "You really didn't think this through, did you? Or did you think you were invincible?"

"You need to go out there and come clean," Bri said. The phone stopped ringing. "Maybe you can rise from the ashes as a reformed man?"

Ashcroft stopped pacing. Impressive quick thinking from Bri. They didn't want Ashcroft to be in a desperate state of mind. Desperate men did desperate things.

"Yes," Layla said, backing up Bri's idea. "You've done wrong, you can't deny that, but this does not have to be the end for your political career."

"How can I make them see?" he snapped, grabbing his gun from the table by the phone.

Layla couldn't see Bri, they were side by side, so she felt the tension in her arms through her own shoulder. Bri had the most to lose, she was with child. Thankfully, there was no bump on show yet, but Blaser would be going out of his mind outside.

"What are you going to do with that?" Layla asked. "You don't have to hurt anyone."

Ashcroft came closer, waving the gun up and down as he approached. "You've ruined my life!"

"This doesn't have to be over! You said yourself you weren't capable of murder, remember? You said it when you came in. You said you didn't want to hurt anyone," Layla said, struggling against her bonds, pushing her body forward to protect Bri on her other side. The pentagram formation they were in meant Lys and Pru wouldn't see what Ashcroft was doing, though they would've had sight on the TV.

"I came here to reason with you," Ashcroft said, grabbing her shoulder and sticking the gun in her face. "You wouldn't see reason."

"Yes, okay, this is my fault. If anyone is going to be hurt today, it should be me. You should punish me."

"No," Bri said. "This is his fault, and he should take responsibility. For once, he has to stand up and take responsibility!"

"Take it out on me," Layla said, panicking when he stepped back. "Please, leave these women alone. This is my fault!"

"He has to take ownership, to be a real man and admit his actions brought us here!" Bri insisted, also pulling on her bindings.

"They're not going to believe me," Ashcroft muttered.

Padget was watching his employer with a concern that worried her.

"They will. They might. These women will back you up," she said, wishing she could separate herself from the innocent women she couldn't bear to see hurt. "Take out your anger on me."

"Bri is right," Pru said in the background. Did the matriarch understand the urgency of the situation? "He is nothing but a pathetic, whimpering creature, blaming everyone else for his own shortcomings. No one will vote for that man. He cannot win until he can have pride in himself, and the country can respect him.

"Ignore them," Layla said.

Ashcroft was still retreating; his expression growing more distant. His attention drifted from the women, but he had to still be listening. "I'll be ruined," he murmured. "I'll be ostracized."

"You'll go to jail," Pru said. The woman still didn't sound upset or worried. She had a lot of faith in her husband and sons but failed to understand they were powerless. "You will have to go to court and be examined under a microscope. If they add murder charges, you may never be free again."

Ashcroft flinched at this declaration and his eyes slowly closed. "I came here to resolve this."

"You came here to intimidate my friend into tucking tail, but she has too much integrity for that," Bri said. "Act with some integrity yourself and maybe you'll find hope when this is finished. Let us go and own up to what you've done."

"You can't manipulate the media," Pru said. "You're not that powerful. Layla is right, the story will eventually come out and scandal always trumps truth in my experience, though in this case the scandal is the truth. You swore to uphold the integrity of your office, but you are not a righteous man. You are selfish and now you must reap what you have sewn. This predicament is no one's fault but your own."

They were really hammering home his demise. She didn't like how his eyes glazed over.

"I can't let them know the truth," he said, his eyes slid up to hers, the childlike fear in them was almost pitiable. Trepidation about his future reverted him back to that primitive state. "I can't face prison."

"Do the right thing," Layla said, softening her demeanor and the tension in her shoulders, giving up her fight. "And maybe you won't have to."

The phone began to ring again, but she held their connection, hoping to break through.

A buzz came from outside before a voice blasted through a bullhorn. "Answer the phone, Ashcroft. Pick it up, or we'll come through those doors. You've got one minute."

The shrill ring of the phone seemed to intensify. In an audio illusion, it got louder and louder, the closer Ashcroft got to her. Their eyes remained fixed. She willed him to surrender. For a few heartbeats, she really thought he was going to give in.

In a snap, he straightened, his expression hardened, and he lifted the gun to his own temple.

"No!" Padget screamed.

Horror erupted, but it was too late. Before Layla could open her mouth, Ashcroft pulled the trigger and his body fell onto the floor. Pru screamed, Lys and Suzette made similar sounds through their gags, and Bri remained silent. Nobody moved. She wasn't sure anyone was still breathing. Padget went over and crouched to feel for a pulse, but there was too much carnage for there to be any hope of life.

"He shot himself," Bri murmured, presumably for the benefit of those without a line of sight.

Men ran in from other rooms and Padget surged to his feet.

"You did this!" Padget said to her. "You! He didn't have it in him! He wasn't a murderer! You did this to him!"

He raised his gun, but the front door burst from its frame, and he whirled around. Law enforcement battered their way through the furniture, and Ashcroft's men were too confused to respond with force.

Padget still had his handgun, but the uniformed men were holding much more powerful rifles. Each had the red line of his precision sight pinned to a different man as they poured in. Orders called for the men to put down their weapons, and all did as they were told.

After the men were cuffed and led out, someone checked for Ashcroft's pulse, but they too found nothing. As it occurred to the officers to cut the women free, the Warner men rushed inside, followed by another bunch of uniformed SWAT officers, probably attempting to hold them back. Each Warner would take a bullet before they'd relent.

Every man had a woman to rush to and Ruger came straight to her. Her arms were freed, and she rubbed some of the gum from her wrists.

"Are you okay?" Ruger asked, crouching in front of her. "There are medics outside to check you all out."

"I'm okay," Layla said. "You should let them check Bri first."

She turned to see Blaser already had Bri on her feet and in his arms. Each of the couples were reunited. Layla noticed that even Gus was here to tend to Suzette.

"Blaser will take her," Ruger said, resting a hand on her face. "How are you?"

"I don't..." Ashcroft's body was being examined by officials. With the gun still in his hand, the forensics, and the testimony of everyone, she was confident they would believe the suicide. "He shot himself."

"Good," Ruger said. "If it got you out—"

"He did it to save himself," she said. "But I've never seen anyone… He was looking right at me."

Lyssa and Colt came into view. Lyssa crouched by Ruger to take her hand, but she could still only stare at Ashcroft's inert form.

"Don't hold in your emotion," Lyssa said. "The only way to process it is to let it out."

Ashcroft's body was blocked when everyone else came to crowd in behind Ruger and Lyssa. There they all were, scrutinizing her with sympathy and understanding. The women were endangered because of her, because of her connection to those who started this. They should revile her, run away and blame her for endangering them. But there was no judgment or anger in their eyes.

"Why aren't you angry?" she asked them.

"We are," Blaser said. "But not at you."

"At Drew? Do you blame my brother for—"

"No," Ruger said. "This wasn't his fault either."

"You're family," Colt said. "When you're one of us, we all take on the risks and responsibilities of each other. Yeah, I'm pissed Ashcroft took the easy way out, but that's not on you. None of this is."

"We're proud of you," Lyssa said. "You were courageous and kept a cool head. That's not easy to do in these situations."

"Drew is on his way," Ruger said, boosting up to kiss her, though she barely felt it through her cloak of shock.

"I think that's the first time you've used his first name," she said.

Her lips began to tingle when he kissed her again. The first sign that she was regaining some feeling.

"I've used his first name before."

"It's the first time you've said it with any familiarity, like he's more than just a colleague."

"I better get used to it if he's going to be family," Ruger said.

"He is?" she asked.

"Like Colt said, you're a Warner now… I'll find a way to sneak a ring onto your finger."

"I might like that," she said and managed to smile.

That was the first time a man had suggested marriage without her recoiling in horror. These people had accepted her. They stood beside her in an atrocious time and still cared about her wellbeing. What was more, she cared about them, all of them, and had been willing to die if it meant saving them. This was family. She was a part of them as much as they were a part of her.

When Ruger kissed her again, she locked her arms around his neck and squeezed so tight that tears began to flood her eyes. She wouldn't let herself lose it completely, there would still be cops to talk to and if Drew arrived to see her in a mess, he would probably start shooting people himself.

"On a less serious note," Colt said.

Layla let Ruger take her onto her feet.

"What?" Lyssa asked.

"The guests are starting to arrive."

"Damn," Lyssa said. "And the terrorists ate our canapés."

This truly was family. Somehow, they managed to find a smile in the tragedy. The FBI was circling them; they would all have to give statements. The scene would have to be processed too, so it was unlikely there would be much time for partying. That didn't help with the overflow of family members.

"You can send them to the salon," she said. "It's not much, but there's space. They could order pizza or something."

"Excellent idea," Pru said. "Ruger you'll run over there with the champagne, won't you? They probably won't let us leave."

"I'll do it," Colt said. "He should be here for Layla."

"Do it at the club," Blaser said. "There's a full bar there."

"If we're talking about making a choice between sending your Great Aunt Ida to Layla's salon or your strip club..., do I really have to answer that?"

"Fair enough," Blaser said. "I'm taking Bri outside to get checked out by the medics."

"I suppose the rest of us should start giving our statements," Lyssa said, clutching Colt's hand and turning to law enforcement.

"Do you need me to stay?" Colt asked her.

With a smile, Lyssa rose to her tiptoes to kiss him. "No, I'm getting good at talking to cops."

"You're good at talking to everyone," Colt said.

Blaser took Bri outside and Colt went to wrangle guests while the rest of them were briefed by the FBI. It was going to be a long night. The questions would be more complicated than those asked after her previous statements to police. She would do what was asked and hopefully by the time Drew arrived they would be finished. In the meantime, she was confident Ruger wouldn't leave her side.

THIRTY-FIVE

"HOW DO YOU FEEL?" Ruger had been asking that same question at regular intervals throughout the day.

Now dark outside, they were alone in the salon.

Drew had arrived with Serendipity not too long after she'd finished talking to the Feds. Because there were so many Warner family members at her place, Drew had taken her to dinner after she was dismissed, but she didn't eat much.

She'd tried to excuse Ruger from the meal because of his other family commitments, but he wouldn't leave her side. He stayed close and held her hand like he was scared to let her go.

She was still trying to come to terms with what had happened. Recounting the story to Drew and Dipity—with Ruger's help—still didn't make events more real.

Drew gave her advice on dealing with trauma, which led to him and Ruger trading "war" stories until she ended up nauseous. Dipity was a great comfort. All the newspapers would be leading with news of the showdown in suburbia, which diluted some of Serendipity and Drew's hard work, but they weren't disheartened. The story was being told. All they'd wanted was for the truth to be made public.

The media had so much to sink their teeth into that they wouldn't focus too much on the ignition of events. Drew, Dipity, and their compadres would maintain their anonymity.

Drew pointed out that the Warners were more likely to be hounded for their eyewitness stories after their brush with death. Her horror was short lived. Ruger laughed off the chances of that—the men wouldn't allow their women to be exploited and Colt had already hired security for their parents' place.

Sweeping the salon floor while Ruger bagged the dirty paper cups and plates brought over from the hardware store for the Warner guests, everything slowed down. The group hadn't had what could be called a party exactly, but the salon gave them a place to congregate, to have a drink and something to eat while catching up on the gossip.

Lyssa and Colt had played hosts with his parents in the fray too. Even Bri and Blaser joined later on. By the time she and Ruger left Drew and Dipity at their hotel and got back to the salon themselves, the core group were tidying up. Feeling terrible that she'd kept Ruger from the fun, she'd insisted on handling the cleanup and everyone else going home. Again, Ruger stayed with her.

"I don't know how to take away your pain," he said with deep frustration. "I wish I knew how to make you feel better."

She stopped sweeping and turned to him. When Ruger had her attention, he dumped the paper cups he was holding into the trash bag then dropped it.

"I'm not in pain," she said. "It's over, the whole mess is done with. It's finished."

"Is that why you've been quiet all night?" he asked, coming to rest his hands on her shoulders. "It's done, so you're planning your next move?"

"Planning? No… I don't know. I suppose I'm still processing everything. I should be elated because it's finished, and no one got hurt… no one on our side anyway."

"You're upset that Ashcroft is gone?"

"It's not that," she said. Ruger took the broom from her and propped it against the wall. In the salon, without blinds on the front window, she felt like they were in a fishbowl. With the lights on inside and the dark dominating outside, their actions played like a life-sized movie for anyone who walked by.

"He killed himself," she said. "Right there in front of me. I saw… I was looking into his eyes when he put the barrel to his head. How could somebody do that?"

"He was desperate," Ruger said. "He probably figured out that killing you wasn't going to get him anywhere. If he wanted to claim he was a hero, all of you would have to die. He would also have to set up his own men to take the fall and that was quite a group of guys to drop a dime on. Even if he'd made it out alive, his men would've sung to save their own necks."

"It just feels… wrong," she said.

Saying these things about the man who'd caused such drama seemed backwards. Exhaling, her forehead dropped to his chest. Selfish as it was, she was happy to have Ruger's strength to lean on.

"It feels wrong because you're a good person. It's not easy for a good person to watch another person suffer."

"He was looking right at me, Ruger, right at me. I was the last thing he saw before…"

"Then he had a beautiful view," Ruger said and kissed her head. "Do you know what we should do?"

"What?"

"First thing tomorrow, we'll go see Lyssa."

"To apologize for ruining her engagement party? Right after that we'll go apologize to your mother for those idiots wrecking her house and stealing her food. Then we'll go and see if Blaser and Bri will forgive us for endangering their future… She's pregnant, Ruger, the stress alone—"

"We can visit everyone if you want, Legs, but they'll tell you the same things they said earlier. No one needs you to apologize."

"So why should we visit Lyssa?" she asked.

"Because she's a therapist. She knows about this stuff."

"I thought she was a sex therapist."

"That's her specialty," Ruger said. "But she went to school for everything. She's a real MD. She coached Bri through a trauma and being best friends with Suzette must be a trauma in itself."

Encouraged to laugh, she tipped her head back. "You think she can fix me?"

"I don't think you're broken. I think everything you're feeling is normal. But she watched her ex-husband die and her stalker too. She can identify with what you're going through, on a human level at least, if you don't trust her doctor skills."

Her head sank to the side until her cheek rested on her shoulder. "I'm so screwed up. Why would you want me to be a part of your family?"

"You already are," he said. "Do you want to take a shower? I'll finish up down here."

"That sounds great," she said. "Make sure you lock all the doors and windows before you come up." Because she hadn't been home since events unfolded, duct tape gum still stuck to her skin. Each time it caught on something, she was reminded of how close she'd been to losing her life.

Ruger carried on with the task as she headed upstairs. Layla tossed her clothes straight in the trash, she didn't want to be reminded of that day at all, and then she tiptoed into the hot spray. The apartment wasn't large, so the shower stall was small, but she enjoyed the security. The steam increased, but she didn't turn the temperature down. She took her time scrubbing herself, determined to wash the memories of the day from her body.

It didn't work, of course. Nothing would make those memories go away. She would have to live with those images in her mind for the rest of her own days.

"Room for another?"

The shower door slid aside, and Ruger joined her.

There wasn't really room for two, but she'd already washed herself. There was nothing to accomplish, other than being close to her man.

The slippery water skidded over their bodies and the pulse of the beads joined the pound in his chest under her cheek. Letting herself relax, the dammed emotion of the day began to seep out and while the water was still hot, she let herself cry. Ruger didn't say anything, didn't offer standard platitudes or try to cheer her up. He let her cry in their private sanctuary, where no one could get to them. There she felt safe, in Ruger's arms, her cheek resting on the beat of his heart.

When the tears were finished, he ran his fingers through her heavy hair and she went with the motion, letting her head fall back to meet his kiss. She didn't have to hear him, to open her eyes and see it, she could feel his intention on her belly. Being naked, steamy, and pressed together brought his arousal up early, but as she cried, they both ignored it, and he was happy to soothe her.

After kissing her, Ruger stroked his fingertips over her eyes, down the sides of her nose and around her lips to her chin. "You are the most beautiful woman I have ever seen."

Now she did open her eyes. He was bullshitting her, he had to be. Her eyes would be red and puffy from the crying. She'd scrubbed her skin scarlet, and any remaining makeup would be smeared all over her face. But he wasn't smiling, didn't even look like he was teasing. His expression was so sincere that she frowned.

"I told Drew I had fallen in love with you," Ruger said, still caressing her face with his fingertips.

"When did you do that? Oh my God, you can't say something like that after the trauma of today."

"It wasn't today that made me feel it," he said. "Being away from you, leaving you under the care of my brothers when I went to Rushe and Flick, I knew I loved you then. I just didn't want to admit it."

"Now you want to admit it?"

"I don't want you to run away," Ruger said. "I've been holding back because I don't want to spook you. But I don't want you to mistake this for something less than it is."

"After today, I don't think that's possible," she said.

Pleased she hadn't dashed for the nearest exit, she was dismayed when he tried to reach past her to turn off the water. She was tired, but that didn't justify neglecting him.

Intercepting his hand, she guided it to her breast and almost laughed when his face lit like a kid being given the keys to his first car.

Ruger bowed to kiss her again and caressed her breasts at the same time. The water was beginning to cool, so time ran short. Bending her knees, she vanished from his kiss and his arms, and opened her mouth wide to take as much of him as she could into her mouth.

On their first night together, she'd told him he wouldn't fit in her throat, and she had no intention of pushing to that limit tonight. Still, he seemed to enjoy her sucking and working her hands up and down his length while not forgetting his other intimate areas.

"Tonight is supposed to be about you," he groaned out.

Every night they had been intimate was about her and she'd been happy to take the pampering. No more taking him for granted. He deserved some pampering of his own. Taking control helped put her insecurities to bed. She was a confident woman but being tethered and tormented had played on her psyche and she didn't want that vulnerability to take hold.

Hollowing her cheeks, she sucked the solid length of him into her and then rose higher on her knees to press her breasts into him. "Do you want more?" she pouted up at him. The shower spray ran in a solid river through the waterfall of her hair into the firth of her back. The tepid temperature was arousing, tickling down her spine and over her ass.

"I sure do," he said.

Bending to pick her up, he guided her legs around him and slid into her all the way on his first advance.

Pushing her clit to his groin, she wriggled against him, stimulating herself as he kissed her again. His hot mouth moved fast, his tongue slid along her teeth then coiled around hers before disappearing only to come back and taste her all over again. His hands kneaded her ass, giving her perfect leverage to work herself against him. But her clit was abandoned when he slid out and in. Pacing himself, he retreated from his brink, taking his sweet time moving within her.

One of his hands skimmed her hip and began toying with her clit, rubbing in gentle circles to torment her. The pressure and rhythm she wanted was far greater than what he gave. Before she could complain, he pressed a finger into her and increased the tempo of his thrusts to match the pace of his finger. He was giving her everything she needed, but with his tongue still battling hers, she couldn't let him know.

His lips slid away; his head stayed close. "Baby, are you—" She screamed and arched into the bulldozer of orgasm that clenched her so hard her knees clamped themselves into his ribs. She didn't need to answer his never asked question with words, her actions spoke for her.

With that permission, Ruger quickened his actions until he too was sated and the two of them hung together in a sopping statue of bliss. The water was cold. Not that it mattered. They remained where they were, wrapped together until their panting slowed.

"Bedtime?" he asked when he straightened his posture, though he kept her in his arms.

"Bedtime," she agreed and this time, let him turn off the water.

The emotion of the day and the workout in the shower left her exhausted. Ruger carried her to the bedroom and set her on her feet, then retrieved towels for them both. She towel-dried her hair and ran a comb through it. Ruger was already in bed and the sight was too inviting. As quickly as she could, she put the towels in the laundry hamper, turned off the light and climbed into bed beside him, more at peace than she'd been in a long time.

EPILOGUE

"DOES ANYONE EVER SAY that the ceremony was horrible?" Layla asked Ruger when he came over with a fresh flute of champagne for her.

"What?" he asked, his face dancing with mischief as it had been all day.

That wasn't supposed to be the happiest day of his life, not that anyone would know that by looking at him.

"All day I've heard people tell Lyssa that the ceremony was beautiful. I'm just wondering if anyone would actually have the balls to say the opposite."

"You would," he said, sipping from his own flute and turning to observe the same scene she was drinking in.

Three months after the devastating engagement party that never really was, Lyssa and Colt had been joined at the altar. Looking at them standing beside the wooden gazebo erected in the Warner backyard especially for the occasion, there was bliss. The three brothers insisted they could build it themselves, so the women had made margaritas and sat on the patio to watch the pantomime. Eventually, their men made good. Two batches of margaritas were made that day, one alcoholic, one virgin.

Bri and Blaser were by the buffet table. The latter talked to his new fiancée as she fed her proud baby bump. For now only family knew, but Lyssa would be sporting her own baby bump soon. She had just hit eight weeks. In another month or so, everyone would know Colt wasn't firing blanks after all.

"Who are they?" Layla asked, nodding toward a couple in the shadows at the back corner of the yard. "They've barely spoken to anyone."

"I'll introduce you," Ruger said.

Dubious of the heightened sense of mischief that sparked and fizzed from him when he snatched her hand to drag her toward the couple, she reserved judgment.

Weaving through others, they crossed the grass. Before they reached the couple, she heard them talking.

"Five more minutes, Lover," the female said, her back to proceedings. The male faced into the yard but was so ensconced in shade that deciphering his features was impossible. "You can stand there and count down the seconds in your head. Just smile and try to look like you're having a good time."

"Smile?" he grumbled.

"Okay, maybe that's asking a little much. Just try not to scare people."

"Hello!" Ruger announced their approach, though she had a sense these people knew they were about to be descended upon.

"Ruger," the female said, whirling around and landing a beaming smile on him as she tipped her head to accept his kisses on either cheek. The male growled. Like properly growled. The menace made her step back. Ruger did the same and held his champagne toward the female. "Drink?"

"You make a very pretty couple," the female said, accepting the glass from Ruger.

"Yes, this is Layla," Ruger said.

"Layla Jansen," the female said. "We had figured that out. She and Drew have the same eyes."

"You know my brother?" Layla asked.

"This is Flick," Ruger said. "And the guy in the background is Rushe."

And all the pieces fell into place. "Ah," Layla said, leaning in to give Flick a hug. She made no attempt to touch Rushe, she wasn't sure he'd put her down in one piece. "Drew saved your life."

"Yes, he did," Flick said without compunction. "He helped me to save Rushe's life too, but we don't talk so much about that."

"Talk so much about what?"

Turning around, Colt and Blaser approached with their women who greeted Flick and didn't attempt to touch Rushe. At least she wasn't the only one. Flick held Bri's hand and rested her other on the baby bump.

"He's going to be beautiful," Flick said, bending down to rest an ear against Bri's stomach.

Bri laughed and held her hands up. Huh, odd. Bri had been demure about her bump and usually didn't like anyone to touch it in public. With Flick, she had no reservations.

"Do you know it's a boy?" Colt asked Blaser. "You never told us."

"Bri knows," Blaser said. "She's not telling me."

"She was the one who wanted it to be a secret in the first place," Colt said. "Women, always reserving the right to change their minds whenever it suits them."

Flick stood up and made eye contact with Bri before hugging her again. Rushe took his girlfriend's shoulders to pull her back to his chest. His arm came around her neck and he relaxed his hand on her shoulder.

"So when are you two getting married?" Flick asked Bri.

"We just bought a house," Bri said. "Give us a chance… You two have been together longer than any couple here, shouldn't we be asking you when you plan to tie the knot?"

Flick opened her mouth, but Rushe spoke. "We are married," he said.

Flick clamped her mouth shut and turned her frown up over her shoulder in Rushe's direction. "We are?"

"Sure," Rushe said. "I have a piece of paper that says so."

"You had one of your contacts forge a marriage certificate? Did I sign it?"

"Yep," he said, and squeezed her closer. "You think I'd take the risk of someone else making medical decisions about my body?"

"He means mine," Flick stage whispered to the group. "There you go. We are married."

"So that just leaves Ruger and Layla," Lyssa said.

All focus switched to them.

"Talk of marriage brings Lay out in hives," Ruger said, looping an arm around her.

"Actually, he hasn't asked me," she said, digging an elbow into his ribs.

He lowered his mouth into her hair but spoke so everyone could hear. "That's because I like having you around. I'm getting used to it. I can't have you running off."

"We're looking at property," Layla said, smiling at his sentiment. Although she shared it with the group, not Ruger. "Now that Dax has sold off everything from Jersey for us, we have a pretty decent nest egg."

She hadn't contributed nearly as much as Ruger, but the salon was booked solid, months in advance, so she was earning more than him at that moment.

"You and Dax seem to be working well at the club," Colt said to Ruger. "Any issues?"

Ruger shook his head. "He's a decent guy, more direct than me, but we each have our strengths."

Every day there were tales of different conflicts the men dealt with. They were a good team. Ruger used his easy charm and humor to defuse possible issues, and if that didn't work out, Dax had the security guys working in tight formation to take out any threats to the women.

"Dax's wife Ivy has taken over the running of the garage," Blaser said. "I only check in once a week now, which has given us the chance to start looking for new premises for a second garage closer to home."

"Home," Ruger said. "Close to your mommy."

"Your mommy too," Bri said. "And she's been a huge help."

"She has?" Ruger asked. "I figured she'd be getting in your way."

"No, actually, she gets Blaser out of my way," Bri said, nuzzling her fiancé's chest. "Without the garage and Risqué to worry about, he's constantly under my feet. But your mom gives him plenty of jobs to keep him busy while I get our new place set up."

"You're all getting your lives together. It's impressive," Flick said. "And I hear you got your book deal, Doctor."

Lyssa's grin hadn't moved all day, but Layla couldn't blame her. She had achieved all her goals. "Yes, it will be published next year," the bride said. "I'll send you all signed copies."

"You can send mine to Serendipity. Rushe and I don't have an address we like to share," Flick said. "But I would love to read about your observations especially in Risqué. I worked in a kind of gentleman's bar myself once."

"We're not talking about that," Rushe said.

The exploits of Rushe and Flick probably didn't belong in any book, at least not one that wasn't R-rated. Rushe had shut down that thread of conversation. The only person who might argue with him was Flick and she said nothing.

Colt moved the group on to a new topic, one that the men were far more comfortable talking about. "Any word on Padget?" he asked, becoming all business, his attention on Rushe, but it was Flick who answered.

"We're watching him," she said. "After he got out on that technicality, we were pissed, but it's worked in our favor because he's leading us straight to all the players. It's sort of fun to circle in on him."

"You're one of the most fascinating couples I have ever encountered," Lyssa said, in a voice suggesting she'd forgotten anyone else was there. "How is your sex life?"

Flick's smile grew coy before she turned it down against Rushe's flexing arm.

"Cherrypop, it's our wedding day," Colt said. "A day off from work."

"Have you ever had one of those?" Ruger asked his new sister-in-law.

Lyssa was always in work mode and asked some of the most outrageous questions, but she'd gotten used to the intrusive and unapologetic nature of her almost sister. Bri was quieter, more careful, but her confidence grew exponentially when Blaser was with her.

Suzette and Gus were somewhere around. Their relationship was public. They seemed to spend most of their time arguing, although they managed the apartments together with amazing efficiency. Suzette had announced their engagement a couple of weeks ago when the gang were having dinner together. From Gus' expression, it wasn't clear if he'd known the news beforehand. It sort of looked like he was learning it at the same time as everyone else. After that, Gus' brother Mattie gifted them the apartment block and everyone was sure that was a positive step.

Since Suzette and Ivy weren't the best of friends, and because Dax was flusher than he had been, Ivy and Dax had moved out of the apartments and into a new house. Since they both spent time in Risqué with their men, Layla had come to know Ivy and loved Mrs. Harrow's straight-talking attitude. On the sly, Layla knew Ivy and Dax were considering having children of their own. Their new four-bedroom house suggested they were close to making it happen.

"So why are you buying a house?" Flick asked her. "Didn't you just buy your salon?"

"We did," Layla said.

"I thought you had an apartment above your salon."

Her relationship with these people was just a few minutes old, but they already knew everything about her life.

"It's too small for us," she said, glancing up at the height of her partner. "Ruger needs more room to lay about."

"She needs time away from work," Ruger said, suggesting the move was for her benefit when in actual fact, he spent most of his day in the salon flirting with the customers from teenage girls to pensioners. Her clients lit up when Ruger came in and she loved to watch him charm them all. He loved being social but working nights at Risqué then spending afternoons in her salon meant he wasn't getting much down time. With them working conflicting hours and living in her place of business, they were in work mode too often. "We'll rent out the apartment and bring in some more dough."

"We'll need more space for when we have kids," Layla said for the shock value and sure enough, Ruger's embrace tightened.

"For what?" he asked.

His ashen expression made everyone in their group laugh, so Layla kept on going. "Sure, everyone else is having kids. It would be great for them all to be close in age, wouldn't it? Then they would go to school together and grow up together."

His mouth opened, but nothing came out. She grinned, triumphant that he would learn not to tease her about marriage unless he wanted to be teased right back.

"I think children would be a great idea," Bri said. "And there's a house opening up on the block behind ours… Pru could put you in touch with the seller."

"Excellent," Layla said.

Ruger took her champagne and downed the rest of the liquid before putting her flute on a nearby table. "Uh, excuse us," he said.

With his arm still clamped around her shoulders, he led her away from the laughing group.

He took her to the fence and cloaked her body with his, probably so no one could lip read their conversation or scrutinize their expressions.

"What?" she asked. "I was enjoying that conversation."

"I could tell," he said. "But it's best not to talk kids when my mom is in earshot. Have you learned nothing in your time with my family?"

"We eat dinner at your mom's nearly every week. If you think she hasn't brought up the idea of more grandkids with me, you're crazy."

"You really think we should have a kid?"

"Relax," she said, cupping his face. "We'll have kids when the time is right for us, not just because everyone else is having them."

"I'm trying not to look relieved in case it upsets you."

She laughed. "You're still settling into your management role at Risqué. I'm still building the business and we've just decided to buy a house. I think we have enough plates in the air."

His eyes slunk down "You know…"

Taking her weight from the fence, concern crept in. "What?"

"I did ask Drew."

"Ask Drew what?"

"If I could ask you, you know, to marry me."

"You did?" she asked. Although she didn't want to be gratified, she was. Asking the head male of the family for her hand seemed archaic, yet there was something endearing about it. "What did he say?"

"That if I hurt you, he'd rip off my limbs and send them to the four corners of the country."

"That sounds like Drew."

"But he also said I could, if I treated you right. He said I could have you… if you said yes."

"Which he probably wasn't holding his breath for," she said.

Her brother knew about her history with men and might assume she'd run for the hills if Ruger asked. But she had been taken on by more than just the man. The family had adopted her as well, enticing for an orphan. Losing any of them would break her heart, but the Warner clan had proven they never abandoned one of their own. If there was heartache to be faced, they would do it together, as a family.

"Maybe not, but I…"

"You what?" she asked, watching his hand slide into his pocket. Holding her breath, she couldn't even blink when he produced a small velvet box. "What is that?"

"What do you think it is?"

She couldn't believe he was smiling at a time like this.

Unable to take her eyes from the box, Layla heard more than saw his expression.

And as her heart picked up its pace, she swallowed away her anxiety. "I don't want to run away from you," she whispered.

"Which is why I'm not going to ask," he said, taking her hand and placing the box in her open palm. "You're going to keep this and when you're ready, if you're ready, you put it on. We never have to talk about it, and I'll never ask. This is a token of my intent, and I won't hurry you. When I see it on your finger, that's when I'll know it's time to make plans."

"You're sure about this?" she asked, seeking out his gaze. "You're really sure you want to be with me, and you won't ever… you won't ever leave me?"

"Legs, there isn't a woman in the world out there like you," he said, tracing his knuckle down her cheek. "I think you were made for me. Once a Warner man picks his woman, that's it. Warners mate for life."

"Sometimes you're just so…" Her smile grew, and her heart stopped hammering. "I love you, Ruge."

"What's not to love?" he asked, opening his arms and stepping back. "The band is set up, there'll be dancing soon. You want to go put that in your bag?"

She had been a bridesmaid along with Bri and Suzette; her dress didn't come with pockets. They had put their gowns on together at the Warner house, with the men getting ready at Bri and Blaser's new house since it was so close. Layla had a backpack containing the clothes and accessories she'd taken off when getting ready for the ceremony, the bag Ruger was referring to.

"No," she said, shaking her head.

Some of the shine left his demeanor.

With her eyes locked on his, she opened the box and slid the solitaire onto her finger. When the box snapped shut, his mischief returned, and he leaped forward to grab her up and kiss her.

Regaining her breath, Layla could only see stars when he finally put her on her feet again. "Now you never get to take it off."

"Good," she said, dropping the box into his pocket then taking his hand. "It's a binding contract, so now you belong to me. You still haven't delivered on your karaoke promise, but you know how I love to dance. There's no way you can avoid it today."

Leading him toward the music and the family, she exhaled her anxiety. He'd tease and protest, but he was hers, and she would never let him get away.

Thank you for reading this tale!
If you can, please take the time to review.

~

Ask your local library for more Scarlett Finn
novels!

~

For all things Scarlett Finn
check out:

www.scarlettfinn.com

www.ingramcontent.com/pod-product-compliance
Lightning Source LLC
Chambersburg PA
CBHW030802200726
48285CB00014B/513